"It's rather a plain church, don't you think?"

Annja glanced around, looking for someone who stood out, someone who was obviously watching her, who had a phone to his ear. The street was quiet. She couldn't see anyone. But they knew where she was.

"Is this a social call?" she said into the phone, still looking up and down the street.

"No. Definitely not. I like to think of it as incentivizing." The man on the other end laughed. In the background, she heard a cry of pain. Garin. Why were they doing this to him? Why torture him? If he knew where the mask was, he would have told them. He wasn't a hero. There was only one thing Garin Braden valued above and beyond the possession of beautiful things, and that was self-preservation. "There's someone here who wants to talk to you," he said.

There was a pause. A second. Two. It felt like forever.

A weak and mumbling voice spoke. "Don't do it… don't give them what they want. Even if you find it…"

It was Garin. The phone was snatched away before he could finish speaking. The next thing she heard was a grunt and the sound of flesh slapping flesh.

"Garin!" Annja called, unable to stop herself.

"You've wasted four hours, Miss Creed. Don't waste any more." The kidnapper killed the connection.

Titles in this series:

ROGUE ANGEL

Alex Archer

DEATH MASK

A GOLD EAGLE BOOK FROM

WORLDWIDE®

TORONTO • NEW YORK • LONDON
AMSTERDAM • PARIS • SYDNEY • HAMBURG
STOCKHOLM • ATHENS • TOKYO • MILAN
MADRID • WARSAW • BUDAPEST • AUCKLAND

Recycling programs
for this product may
not exist in your area.

First edition January 2015

ISBN-13: 978-0-373-62172-9

Death Mask

Special thanks and acknowledgment to
Steven Savile for his contribution to this work.

The
LEGEND

...THE ENGLISH COMMANDER TOOK
JOAN'S SWORD AND RAISED IT HIGH.

The broadsword, plain and unadorned,
gleamed in the firelight. He put the tip against
the ground and his foot at the center of the blade.
The broadsword shattered, fragments falling
into the mud. The crowd surged forward,
peasant and soldier, and snatched the shards
from the trampled mud. The commander tossed
the hilt deep into the crowd.
Smoke almost obscured Joan, but she continued
praying till the end, until finally the flames climbed
her body and she sagged against the restraints.

Joan of Arc died that fateful day in France,
but her legend and sword are reborn...

PROLOGUE

Late-night traffic roared along Madrid's Gran Vía. These cars were status symbols driven by men in the throes of their midlife crises. Overpowered engines strained in the chassis of superlight metal. Beautiful people stumbled in and out of bars. There was no room for ugliness or poverty in this make-believe world that pretended not to be in turmoil. They partied hard and loud, the constant babble of noise disguising the rotors of the approaching helicopter.

It was a quarter to midnight, not quite the magical hour when the luxury sports cars would turn into pumpkins and the men behind the wheel into the rats they were deep down.

The men on board the helicopter paid no attention to the world below. They had their mission objectives and wouldn't be distracted from them by little black dresses. They had the job timed down to the second. They had covered every possible parameter and were prepared for every eventuality. They would be long gone before the first alarm sounded.

The helicopter circled what passed for one of the

only skyscrapers in the downtown area, giving the six men on board time to confirm they were good to go, and then they pulled ski masks down over their faces. This was a well-drilled team, used to dealing with high-risk ops, infiltrations and extractions, scenarios which could turn on a dime. That killed complacency before it could get a foothold in their ranks. Every op carried danger. Planning minimized the risk but never truly took it away.

The first man jumped out seconds before the skids had settled on the roof of the office block. Head down, he ran hard, arms and legs pumping, toward the infiltration point. The arrogance of money had made their job so much easier. A helipad on the roof of an office block? It was like taking candy from a baby.

Nine seconds after the initial breach lines were tethered to the building, the first three men stepped off the edge of the roof, beginning to rappel down the side. The second trio was nine seconds behind them. The building's panoramic windows were made from high-tensile glass, essentially bulletproof. The men drew level with the target's floor, pulling off to pause on either side of his office. The front three men attached devices right, left and top-center on the huge window. Bullets were one thing, concentrated explosives quite another. A hand went up, each finger closing one second after the other, counting down to the detonation. Noise-reduction earbuds saved their hearing as the charges blew, and the men turned their faces away to protect their eyes as the glass shattered.

The window blew inward, showering the three men deadlocked in a late-night meeting in the Rojo International offices with deadly rain that cut through their designer threads as if they were paper.

Less than a minute had passed since the team had rolled out of the helicopter. Fifty-five seconds, to be precise.

All six team members swung inside the gaping wound in the side of the skyscraper before the last glass fragments had started their downward spiral to the street below.

A hail of gunfire tore into the ceiling, meant purely to terrify.

It had the desired effect.

A second volley of gunfire had two of the suits dancing in jerky rhythm as their bodies were riddled with bullets. Blood spattered the wall behind them, leaving silhouettes of the dying clearly visible.

The third man sat motionless in the midst of the carnage. Well, not quite motionless, the team leader realized, seeing the man's eyes dart to the Mark Rothko painting on the wall that had caught some of the blood spray. The arc of red was incongruous with the blocks of color. The man seemed more concerned about the damage to his painting than he was about the two men bleeding out on the expensive silk rug.

He said nothing.

The boardroom door burst open and another man—broad, burly and dead before he took his first step inside the room—managed a single shot before a hail of bullets took him down. The bullets cut through his torso, the impact driving him back through the doorway.

"Two more," the leader said, motioning left and right for two of his men to go on the hunt while the other three followed him.

The man at the table didn't so much as flinch as cable ties were slipped around his wrists and cinched so tightly they drew blood. He looked up at the security camera high in the corner of the room, making sure it saw everything. The red light winked back. It was recording.

"You," the leader said to one of his men, who crossed the room quickly and blacked out the lens with spray paint.

Ninety seconds had passed since the helicopter had touched down.

Everything was on schedule. Clockwork precision. The silent alarm would have been tripped the second the window shattered. Police response times were fast when it was big money they were protecting, but there was no sign of any kind of armed response yet. The leader had it timed to two minutes twenty-five for the first siren. Anything after that was sloppy, and he wasn't about to let sloppiness carry the day. He'd planned for two twenty-five; he'd stick with the plan. More gunfire ripped through the office, followed by the crash of furniture being tipped over.

There was a single shot after that, then silence.

The two men sent on patrol returned to the boardroom as a harness was being strapped to their target's chest. One of them gave a single nod, confirming that everything had been taken care of.

No one had imagined an "unbreakable" window on the thirty-second floor posed a substantial security risk. Not the architects. Not the men who had taken up residence in the high castle of Rojo International's offices. And most importantly, not the man being strapped into the harness by his team.

"Move," the team's Number Two barked, hauling their captive to his feet.

The man resisted, but that only resulted in pain as Number Two delivered a punishing blow to his gut that doubled him up, and as his head came down, a crunching right uppercut that sent him staggering sideways. "Move," Number Two repeated, and this time the man did as he was told.

"You are going to pay for this," he snarled. Rather than another blow, his defiance was paid back with silence—a wad of tissues forced into his mouth and a strip of gaffer tape slapped across it. Number Two dragged him to the window and stood only inches from the edge, grabbing a fistful of his hair and forcing him to look down.

The drop was dizzying.

"A spectacular view, I'm sure you'll agree, Mr. Braden?" the team leader said, bracing himself against the window frame. "An entire city quite literally at your feet. Look at it. Drink it in. It could well be the last thing you ever see. I'd hate for you to forget it."

GARIN BRADEN WASN'T used to people treating him like this. He wasn't a victim. He'd lived his entire long life by one simple credo: "Do unto others before they can do unto you." A man didn't get to Garin's age by being a victim. He pushed back against the hand on his head, but the man didn't relinquish his grip. Garin felt the air rush into his face. It was all too easy to imagine the sidewalk rushing toward him. He swallowed. He wasn't in control. He didn't like that. He tried to run through his options, but with the harness pinning his arms, and the assassin's fingers tangled in his hair, there was little he could do. Sadly, learning how to fly wasn't possible, though it was looking increasingly like a necessity. Lacking wings, Garin felt hands on the center of his spine and then he was kicking against nothing, falling.

For a second—the silence between terrified heartbeats—he was suspended in the air thirty-two stories above the Madrid streets before the line hooked through his harness snapped taut and stopped his plunging descent. And then he was *rising* as he was hoisted toward the roof.

Less than a minute later, a battered and bloody Garin Braden was secure in the helicopter, the last of the team clambering in to join him; another thirty seconds and they were airborne.

They were more than half a mile away before they heard the sirens of the first responders.

All the money in the world hadn't been able to keep Garin Braden safe.

The clock was ticking.

1

24:00—Madrid

The drumming vibration of her cell phone on the night-stand dragged Annja Creed out of sleep. For a moment the noise had been part of the surreal landscape of her imagination, but as she opened her eyes she completely forgot what she'd been dreaming. Annja had been in Valencia for a week working on a piece on gargoyles for *Chasing History's Monsters*, and now she was in Madrid, recharging her batteries. There was nothing like the mix of modernity and history as a backdrop for a little R & R. She looked at the alarm clock and saw it was ungodly early, for a vacation day. Who in their right mind would be calling? Then she realized it was probably Doug Morrell, completely forgetting she'd booked the next few days off. Her producer could be a pain when she was overseas, always wanting an update, querying her expense claim or just reminding her the show needed to be *sexy*. That was the nature of the beast, after all. Sexy television. Sexy history. Sexy monsters. Sexy claims of links between the two. She'd just turned the latest segment in. Doug could wait. She rolled over and closed her eyes again, but a second and a third call came in quick succession.

She gave in and picked up.

"What do you want, Doug? It's the middle of the night."

That wasn't quite true. The morning sun filtered through the too-thin hotel curtains, picking out the cigarette-smoke discolorations on the fabric.

It wasn't Doug. "Check your email. Click on the link. I will wait," the voice said. She couldn't place it.

"Who is this?" Annja heard another voice in the background but couldn't catch what was being said. The line went dead. She checked her recent calls, but the number had been blocked. Annja pushed the covers back and sat up. It was almost seven, and the cleaners were already moving around outside her room, no doubt wishing she'd go down for breakfast so they could do their jobs.

She got out of bed reluctantly and headed through to the bathroom. She'd check her email, but not before taking a hot shower to help wake her up.

When she emerged, one towel wrapped around her and another making a turban around her wet hair, she crossed the floor to her laptop on the dressing table and powered it up.

She had a single new email.

The subject line said Urgent, and the sender was Garin Braden.

But it hadn't been Garin's voice on the phone.

If you want to see Mr. Braden alive again, follow this link.

Annja clicked.

A window opened on her screen and a few seconds later the image resolved into what looked like a live video feed. The sole image on the screen was a digital clock that read 23:52:27. It took her a couple seconds to realize it was counting backward from 24:00:00.

"Hello, Annja, so glad you could finally join us," a voice said. It sounded different through the tinny speakers than it had on the phone. There was no sign of the male speaker on the screen."Time is precious. You have already wasted seven and a half minutes of it."

Wasted?

She didn't know what was going on, and the steaming-hot water had only dragged her so far from sleep. "Stop messing around, Garin. I'm tired and in no mood for your stupid jokes."

The camera zoomed out, gradually revealing that the clock was in the middle of a man's chest. He was slumped in a chair, his hands tied behind his back. He was breathing, but he was bloodied and bruised, and Annja couldn't tell if he was conscious. Wires ran from the clock to a box beneath the chair he was tied to. Water was thrown from off camera, soaking his blood-streaked shirt. The man lifted his head slowly, staring at the camera through one swollen eye. His mouth was smeared with red. Still, he was immediately recognizable.

"Garin!" Annja said, his name catching in her throat.

His eyes didn't seem to register his name or Annja's voice. He was dazed and confused and clearly had no idea what was going on.

"What do you want?" Annja asked.

"I like that," said the off-camera voice. "Straight down to business. No pretense of bargaining. No bluster or demands that I let him go. We can work together, Miss Creed."

"What do you want?" Annja repeated.

"The Mask of Torquemada."

"The what?" She knew exactly what the voice had said, and had a good idea what it had meant. But that didn't mean she'd be able to meet this person's demands.

"Do you really want to waste time pretending you don't know what I am talking about, Miss Creed?" the voice said. "Nine minutes. Ticktock. Ticktock. The more time you waste now, the less time you will have to save your friend. Find the mask or your friend dies. Is that incentive enough for you? Twenty-three hours, fifty-one minutes."

"You can't expect me to find something that's been lost for centuries in a single day. That's impossible."

"You better hope not, for Mr. Braden's sake."

"This is insane! I don't have the first idea where to start looking…or what I'm even looking for. You can't just say 'Find it.' I'm not a miracle worker!"

"Well, there's one man here who is desperately hoping you are, Miss Creed. His life depends upon it. I will call you again in a few hours to see how you're getting on. Godspeed, Annja Creed. Ticktock. Ticktock." The camera zoomed in to focus on the clock in the middle of Garin's chest, then panned up to his face. "Just in case you need reminding."

Annja couldn't look away.

Garin looked at her with dead eyes.

She wondered if he had been drugged or just beaten so badly he couldn't focus.

His head slumped forward again. This time it stayed down.

Annja watched as the clock ticked down another minute. She had less than a day to save Garin, with no idea where to begin, no clue as to where he might be. Normally there was one man she'd turn to if she needed technology to help her find someone—Garin. He wasn't going to be able to help her now.

She continued to stare at the screen, trying to learn as much as she could about the place he was being held, but there was precious little to be gleaned from it. The light was artificial, the walls behind him were bare brick. It could have been, quite literally, anywhere in the world.

Another minute passed by and she knew she had to do something; anything.

She'd wasted ten minutes of his life already.

Ticktock. Ticktock.

2

"Annja? As much as I adore you, my dear, I adore my sleep much *more*."

"This is work," Annja said.

"A four-letter word," Roux said. She could imagine the smile playing across his lips as he grumbled. He could be a crank at the best of times. "And not one of the more amusing ones."

"Have you heard from Garin?"

"Not recently. Last week. Why?"

"I was just sent a link to a video chat. Garin was on the other end. There was a clock strapped to his chest and a bomb under his chair. He was in a bad way. Beaten bloody."

"Couldn't happen to a nicer chap."

"This is serious," she said. "In less than twenty-four hours that clock hits zero and the bomb detonates, taking Garin with it. That's the threat."

"I assume this is a kidnapping? So what do they want?"

She heard him moving around the château, talking with her as he made his way to his study.

"They're asking for the Mask of Torquemada," she said. It came out in a more matter-of-fact way than she'd expected. Everyone knew who Torquemada was—a Dominican zealot who rose up to become the first Grand Inquisitor of the Spanish Inquisition, rabidly anti-Semitic, the scourge of the Moors—but in all the stories she'd heard of his vile purge, there had never been anything about a mask.

"Good luck with that," Roux said dismissively. "It's been missing for more years than I can remember."

"So there *is* a mask. But you were there, weren't you? You and Garin."

"I may have been," Roux said, not giving anything away. "But I had other things on my mind than a mad Dominican obsessed with religious purity. I'd already had a lifetime of that. I was in France. It's not like we had CNN giving us hourly updates as the atrocities rolled on, but yes, you heard things, obviously. It was easy to throw accusations around, and you know the old adages about mud sticking, no smoke without fire. People were willing to believe anything if it meant they were safe from the worst of it, that it couldn't happen to them. Torquemada was a Christian zealot. He was the driving force behind maybe as many as two hundred thousand Jews fleeing Spain. His priests *encouraged* another fifty thousand to convert to Christianity. Though I use the term *encouraged* in its most liberal sense."

"And the mask?"

"If it ever existed, buried with him."

"So we're just talking about a little tomb-robbing here. I guess I can deal with that. Wouldn't be the first time. Where's he buried? Do we know?" She had already forwarded the email to Roux, along with the link.

"Yes. It's a matter of public record. Unfortunately, his grave was ransacked only a couple of years before the Inquisition was disbanded." Meaning the task had already become exponentially more difficult than she'd thought it would be in the matter of a few seconds. "They took everything in the tomb. Burned his bones, mask, everything destroyed in an auto-da-fé. An act of faith." He fell silent and she knew he was waiting for her, giving her the chance to respond and draw her own conclusions.

"Okay. Well… If it was destroyed, then that's a death sentence for Garin, so I'm going to ignore that option for now and assume that the mask was stolen and is still intact. People are greedy. If it was worth something, someone might have taken it." She took the old man's silence as agreement. "Where was he buried?" It was a starting point. Nothing more than that. But it was better than sitting around waiting for inspiration to strike. Five hundred years was a long time, but Annja hoped the normal logic of a search would hold true: the best place to start looking for something that had been lost was the last place it had been seen.

"The Monastery of Saint Thomas Aquinas in Ávila,"

he said. "I'll join you there as soon as I can, but first I think I shall pay a visit to Seville."

"What has Seville got, apart from a barber and some oranges?"

The old man chuckled down the long-distance line. "It's where so much of it began, my dear. As you say, for want of a better place, why not start at the beginning? Seville is where the first of these so-called acts of faith of the Inquisition took place in a particularly grisly sacrifice. Six people were burned alive."

"That's barbaric." The history of the Inquisition was fascinating in and of itself, but she'd never considered it for the show. There were plenty of human monsters from that time, without the need to invent others for public edification. Using religion and ethnicity as a means of population control turned her stomach. It didn't matter if it was five hundred years ago in Spain, sixty years ago in Germany or twenty years ago in Rwanda. Genocide was one of the few horrors that didn't lessen with time.

"Yes, it was. Just as all forms of human sacrifice are," Roux agreed. There was a pause. He was obviously thinking. "I won't touch down for at least three hours, even if I get airborne in the next thirty minutes. I'll contact you as soon as I land. In the meantime, I'll make a call. Garin isn't the only one with a little black book. I know a guy…he might be able to pinpoint the IP address from the webcam. See if we can't find a source. You look at finding the mask, I'll try to find

Garin—hopefully, we'll meet somewhere in the middle. Twenty-four hours is a long time."

"In politics, maybe. In kidnap and ransom? I'm not so sure."

"Just concentrate on getting to Ávila. I'll give my guy your details and have him meet you there." Roux hung up without waiting for her response. There was no "good luck." He was all business, which was exactly what she needed from him right now. There wasn't a moment to lose. She pillaged the hotel room of anything useful, throwing a change of clothes into a backpack, then zipped herself into her motorbike leathers and headed down to the hotel's underground garage.

The Triumph Rocket III Roadster was where she'd left it.

It was a beast of a machine. She loved it. Annja slipped her bag from her shoulder and stowed it inside one of the panniers, then straddled the bike. It was bigger and heavier than she was used to, but the Roadster had so much pent-up power as she gunned the engine, she couldn't help but grin at the thrill when it roared to life beneath her. There were perks to being a celebrity of sorts: companies bent over backward in exchange for a little publicity. She was a great ad for the bike. As Doug said, there was something inherently powerful about a great bike and a leather-clad rider. He would have called it sexy. She liked to think of it as iconic. Giving the Roadster up when she left Spain was going to be tough. She intended to hit the open road and see as much of the countryside as she could before then.

The bike roared up the ramp and out of the garage, banking sharply as she took the turn into the street. She was strong, but still, the muscles in her shoulders and forearms tightened as she leaned to keep the bike upright. She opened up the throttle, slipping into the early-morning city traffic. In a car, the congestion would have been a problem, bumper-to-bumper impatient drivers trying to cut in and out of lanes. But even though the Roadster was designed for the open road, it was maneuverable enough to weave in and out of the snarl of vehicles.

She accelerated ahead of the traffic jam, hitting the lights just as they changed from red to green, and left the line of cars trailing in her wake. They couldn't match the bike's speed in these conditions.

A few minutes later, she was more than a mile outside of the city, but the road ahead was blocked by a pair of trucks struggling uphill side by side, slowly losing momentum as the incline increased, neither one prepared to slow down or change lanes in case they couldn't make it to the top of the hill. A snake of frustrated drivers had built up behind them.

Annja didn't have time to waste.

She leaned to the left, letting her weight steer the bike into the narrow space between the lanes, and raced toward the gap between the two trucks. Drivers vented their frustration at her gambit, but that voice and its damned "ticktock, ticktock" was all she could hear. Annja twisted the throttle hard. Her grip tightened as she leaned forward, and the rush of air battered her.

Still, she accelerated, surging past the barely moving cars. A chorus of horns bade her farewell as she disappeared between the trucks, her shoulder blades inches from the high-paneled sides of both. The huge vehicles drifted closer together as she sped between them.

She caught a glimpse of one of the drivers in his wing mirror. There was no mistaking the panic in his eyes. She grinned, but realized there was no way he'd be able to see the expression through her helmet's black visor, which, all things considered, was probably for the best. He veered away suddenly, widening the gap for Annja, who surged ahead of the trucks and into the freedom of the open road.

She hit a hundred and thirty-six miles an hour in a few seconds, topping out the engine. The landscape blurred in her peripheral vision. Annja kept her head down. Speed limits didn't matter. She'd take the ticket, if the cops could keep up with her. Ticktock. Ticktock. It was just her and the road, but she didn't have time to enjoy it. She only had eyes for the dashed line leading all the way to the horizon.

She could feel the heat of the engine through the leathers on the inside of her right leg by the time she pulled up outside the high stone walls of the Royal Monastery of Saint Thomas Aquinas in Ávila.

She'd ridden as if the devil was on her tail.

The journey hadn't even taken an hour.

She checked her phone. There was a message from Roux's hacker giving her the name of a café—Giorgio's—and instructions to meet her there in forty-five minutes.

The message was fifteen minutes old. That gave her half an hour to unlock the secrets of the Grand Inquisitor's shrine.

Ticktock.

3

Ávila, the City of Stones and Saints.

That was how the place was described in the tourist brochure Annja picked up from the dispenser just inside the monastery walls. Footsteps echoed deeper inside the medieval building. She thumbed through the leaflet. It was the standard tourist fodder, ready to guide her to all kinds of attractions inside the city. She was only interested in the monastery. She handed over five euros at the glass window and put the change in a tip jar for renovations. Annja couldn't tell whether the look the young museum worker gave her was admiring or disapproving, but the way his eyes lingered was most certainly lacking piety.

She gave him a smile that raised the color in his cheeks and followed the sign that led inside.

The monastery consisted of two floors built over three cloisters, and according to the floor plan, the initial building had begun in 1482 but only been completed in 1493. She skipped through much of what came next, looking for the name Tomás de Torquemada. It would be too much to expect any kind of reference to a mask in the literature, but she found plenty of the usual tourist facts broken down for easy consumption. A simple engraving showed him in profile, bearing the familiar tonsure of a Dominican friar. He looked…ordinary. It was hard to believe she was looking at the man behind one of the most ruthless religious purges of all time. There were a few cursory details about the Inquisition and the fact that Torquemada had lived out his final days here, being buried within the grounds of the monastery five years after its completion.

Two elderly washerwomen busied themselves with mops, sluicing them across the stone floor of the cloister of Silencio. They worked in silence and Annja had no intention of making them uncomfortable by asking questions. She walked quickly across the wet floor, shrugging in apology to the women. There was no sign of anyone remotely official, which would have made asking questions easier. She worked her way slowly around the room, looking for any kind of visual clue in the decor.

"It's quite plain compared to the Reyes cloister," a man said behind her. She hadn't heard his footsteps on the tiled floor.

Annja turned, expecting to come face-to-face with a monk. He wasn't. Or at least he wasn't dressed like one. He wore a lightweight charcoal suit with a matching shirt. "Sorry?"

"The Cloister of the King. You were looking at the ceiling?"

She glanced up at the vaulted Gothic-style ceiling above her, surprised that it hadn't been the first thing to catch her attention when she entered the cloister.

"There was a beautiful mosaic in the dome, the work of a Mudéjar—a Moor who remained in Spain after the country began to be reclaimed for Christians—but it's long gone now, I'm afraid. Lost to time and vandals. The Mudéjars kept their faith even though they couldn't make their devotions publicly. Such a sad time for our country. Our great shame. And yes, I say that with no hint of irony, given who is buried next door." He offered her a wry smile. "The word *Mudéjar* also refers to the style of architecture, but in this case the ceiling was the work of a single man, or so we have come to believe. Sadly, as I said, it has long since been lost. Of course, not all Moors remained faithful—many converted to Christianity. They were called Moriscos, but that was a title that came loaded with contempt and mistrust."

So many Moors and Jews had been driven out of the country or forced to renounce their own faith under fear of death, and yet others were allowed to continue with their lives. But why? The cynical side of Annja wanted to say money. So often it came down to money. People bought their freedom with it. Was that what had happened all those years ago? The Mudéjars had paid off the Inquisition?

"Might I ask, are you planning on making a program about us?"

"Sorry?" she said again, running about three steps behind the man as he moved from subject to subject.

"You are Annja Creed, aren't you? I may be speaking out of turn, but I rather hope you aren't planning on featuring Friar Torquemada in an episode of your *Chasing History's Monsters*. He was one, of course, but he was a very human one," he said, holding out a hand. "Francesco Maffrici. I am the curator here."

She smiled, shaking his hand. His palm was soft against hers. "No, no, this isn't exactly work, more a personal interest."

"Excellent, then anything I can do to help, I am at your service."

"Well, obviously, I am interested in Torquemada, but not for the show."

The man nodded, offering her a wry smile. "The man and the Inquisition. They provide our daily bread."

"I can well imagine. Actually, I'm interested particularly in the Mask of Torquemada. I understand that it was buried with him?" She offered it as a question rather than a statement, inviting him to correct her.

"That rather depends on which version of the legend you want to believe."

Annja was intrigued. Two legends meant a mystery. Not that she had time for one.

"It wasn't uncommon for a death mask to be made to capture the features of the recently deceased. Generally they would use wax and plaster. And perhaps that was so with Torquemada, but then you have to ask yourself—why would something like that be buried with him? That's not so much a legend as a rationalization. The second hypothesis suggests that a mask was cast in metal some time before his death so that others could act in his place while he was ill. It would have meant that anyone could have overseen the tortures of the Inquisition, making it clear that they were acting in his name. Of course, once he was dead there was no need for it. None of his successors found the need to follow his example. Perhaps they were not quite so driven to inspire fear or could more easily hide the delight they took in their work?"

"You think he enjoyed it?"

"Oh, absolutely. Without doubt. His interests lay far beyond driving non-Christians out of Spain. It might have begun that way, a means of driving Jews and Muslims out of our land, but it lit a fire in the dark places of his soul. In the earliest days of the Inquisition, the Moors and Jews were given the option to convert, which meant they were able to remain in the country as second-class citizens. Later, their conversion offered no protection. The Inquisition turned on them and on other minorities that were considered to be outside the teachings of the Bible."

"If only they'd been the last ones to take that approach," she said. She hadn't meant to say it aloud.

"We never learn the lessons of the past, despite the threat of being doomed to repeat it," he said. "But I suppose you know that as well as anyone."

They both fell silent for a moment as they considered the wider implications of what they'd been saying. It was a comfortable silence, interrupted only by the clatter of metal buckets and the spilling of water. The two women seemed to bicker rapidly, but the words quickly turned to laughter and they set about mopping up again.

"We should leave them to it," the curator said, turning his back on the women. "I have something interesting you might like to see."

Maffrici led the way out of the cloister toward the church that stood inside the monastery walls. He opened the door for her to follow. Annja noticed he was wearing white gloves, and assumed he was being careful not to leave greasy fingerprints on the relics here. It was a good precaution, with so many enzymes secreted by even carefully washed human skin. Years and years of handling would damage just about anything, and why risk making a further impact?

Annja was only half listening as Maffrici talked her through the architecture of the building. Garin was still sitting in that chair somewhere, battered and bloody and needing her help…help that, right now, she was in no position to give. She needed help of her own to find the mask before the seconds ran out.

That meant being direct, even if it felt rude. "Is there any more you can tell me about the mask?"

"Not really. I'm afraid that there are no pictures of it, not even a drawing from the time, as far as I am aware."

"But you are sure it was buried with his body?"

He nodded. "Assuming it actually existed, yes, but you know how it is—stories get passed down from generation to generation, records get lost. A lot of truth becomes legend, but much more legend becomes truth. What we believe has a tendency to change over the generations. There is almost always a kernel of truth at the core of any enduring story, but it is so much harder to identify it among the embellishments that come later."

Annja tried to read between the lines. "Are you suggesting Torquemada might have not been as bad as he's currently portrayed?"

"Quite the reverse, actually—that he was perhaps not as pious and devout as he is now remembered to be. For a man who was a scourge on nonbelievers and heretics, isn't it peculiar that he carried what he believed to be the horn of a unicorn for protection?"

"No more crazy than the zealots who think they're carrying a piece of the True Cross," she said.

"Ah, perhaps not, but does a man wielding supernatural protections—the objects of witchcraft—strike you as someone who believes absolutely in the protection of his God?" The curator came to a halt. "His tomb was broken into in the 1830s, his bones removed and burned here, on this spot, mimicking an auto-da-fé, the kind of act of faith Torquemada would have ordered during his lifetime. It was something in the nature of poetic justice. The Inquisition had fallen out of favor and the people were no longer afraid of the Church in the way they had been for hundreds of years. So much of the monastery was destroyed thanks to those revolutionary hammers. Which is of course how we lost that wonderful Mudéjar ceiling."

"And that was when the mask was removed?" Or more likely destroyed, she thought.

"There is no record of anything other than his remains having been removed from the tomb, but that was not the first time his rest had been disturbed."

"The tomb had been broken into before?"

"Indeed, yes. Only a couple of years after his death, in fact. Records indicate that a ring was taken from the remains. It was recovered and returned to the corpse. The thief was given the same treatment as many of Torquemada's own victims. Of course, that doesn't mean something else wasn't taken and never returned."

Annja was already running the permutations in her head. If the mask had remained in the tomb until the 1830s, then it had almost certainly been destroyed in the desecration or fallen into the possession of some rich private collector with a penchant for the macabre. The latter possibility would only make the treasure hunt more difficult. Theft a few years after the dead man's burial was preferable, since it meant there was much more time for the mask to have become lost and ultimately forgotten. But its chances of survival increased markedly if it had been stolen in the nineteenth century. The question was, where was it most likely to have gone next?

"There is a plaque," the curator said. "Let me show you."

The man led her through to what remained of Torquemada's tomb. It was little more than a symbolic plaque.

"'Here Lies the Reverend Tomás de Torquemada,

One of the Holy Cross, the Inquisitor General. This House's Founder. Died 1518, on 16 September,'" Annja translated from the Latin inscription.

"Very impressive," said the curator. "It's rare to find a—" he checked himself before saying *woman* "—person these days with a fair grasp of Latin."

"I'm all about the dead languages." She laughed, spotting another inscription on the wall. "They look great on the dating profiles." That confused the poor guy for a moment, reminding her that they were communicating in what was obviously his second or even third language.

She mouthed the next words without actually making a sound. *May This Plague of Heretics Pass.*

"I don't think he really wanted to be buried here. It was more of a political decision than anything else," Maffrici said. "He was born in Valladolid and never really severed ties with the city. He established a tribunal for the Inquisition there and remained connected to the Convent of San Francisco until his dying day. The strange thing is…" He broke off suddenly, as if not sure he should be speculating so freely in front of her. Annja waited patiently while he considered whatever it was he was about to say—or not say.

"What is it?" she asked eventually, breaking into his private world.

"There's a novel," he said. "*El hereje. The Heretic* by Miguel Delibes, one of our most celebrated novelists. Perhaps you've heard of it? The inscription there reminds me of it. The book is set in Valladolid and describes something called the path of the heretic, or the pass. But that is not what I just realized…what…stopped me. I haven't really thought about this before, but it has been staring me in the face for such a very long time." He rubbed his white-gloved hands together as though in appreciation or greed. "The ceiling, the one that's missing from the dome…that depicted Valladolid, too."

"So what you're saying is, in terms of Torquemada at least, all roads lead to Valladolid," she said, grinning. It was too much for this all to be coincidence. Of course, there was no guarantee that the mask had been taken there, but there was a strong connection between this place, the Grand Inquisitor and the city of Valladolid. She checked her watch. She could make the ride in an hour, ignoring speed limits, but first she had to meet Roux's hacker.

4

Annja had to ask for directions to Giorgio's. It wasn't on the main drag, but rather tucked away on a quaint side street that, as she walked down it, gave her the distinct impression of time travel. Each step seemed to take her back a decade until she was somewhere around the fifteenth or sixteenth century, surrounded by amazing buildings that had withstood the Inquisition and the civil war and the ravages of change. Giorgio's was one of those hip spots where the beautiful people went and made sure that everyone else knew just how hip it was.

Annja checked her reflection in the Roadster's side mirror, the bike helmet in her hand, long hair spilling over bike leathers. She grinned. She certainly didn't resemble some young, upwardly mobile stockbroker, or a woman in search of one.

She opened the door, and even before she'd taken her first step inside, she received a mixture of looks from the clientele that could have frozen a penguin on an ice floe. The women scowled in disapproval, sneering at the skintight leathers, while the men leaned forward, interested, engaged. She ignored both. She was used to being stared at. It was part of being a celebrity. Even if she wasn't a big star, there was always someone on the street who would do a double take, obviously thinking, Aren't you the woman from the TV show?

She scanned the room. There were at least a dozen guys sitting alone in different parts of the café. A few had shot a glance—or more than a glance—in her direction, but none of them had raised a hand in recognition. She didn't hold any of their gazes, and it didn't take long for most of them to look away, drawn back to their computer screens and cell phones. As she walked toward the counter at the far side of the café, she noticed that one man was still watching her. There was a paperback copy of Howard Fast's *Torquemada* next to his untouched cappuccino. That was enough to convince Annja he was her guy.

She walked to his table and sat down.

"Annja," the young man said. He didn't rise to shake her hand. And unlike the rest of the men in the vicinity, he didn't appear to be mentally stripping her leathers. "You made good time. I'm Oscar."

She sat down across from him. He was barely old enough to be out of university, but when it came to tech wizardry it was a case of "the younger, the better" these days. His tousled, sun-bleached hair was stylishly unkempt. He fit in here far more than she did. His olive skin was offset against a white cotton shirt. Not that she was one to judge a book by its cover, but this kid was the polar opposite of every computer nerd she'd ever met. She didn't know what to make of that, but Roux trusted him with Garin's life. She knew that much.

"So, the old man said you needed to trace the source of a video stream, right? Shouldn't be too difficult." He held his hand out across the table. For a weird second she thought he was asking her to dance, but then she realized he wanted her phone. She handed it over. "You go order a drink," he said. "I'll see what I can do."

She watched as he connected the phone to his laptop via USB cable. As soon as the jack went in, Oscar was lost in concentration. Stylish or not, he was definitely a tech nerd.

Annja ordered herself a latte from the barista. Drink in hand, she rejoined him at the table, but didn't say a word. The meeting wasn't about social niceties; it was about helping Garin, plain and simple. And in any case, the kid was absolutely oblivious to the rest of the world, his entire focus zoned down to the screen in front of him. The coffee was hot but good and went down creamy.

"Okay," Oscar said after a few seconds, though he wasn't talking to her. "Good. Yes. Okay…no. Not good." He looked up at her across the top of the laptop. "Whoever wrote this code knows their stuff. And they're determined to stay hidden. The signal is being bounced through half a dozen countries, via anonymous routers, and each connection in the chain is changing its IP addresses every minute or so. It's not impossible to trace, but it's not easy. For a start, it's going to take time to crack the algorithm they're using to cycle through IP addresses, so we can predict where they're going to switch to next and keep the line open long enough to trace it all the way back to source."

Annja had a decent idea what he was talking about, but there was a huge difference between a decent idea and the kind of understanding the hacker obviously had.

"But you *can* trace it?" she asked.

He nodded.

"Good. That's all I needed to hear."

His fingers moved quickly across the keyboard, picking out commands in rapid-fire succession, then pausing a beat as he waited for responses to come back to him.

Oscar swore under his breath, suddenly working faster.

"There's a worm embedded in the file," he said. "It's trying to take over my system. It's got the processor going crazy, and the core temp is rising. I think it's trying to blow my battery. Ingenious bastard. Well, at least this is going to be *fun* now."

He turned the machine slightly so Annja could see what was happening—not that she knew what she was looking at beyond a guy hammering out what seemed to be random letters on a keyboard.

"I'm just making sure I've got a backup of everything here. Assume the worst," he said, but even as he spoke, streams of numbers and letters filled the screen, superimposed with picture after picture. The deepening furrow in the hacker's brow worried her. So much for "shouldn't be too difficult."

He swore again and killed the Net connection, disabling the Wi-Fi. That didn't slow the virus now that it was in his hard drive, and it continued chewing up data and spitting it out again, faster and faster until trying to focus on it hurt Annja's eyes. The fan whined as the first faint whiff of smoke curled up from beneath the laptop.

Oscar acted quickly, closing the lid and flipping the machine over.

It took two hands to release the catch and pop the battery, but the second he did it heads turned, drawn by the stench of burning.

He dropped the battery, staring at the smoldering plastic housing as if his entire understanding of the world had just been betrayed.

"What the hell just happened?" Annja asked.

"Some serious piece of code. Some seriously serious piece of code. The virus overloaded the system resources, then created a surge back into the battery. That's not an easy thing."

"So we're up against someone who knows what they're doing—IP masking, making computers burn up…"

"Yep, we're not talking spotty teenagers in their bedroom, that's for sure."

"Is there anything you can do?"

He looked at the sorry state of the battery. "This thing's fried, but there's always something that can be done if you're resourceful enough," he said, fishing inside his laptop bag for a small device that he connected to her phone. "I'm going to make an image of your phone—basically clone it—and see if I can trick the code into thinking it's your phone that's trying to access the file, not my laptop. It could take me a while, but sooner or later I'll crack it."

"Unfortunately, time's the one thing I don't have."

"This is personal now. Trust me. I'll get you what you need. There's something I can tell you right now, though."

"What's that?"

"You were watching a recording. It wasn't a video chat."

5

Plaza Mayor was already a hive of early-morning activity, bustling with tourists and locals when Annja reached Valladolid.

Even with the steady hubbub, the huge plaza still felt like a wide-open space in the claustrophobic Old Town. The city wasn't what she'd been hoping to find, even if she wasn't entirely sure what that had been. The buildings might not have been as thoroughly modern as many of the cities she'd visited around the world—all glass, concrete and steel—but everything here was still far too new to be hiding any ancient secrets. Almost all of the buildings appeared to have been built in the past hundred and fifty years. There was absolutely nothing amid all of the banks, gift shops, cafés and restaurants that could have been standing even two hundred years after Torquemada's death, never mind the early days of the Inquisition.

Annja slammed down the kickstand and parked the bike up. She walked around the outskirts of the plaza, taking a closer look at each building, but no matter how desperately she willed it, she found nothing of interest. Feeling her mood darkening, she realized she hadn't eaten all day. She didn't want to stop the search, not when time was so short, but she wasn't going to be any use to Garin if she starved herself, so she went inside the nearest café and ordered a coffee and a Caesar salad. It would be enough to keep her going.

There were a dozen metal tables and chairs outside the café, so she picked one and, like a tourist, stretched out her legs to ease the cramped muscles and soak up the sun while she waited for her meal. On any other day, she could have happily wasted a couple of hours just drinking in the ambience, but today wasn't a day like any other. Today she had a job to do. She pulled out her phone and called Roux. She knew he'd be in the air. All she wanted to do was leave a voice mail he could check as he landed. Her message was to the point. "I'm in Valladolid. Following leads I picked up at Ávila. Everything points to this place being central to Torquemada's tale. I'm not sure what I'm looking for. I'm just hoping I'll recognize it when I see it." She killed the call.

A flyer on the table caught her eye. She picked it up. The flyer showed the same image as the billboard outside a theater on the opposite side of the square—a woman dressed in nothing but black underwear, smoking a cigarette from a long holder, obviously advertising some kind of burlesque show. It seemed out of place among the restrained buildings. It took Annja a moment to realize that the woman was actually a man. That brought a smile to her lips; clearly things weren't always what they seemed to be. There was a good lesson there. First impressions could be deceptive. She flipped the leaflet over and read the small blurb that explained the show was taking place at the Teatro Zorrilla.

"It's very good, even if you can't speak Spanish." Annja looked up to see a waitress clearing plates from one of the neighboring tables. She was surprised that the waitress spoke to her in English until she realized she must have overheard at least part of the message she left for Roux.

"I'm afraid I'm not going to be around long enough to take in a show."

"Ah, that's a shame."

The girl smiled and started back toward the door, balancing a tray of dirty cups.

"I know this might seem like a stupid question," Annja said. "But I don't suppose you know where the Convent of San Francisco used to be?"

The girl shrugged. "Sorry. Was it around here?"

"I was really hoping so, but I can't see anything to even suggest where it might have been."

"Well, it depends how old it is. Most of the buildings around the plaza were built in the 1800s, I think, and some of it is more modern than that. A lot of the old buildings that were here before that were demolished to make way for the new. There's some kind of plaque on the theater—one of those historic-landmark things—but I can't remember what it says. Sorry."

"That's okay. Thanks, anyway," Annja said. "I'll go take a look."

The theater was closed, its front doors locked and everything inside dark. Even the box office. The plaque was on the wall beside the main door. It detailed how the Zorrilla had been built on the original site of the Convent of San Francisco.

A dead end, Annja thought miserably, realizing how much time she'd wasted only to reach a standstill.

She was already three hours down and all she had to show for it was a burlesque theater built on the site of an old convent. That wasn't going to help Garin.

Or was it?

That very much depended upon what had happened to the convent and whether the theater had been constructed in its place or on top of its partial remains. She'd seen enough buildings that had been built directly on top of previous ones to know that there was a chance the foundations and any lower levels might— just might—have survived beneath the new one. There was an entire city beneath Chicago, for instance, not that you could access it. Annja had no guarantee that there was anything of the convent left, not even a few broken stones. There was a chance, though, and in the absence of any other leads, she was going to take it and hope the old builders had simply chosen to bury the convent, or the cellars and mausoleum level at least, rather than waste time and resources demolishing it. Hell, it was even possible the lower levels had been used in the construction of the theater's foundations, but she doubted she'd be that lucky. Given the way her day had been going thus far, the place had probably burned to the ground.

Hammering on the front door brought no response.

She headed around the side of the building in search of the stage door, hoping there'd be someone inside the building who'd let her in, assuming she could make herself understood—though how convincing her Spanish would be was anyone's guess.

Unsurprisingly, though, the side door was locked, as were some larger doors at the rear where stage equipment was likely delivered.

Having exhausted her options at ground level, Annja looked up. There was a small window ajar more than twenty feet above her, so she couldn't simply make a jump for it, but there was an inviting drainpipe that would take her up to a ledge from which she could probably reach it. The drainpipe flaked paint and rust when she tested it, but she thought it might just hold her weight. She glanced back down the alleyway and into the plaza to be sure no one was watching her, then she shimmied up the pipe. A small boy turned in her direction, an ice cream in one hand, his mother holding the other one. He gave her a white-smeared smile and then disappeared, dragged out of sight by Mom.

Annja hauled herself up, finding her first foothold in the grouting as she scrambled upward. Less than thirty seconds later, she was inching along the ledge. She pressed up against the glass and reached inside to open the window wide enough to flop inside.

She found herself in a janitor's cupboard, full to over-flowing with the clutter of cleaning supplies—buckets, brushes and disinfectants all promising the reek of summer forests and autumn meadows, and enough toilet rolls to keep a small army clean and fresh. Annja managed to negotiate the obstacle course without sending the precarious piles of chemicals and cleaning fluids sprawling. The door opened—mercifully, it wasn't locked—to reveal a heavily carpeted hallway. The carpet was one of those old red faux-Chinese patterns that cinemas and theaters around the world loved so much in the seventies. She wasn't going to find anything ancient on this floor, so her first job was to locate the stairs. She followed a sign for the emergency exit, figuring it would offer the most direct route down. The stairwell was undecorated, showing the weeping brickwork of the old theater. It opened up onto the front of the auditorium, stage left.

The auditorium was in near-absolute darkness; only a strip of low-level security lights was on, giving enough of a glow for Annja to approach the stage without falling over.

She was certain there would be a space beneath the stage, and with luck, that would lead into the bowels of the theater, where she'd find the remains of the previous building…if they even existed. The curtain was down, so thick it gave no hint of the burlesque backdrop it hid.

A door with a glowing sign displaying the word *Salida* took her in the right direction.

Another door led her to the backstage area, where

a flight of wooden stairs led down into the darkness below.

No one challenged her as she moved through the old theater.

She'd been reluctant to turn on additional lights in case they alerted anyone connected to the theater, inside or out, but once she started descending she had no such reservations about turning on the first light she found.

Annja detected the faintest odor of damp as she reached the bottom of the staircase.

The glow of the strip lighting failed to illuminate much beyond the stairs, but she saw a flashlight standing upright on a small desk close by. It didn't take long to sweep the entire area with the beam. She made her way back among the scenery boards, playing the flashlight beam between them, searching for a sign, anything, that hinted at another way down, deeper. Cobwebs clawed at her face as she made her way into the gloom. Annja peered behind stacked boards, moving them so she could see behind them properly.

The shadows gathered around her feet masked the step. Her heel caught, but she stopped herself before she went sprawling to the ground. She took more care as she moved on. There was another step only a few feet away. And another beyond that, turning slightly. She followed the spiraling steps, descending into a space below the theater's storeroom.

Her heart raced as she realized this space was *much* older than the Zorrilla itself—which had to be a good thing. Surely that meant the theater had been built on top of the old convent, didn't it? The room before her extended far beyond the walls of the theater. Annja tried to orient herself with the world above. As best she could tell, the vast chamber seemed to lead away from the plaza, running beneath other buildings that now occupied the land where the convent had once stood. Meaning she was standing in whatever remained of the ancient building.

Playing the light around the room, she spotted a passage. It was the only one. She followed it, but before she had moved too far along it, her way was blocked by a stone wall with a stout iron-banded wooden door set into it. A heavy iron ring hung as a handle.

She pushed against the door. It didn't give.

Locked, or bolted from the other side? She put her shoulder against it and pushed again, harder this time. The door gave a little, the creak echoing through the low-ceilinged passage to the cavernous room behind her.

Annja held her breath, sure the noise would summon someone, and counted to ten before she pushed again. No one came. She put all of her strength behind the next push. This time the rotten wood splintered and the rusted metal snapped, the entire frame giving way under the force. The door scraped open into the room beyond, releasing a rush of air that hadn't been breathed for probably two hundred years or more.

Annja paused on the threshold, shining the flashlight inside.

The beam illuminated dust-and-cobweb-covered shapes that made no sense at first.

Then Annja realized she was looking at bones covering every inch of wall from floor to ceiling. On and on, as far as the light shone, bones. Annja had visited the catacombs beneath Rome and other ossuaries in and around Vienna and Prague, but they never ceased to take her breath away.

She paused while the dust of centuries—which she'd shaken up simply by breaking the seal of the door—settled again before she entered. It was an unconscious act of reverence. She lived for places like this and had no desire to disturb the dead if she could help it.

She took a deep breath before she entered the chamber of bones.

The long, narrow passage stretched deep inside this new—or rather, much older—section of building, reaching at least thirty feet ahead of her before another corridor crossed it. The walls of this second corridor were shored up with bones, as well. It was as if the entire catacombs had been constructed from bones, but of course there must have been stones somewhere beneath the skeletal remains, now yellowed and calcified with age.

Annja's footsteps echoed back to her as she advanced slowly through the passageway. She kept one hand held out in front of her face, brushing away the strands of cobweb before they smothered her face. So many bones, so many bodies piled atop one another, all of them becoming one in death, abandoned and long forgotten.

She was sure no one even knew that they were still down there.

The tunnel stretched far beyond the flashlight's beam. She continued on, one step at a time, checking every inch of the damned place for a clue, for something that would link to the mask and give her a chance to save Garin. That was all she wanted. She'd already done the impossible and found the Convent of San Francisco, a building that hadn't existed for the best part of two hundred years, but that wasn't enough. She needed to find the mask. And if not the mask itself, something that would lead her to it. She was wasting her time. There was nothing here.

She walked on, her boots grinding dust and grit into the stone floor with each step.

She passed another intersection and another and she began to grasp the sheer scale of what lay down here.

She was tempted to try one of the many passages branching off the main corridor, but knew that if she ventured off the central path, she risked walking into a labyrinth of bone and becoming disoriented. So she continued going forward, trying not to think about how many thousands of people must have died to make these walls.

A few minutes later, Annja was grateful she hadn't deviated from the main passageway.

Bones gave way to rows of stone coffins set in alcoves in the walls.

Coffins meant a more important kind of dead. She walked down the line, fingers lingering on the crosses and tracing the inscriptions that told the briefest stories of the lives they contained. The coffins held the remains of women who had held office within the convent. But the farther along the line she went, the more male names she encountered, until she realized she was standing before the tombs of men who had served the Inquisition.

One coffin stood out because it didn't bear the cross or any Christian blessing meant to serve the deceased in the next life.

It bore only a single word: *Morisco.*

That was the word the curator had used at the monastery in Ávila, the term for the Moors who'd converted to Christianity rather than fleeing the country from the Inquisition.

But why would a Muslim, even one who'd changed his religion—in public at least—be buried in such an obviously Christian place? The curator had said the word was an insult, hadn't he? She lingered in front of the stone sarcophagus. There was definitely something wrong about its presence here, amid the tombs of the Inquisitors and the sisters of the convent. It fairly screamed at her.

Annja wasn't going to learn its secrets just by staring at it, though. She needed to look inside. She placed the flashlight on top of the stone lid, then took a deep breath before pushing hard. She was rewarded with the sound of stone grinding on stone until it had opened a crack.

She picked up the flashlight once more and shone it into the coffin.

She could never have imagined what its beam revealed.

6

Roux stepped onto the tarmac and into the sudden heat. It was fierce enough to drive the breath from his lungs after the unnatural cool of the air-conditioned private jet. He was glad to have something solid beneath his feet even though the flight had been relatively short. It certainly hadn't been smooth. Long ago, he'd realized that as luxurious as the Gulfstream was, it was still just a tin can hurtling through the sky. It didn't matter whether he owned it or an airline did, the plane was still going to get battered around by the elements on any given flight.

The old man was a frequent flier.

Although he kept an overnight bag on board, packed with the essentials of modern living, he left it behind. Sleep wasn't on the schedule. Walking across the landing strip, he listened to Annja's message. He returned her call, but it went straight to voice mail.

"It's Roux," he said. "I'm in Seville. I'll give you a call when I have news. Check in when you can."

He slipped the phone back into his pocket and pulled out his passport, ready to present it to the immigration officer. There would be no complications; there never were when you paid the kind of money he had to arrange this short-haul flight. A car would be waiting for him when he stepped out of the terminal. Money made the world go round.

He wasn't disappointed. Less than ten minutes after the cabin door had depressurized, Roux was sitting comfortably in the back of a chauffeur-driven black Mercedes Benz. He could have rented a car and driven himself, but it was just easier to take the driver.

"Where to, sir?" the driver asked in flawless English. The company Roux had contracted had offered a selection of drivers able to speak a wide range of languages, anything to suit his needs. He learned forward, checking the man's name against his license. Mateo.

"First stop, the remains of the Castillo de San Jorge, Mateo, there's a good man," Roux said, assuming that the driver knew where it was.

"Of course, sir. Is your interest in the Inquisition?" The driver had struck on the connection straightaway, but then no doubt everyone who visited the place had that particular interest.

"One of many," he said. "Do you know it well?"

"I worked there as a tour guide during my studies. Unsurprisingly, people only ever wanted to hear the goriest details of tortures."

Roux smiled. "Human nature, my friend. And, you must admit, there's plenty to keep them entertained."

"Oh, yes, but it was always more fun to make up something particularly awful, just to watch them squirm." He laughed.

Roux liked the man. Sometimes there was too much truth in the world. A guide having a little bit of fun at the expense of a few tourists wasn't that big a crime... all things considered.

"You're more than welcome to come inside and revive your fledgling career as a tour guide," he offered.

"It's your dime, boss," the man said. "Doesn't matter to me if I'm kicking back in the car waiting for you to come back, or if I'm giving you the grand tour of the ruins. Costs the same for you. But are you sure you want me making stuff up?" He grinned in the rearview mirror as he pulled into traffic.

The journey was short, the private landing strip only a few minutes outside of town. The driver didn't take any risks, waiting patiently for the lights to change before indicating and turning right, going against the flow. The entrance to what remained of the Castillo de San Jorge lay next to the market in the center of Seville, though the remains themselves were buried beneath the "new" market, close to the river Guadalquivir. *New* was a relative term. There'd been a market on the spot for over a century. Roux could remember what it had been like before. Sometimes his longevity weighed heavily on him. He could look at the ever-changing world and realize just how little of it was actually permanent, and no matter how much it changed, none of those changes lasted all that long.

It was going to be damp in the ruins, moist and clammy, especially where they butted up against the riverbed. There was no guarantee he'd even be able to get that far. He couldn't remember what the Castillo de San Jorge had been like in the late 1800s when he'd last been there. There certainly hadn't been a visitors' center, though, or tour guides to answer his questions.

Mateo dropped him at the entrance, then went to park the car.

By the time he returned, Roux had worked his way through the selection of brochures without finding what he needed.

The driver slipped his phone back into his jacket pocket as he approached. Roux nodded, assuming the man had taken a few minutes to chat with his employers or the significant other in his life. In the past fifty years or so, the world had changed so much he didn't even automatically think "*woman* in his life" when he looked at a handsome guy like the driver.

"Everything okay, boss?" Mateo asked. "You look… troubled."

"I'm reading about how the trials actually took place in the Town Hall."

"The Ayuntamiento? That's right. But this is where the first auto-da-fé took place, making it very much the birthplace of the Inquisition. The first executions happened in Seville. Those poor souls who fell foul of the Inquisition were burned alive on a platform designed just for the purpose."

Roux sighed deeply. "There's no end to the ingenuity of men who want to make others suffer."

"Spoken like a man who knows his stuff," Mateo said. "Do you want to know what the real irony is?"

"Go on, amaze me," said Roux, expecting to hear one of those little lies the driver had used to spice up his guided tours.

"The guy who designed the burning tables they called the *quemadero* was a Jew. He became a victim of the Inquisition himself."

"So his ingenuity bought him no favors with the men in power."

"None."

It was no different from Joan of Arc's France, Roux knew. There, the executioner might have had mercy on the "witch" and snapped her neck before she burned. It was barbaric and brutal, and the horrors he'd seen over the centuries still lived on inside his head.

They moved through the room, toward a display that showed a reproduction of a painting by Goya along with sketches of suspects wearing pointed hats and tabards bearing a cross that marked them as being under investigation by the Inquisition. Roux had seen the original many times, and not only on the walls of the Royal Academy of Fine Arts of San Fernando in Madrid, where it hung. He had spent almost a year in the artist's company after he fled to Paris. The last time they talked had been only days before Goya suffered his fatal stroke. It brought back so many memories, some of which he would much rather forget.

"You think it was really like that?" Mateo asked.

"Not at the beginning," Roux said. "But by the end, certainly." He spoke with more certainty than the driver could have expected. But then, the man could never have guessed the old man he was talking to had witnessed many of the Inquisition's horrors firsthand.

"There are some more of his drawings here in Seville," Mateo said. "Some of them are studies that may have led to this painting."

"Are there?" Roux had thought the artist had destroyed everything related to his dark pieces. This was news to him. But did it matter? Was this the important thing he'd been hoping to find? A few sketches by a lost friend?

"They are in the Museum of Fine Arts. Fifteen minutes' walk from here, not even half that in the car."

"Then what are we waiting for?"

"They aren't on display—they're only brought out for special exhibitions."

"There are always ways and means," Roux said.

He suddenly had a hunch and was curious to see what of his old friend's art had survived. He remembered Goya's fascination with the darkest days of his country. The man was a scholar with a passion for learning and a habit of hiding those things he had discovered in his art—especially in the sketches that formed the foundations of the finished paintings. There was no telling what he might have hidden on those charcoals. Roux hadn't planned on this detour, but the few minutes it would add to the search could prove invaluable in the long run.

Roux didn't waste his time calling some petty bureaucrat in the museum. He cut to the chase, speed-dialing one of the movers and shakers in the country. The woman was on the board of a number of museums and art galleries and could pull strings quickly. She was also an ex-lover, which made the first sixty seconds or so of the conversation a little awkward. It had been more than thirty years since they'd spoken, and although she sounded much the same, she couldn't be the young woman she had been, even if he was exactly the same man he was that last time he'd lain down beside her. The phone line was like the dark, though. It hid the truth of the years between them.

She promised the pictures would be waiting for him when he arrived. He promised to come visit her soon. One of them was lying and they both knew it.

The traffic made the journey slower than Mateo had suggested, but only by a few minutes, and it gave the curator time to set up a private room with the sketches displayed for Roux's viewing. The curator, a short, balding man, met them at the door as they arrived, a hand held out in welcome as if they were old friends.

"Welcome," he said, ushering Roux inside. "I was given to understand you only have a limited amount of time, and with the very short notice, well, the space we've been able to make available for viewing…isn't optimal. The lighting, et cetera… I hope you understand."

"Of course," Roux said, waving away the apolo-

gies. "I'm sorry it was such short notice and appreciate your efforts to accommodate a demanding old man."
He smiled wryly.

"Please, please," the little man said, "let's just forgive each other, then. This way, *gentlemen*." He offered
a mildly disapproving glance in Mateo's direction as the
driver climbed out of the car to follow them.

"It might be better if you wait with the car, Mateo,"
Roux said, deciding he'd rather not have a witness.
There was a chance money might well need to change
hands, if the curator was holding out on anything, and
a man was always more susceptible to a bribe if he
wasn't being watched.

Once they were inside the room it was clear why the
curator had been reluctant to have the extra body inside. The private viewing room was barely larger than a
broom cupboard—a particularly small one, at that—and
was obviously set up for restoration work rather than
viewing. A woman Goya would have dearly loved to
have painted waited for them inside the room.

"Our collection of Goya drawings is really quite remarkable, the pride of our humble little museum," the
woman said. "We were incredibly fortunate to have
these willed to us in a patron's estate many years ago.
They are by far the most precious treasure we have in
our care." She waved an open hand toward a folio on a
workbench that had been cleared. "Please." She slipped
on a pair of cotton gloves before she opened it. "Just let
me know when you are ready, and I'll turn them over."

Roux was momentarily disappointed he wasn't going

to be able to touch the drawings himself, but then they were the property of the nation, and she had no idea Roux's own face could be hidden away inside one of them, just another one of the artist's little jokes.

She opened the folder to reveal the first of the pictures.

It was a study of a man's face beneath a pointed hat.

The second was the face of a monk.

The third was of a row of officials sitting in judgment.

None of them were significantly different from the final pictures he'd seen in Milan.

But as the woman revealed the fourth picture, Roux's breath caught.

The sketch was of a mask, or rather, a face wearing a mask.

This was what he'd been hoping against hope to find. He'd half expected it not to be here. His friend had been obsessed with the Inquisition, and it was no surprise that Tomás de Torquemada figured into this. Still, he hadn't dared to hope Goya had known anything about a mask because there was no way for him to reach across the years and ask him. Francisco Goya, though, had reached across the years to talk to Roux the only way he knew how—through his art.

"What can you tell me about this?" Roux asked, trying not to make the inquiry sound as urgent as it felt. He wanted to hear it from their lips, but it was hard not to jump to conclusions. It had to be the Mask of Torquemada.

"Ah, this one. Quite…haunting, isn't it? Certainly one of his darker studies. There is, of course, the possibility this study has nothing to do with his Inquisition sketches," the curator began, but the woman cut him off.

"There were stories, none of them written down at the time, sadly—at least none that have been recovered—and many of them conflict, but it is believed that the Grand Inquisitor, Torquemada himself, wore a mask when he witnessed interrogations." The woman pursed her lips, clearly not comfortable bringing anything as sordid as torture into the conversation. The art was all that mattered to her. "There is one school of thought that believes he wore it chiefly to terrify, but there is another that believes it was to hide his own fear."

"From what I know of the man, that doesn't seem likely," Roux said. The many religious zealots he'd encountered in his life had all relished their work. It was the one thing they all had in common.

"As I was saying," she continued as if he hadn't spoken. "There is an alternative theory, that the mask was actually a torture device itself."

"Interesting."

"Indeed. It may even have been the inspiration for Alexander Dumas's *The Man in the Iron Mask.*"

"Or Dumas's mask might have helped create some of the myth around Torquemada himself," the curator suggested.

It was possible, of course. And from what Roux remembered about Goya in his final years, it was likely the artist would have made that kind of connection, too.

In 1847, Dumas had popularized the story of Eustache Dauger, held in jail in 1669. Roux had never particularly liked the man. Dauger was a poseur, but then, by the time they had rubbed shoulders in the royal court of Versailles, Roux was long past the part of his life where he'd craved any sort of notoriety. He was a creature of shadows by then, moving silently, obsessed with the search for the lost fragments of Joan of Arc's shattered blade.

"When do you think these were drawn?" he asked.

"Goya started work on *The Inquisition Tribunal* in 1812, so these sketches must date from earlier than that."

More than a decade before he'd first met the man. "The mask did not make it into that painting," Roux noted.

"Which is not particularly unusual for an artist like Goya. He made hundreds of preliminary sketches, working on countless details that didn't make it into the final works for whatever reason."

What she said was quite true, but there was something about the drawing that made Roux think the artist had other reasons for not including it in the final painting. Certainly this wasn't something conjured from his imagination. Goya was quite grounded in his studies of the Inquisition pieces. He wasn't given to flights of fancy. No, the old man couldn't shake off the feeling that Goya had drawn this from life, right down to the ribbon that tied the mask in place.

"Is there any way I could have a copy of this?"

"I'm sorry, that's quite out of the question," the

woman said, but this time it was the curator's turn to step in, not wanting their unhelpfulness to get back to the board member who'd facilitated Roux's visit. She was that powerful in this world.

"I'm sure there's some way we can accommodate you, sir."

The woman gritted her teeth, determined to put herself in between the man and her treasure. "These cannot just be placed in the photocopier, you know."

Roux had no idea if that was what the curator had in mind, but he had a simple enough solution and one that would be far more efficient, while leaving the drawings untouched. He fished his phone out of his pocket and held it up like a flag of truce. They both looked at him as if they couldn't quite comprehend what he was thinking. He spelled it out for them.

"If I could just take a photograph? That would be quite incredible. I would be forever in your debt."

"Of course," the curator said, fussing around to make sure that Roux had enough room.

Roux glanced at the woman. While she didn't seem enamored by his request, she didn't object.

He captured a single image of the sketch. There was nothing else he was likely to learn here, so he gave his thanks and made his farewells, promising to put in a good word with his friend when he saw her next.

The curator couldn't hide his pride. "Our pleasure."

The woman forced a smile. She clutched the portfolio close to her breast. It would be hidden away again, lost to the world until the next exhibition. There was something sad about that, but it was equally wonderful that new generations would discover these treasures and keep on discovering them as long as there was someone like her to cherish them. He smiled his thanks and followed the curator back out through the warren of corridors to the main glass doors.

Stepping outside, Roux had to look up and down the street several times before he spotted the car, and Mateo standing beside it. The driver waved and slid back behind the wheel, driving up to him. As he got in and closed the door, Roux heard the sound of an engine starting up close by.

"Did you find what you were looking for?"

"I think perhaps I did," Roux said, studying the picture on the phone's screen.

He forwarded the photograph to Annja, then tried to call her, but it went straight to voice mail again. He hung up without leaving a message. Roux put the phone back into his pocket. He glanced through the rear window, taking one last look at the museum. All this time, it had held a secret without even knowing it. Annja would appreciate that.

Roux was still looking out the rear window as the car took a slow right turn. The driver in the car behind them was staring back at him far too intensely for comfort.

This wasn't the old man's first time at the rodeo.

He was being followed.

7

Annja had expected bones. Bones or dust. Or fragments of one and a gathering of the other. A few rags, perhaps, untouched for generations.

Deep down, there'd been a tiny part of her that had hoped it'd be easy, that she'd push back the lid and see a silver mask lying on some moldering cushion, just waiting to be found. That would have been all of her lottery-ticket, late-running-for-a-train and traffic-lights-in-her-favor luck for the rest of her life all rolled into one.

But it wasn't to be.

She wasn't that lucky.

Which was bad news for Garin.

The flashlight beam played across the only thing the stone casket contained: a key. A small brass key with worn teeth.

Annja reached inside for it.

She assumed the metal would feel rough, pitted with corrosion given its obvious age, but it was surprisingly smooth. There was the obvious coarseness associated with something made so long ago, but it had weathered the passage of time relatively unharmed, no doubt because of the near-vacuum seal the sarcophagus lid provided. It had been hidden for a reason. More than that, it had been hidden *here* for a reason. Why, though, had it been placed in an empty coffin marked for a Moor and surrounded by tombs of the Inquisition's most faithful? That only opened a nest of questions, the most immediate being: What did it unlock?

She heard a sound originating from the direction she'd come. The unexpectedness of it caused her heart to skip a beat.

Someone was heading her way.

Had she been followed down here?

She could make herself known, avoiding an unpleasant confrontation—but that would mean having to explain herself, and it wasn't as though she had a right to be down here. It would eat up valuable time she couldn't spare. Or, to be blunt, time Garin couldn't spare.

She turned off the flashlight and did her best to slide the lid of the sarcophagus back into place without making enough noise to wake the rest of the dead down here. Even so, the grating of stone-on-stone echoed through the chamber.

A voice cried out.

She didn't like the sound of it.

Annja crept deeper into the catacombs, not wanting to be discovered by whoever was down there with her. She could only hope she'd be able to find another way out of this charnel house, but the odds weren't in her favor.

She edged forward in the dark, trying not to make a sound.

She was lucky the avenue was straight and that the person moving toward her was carrying a hooded lantern, which spread its glow across the floor without lighting the entire tunnel. She was going to have to get out of there, though. There was no way her luck was going to hold. Annja crept along the passageway, trying to time her footsteps to those of the newcomer. It wasn't easy, but thankfully, the other person wasn't trying to be quiet.

Annja almost missed the narrow flight of stairs—old stone steps with well-worn edges leading upward.

She held her breath as the lantern swung in the darkness.

A muffled voice called out, too indistinct for her to make out any words.

She stopped moving.

She could wait and hope the newcomer missed her, or trust to whatever god looked after reckless explorers in ancient crypts, and take the stairs, praying they'd lead her out of there and not into trouble. Fortune favors the brave, she thought. She took the first few stairs as fast as she could, making sure that she got her body out of the line of sight in case the hooded lantern's light got too close too quickly. When she was high enough up the staircase, Annja turned on the flashlight. The time for stealth was over. She broke into a run, her boots clattering on the stone.

"*¿Quién es?*" the newcomer shouted from below. Annja took no notice. She needed to get out, fast, and hang on to the key. That was the most important thing right now. That key opened something, somewhere. A Moorish tomb in a Christian burial ground—that had to mean something. She wasn't far enough down the path to know what, yet, but she would. Did it have anything to do with the mask she was looking for? Impossible to say. She couldn't worry about that now. All she could do was run. And she did, clutching the flashlight in one hand, the key in the other. She wasn't about to risk it falling out of her pocket.

An icy thrill of fear coursed through Annja when she saw the heavy wooden door blocking her way at the top of the stairs. She hit it hard, expecting it to bounce her back, but it swung open easily. Without hesitating, she stepped through and slammed it closed behind her. There was a key in the lock. She turned it, locking it on the person in the crypt.

It took a moment for Annja to realize where she was. She hadn't emerged in the Zorrilla Theater, but, perhaps unsurprisingly, in a church.

Her phone rang almost as soon as she took her first steps down the aisle toward the door that would take her outside. The only worshipper, a woman kneeling at the altar, turned and offered her a withering glance. Annja was getting a lot of those these days. She hurried down the aisle and out into the fresh air before she checked her phone.

Number withheld.

"Hello," she said.

"Well, well, well… Am I to take it you have found religion?" the voice in her ear mocked.

It took her a moment to realize she was speaking to Garin's kidnapper, the voice from the video feed. The fact that he knew where she was located was unnerving, to say the least. Were they watching her? Using satellites to track her like Garin had in the past? GPS on her phone? She glanced back inside the cool confines of the church. The woman had returned to her devotions and had absolutely no interest in Annja. There was a priest in the chancel now, lighting candles. Assuming it hadn't been the priest himself, there was no sign of the person she'd heard in the catacombs.

"It's rather a plain church, don't you think?"

She glanced around, looking for someone who stood out, someone who was obviously watching her, who had a phone to his ear. The street was quiet. She couldn't see anyone. But they knew where she was.

"Is this a social call?" she asked, still looking up and down the street.

"No. Definitely not. I like to think of it as incentivizing." He laughed. It wasn't a maniacal sound, not the *mwahahaha* of a cartoon villain. It was filled with genuine mirth. In the background, she heard a cry of pain. Garin. Why were they doing this to him? Why torture him? If he knew where the mask was, he would have told them. He wasn't a hero. There was only one thing Garin Braden valued above and beyond the possession of beautiful things, and that was self-preservation. He would have given them what they wanted if he thought it would buy his freedom. Once he knew he was safe, then he'd figure out how to get it back. That was the kind of man he was.

"There's someone here who wants to talk to you," the voice said.

There was a pause. A second. Two. It felt like forever.

A weak and mumbling voice spoke. "Don't do it… don't give them what they want. Even if you find it…" It was Garin. The phone was snatched away before he could finish speaking. The next thing she heard was a grunt and the sound of flesh slapping flesh.

"Garin!" Annja called, unable to stop herself.

"You've wasted four hours, Miss Creed. Ticktock. Ticktock. Don't waste any more." The kidnapper killed the connection.

Annja looked around again, phone still pressed to her ear.

She tried to think. Yes, they knew where she was, but she couldn't see anyone watching her. There was no obvious tail. Her first thought when the phone rang had been that they were close, maybe even behind the light in the catacombs, but there was no proof, only paranoia. Her phone hadn't worked down there, which meant the kidnapper's couldn't, either. It was much more likely they were using the same kind of technology that Garin would have. They had her phone number. Maybe they had a way of monitoring her SIM? She thought about pulling the battery out of the phone, but she needed to stay in contract with the old man.

She called Roux.

He answered on the third ring. "I've been trying to reach you."

"I went on a little trip. Underground."

"Find anything?"

"Maybe. The old Convent of San Francisco is gone, but the builders got lazy. They just leveled the land out and built over the old foundations. I found a way down into the catacombs. In among all of the tombs of the sisters and the good Christian servants of the Inquisition, I found a single sarcophagus that was out of place. It was marked Morisco."

"Interesting. A Moorish grave hidden in the heart of a Christian shrine."

"Exactly."

"I'm assuming you opened it?"

"I did."

"And?"

"No bones. No body."

"It was empty?"

"I didn't say that. There was a key inside."

"A key? That seems like a lot of trouble to hide a key, don't you think?"

"I do. Which makes it important. I don't know what it opens or why it was hidden, or even who did the hiding, but I'll work it out. That's what I do. How about you?"

"If you check your texts you'll find a picture of a preliminary sketch by Goya. Like your key, it has been hidden away, this time in the archives of a gallery here. It's a drawing of a mask. I'm sure it's the one we're looking for. I'm also sure it was drawn from life."

"Which would be proof that the mask exists."

"Or at least existed," he agreed.

"Well, it's a start."

"Indeed it is. The other thing that makes me think I'm on to something here is the fact that I'm being followed."

Annja felt the fine hairs on the nape of her neck prickle.

It was one thing for the kidnappers to know where she was and what she was doing, but they were keeping tabs on Roux, too? That meant they knew about them, how they worked. Knowing their enemy, knowing how they'd act and react, gave them a distinct advantage over Annja and the old man.

"Funny you should say that," she said.

"Are you being followed?"

"As good as. I just had a call from the kidnappers. They knew where I was. Pretty much described the church I'd just walked out of." She looked back at the woman who was still kneeling in prayer, but it was the reredos that caught her attention, an ornate altarpiece depicting Saint James killing Moors. The image was enough to trigger a thought inside her head. The sarcophagus, and by extension the key, was a Moorish relic hidden away beneath a Christian church. What if that was the clue itself?

She was going to have to think about that. And she wasn't going to risk saying it over an unsecure phone line, not if the kidnappers were as tech-savvy as she feared.

"Don't tell me where you're going," she said. "Don't tell me what you're planning to do next."

"You think we've got unwanted ears listening in?"

"It's not worth the risk."

She pictured him nodding. "Look after yourself, kiddo."

"I always do," she said, hanging up.

She already had an idea fermenting inside her brain.

The curator back in Ávila had said that Torquemada had founded a church here in Valladolid. That had to be her next port of call.

Annja crossed the city to find the church. Without a map it wasn't easy, as Valladolid was a city seemingly constructed on the foundations of faith, with spires every few streets denoting yet another place of worship. It was like looking for a particularly sanctified needle in an already consecrated haystack. But after fifteen minutes of driving around and several stuttering conversations with helpful locals, she found herself standing outside the incredible building, wondering how she could possibly have taken so long to find it. The great Gothic frontage was imposing. It wasn't difficult to imagine how the people of Valladolid would have reacted to its construction at the time: with awe. The church was built to the glory of God.

She was glad she hadn't come straight here, even

though it was a more logical starting point for her search. She wouldn't have discovered the key if she had, and there was no way of telling how important that key might turn out to be before the day had run its course.

Annja retrieved the flashlight from her panniers. She wasn't going to pass up the chance to take a look at what lay beneath this church if the opportunity arose.

There were more than a dozen people milling around inside, most of whom appeared to be tourists rather than worshippers. Beside a box inviting donations, several piles of leaflets provided information for visitors in a variety of languages. Annja skimmed the English one. It was crammed with tiny print and facts about the church and other religious buildings in the area. As she pocketed it, her attention was captured by an information board that gave a brief history of the church.

The first line sent a shiver up her spine.

She was wasting her time.

The San Pablo church had indeed been commissioned by Torquemada, but not *Tomás*. She could have screamed in frustration. This church was founded by Cardinal Juan de Torquemada, the Grand Inquisitor's uncle.

She was already looking in the wrong place.

She felt like banging her head against a brick wall.

But she didn't stop reading. Hoping. She didn't want to give up. She closed her fist around the key. The information board went on to explain how the facade, the final element of the church, hadn't been completed until the year 1500, even though the cardinal had died in 1468.

It seemed like an easy mistake for someone unfamiliar with the two men to make, but the curator must have known better, surely? He wouldn't have simply assumed the familial name meant the same man was behind the construction. Annja stared at the information, absorbing it, thinking, and made a connection; the building was completed two years after the Inquisitor's death.

The same year that his tomb had been broken into for the first time.

Perhaps there *was* a connection, after all.

Just not the obvious one.

When she read that the church had been built on the ruins of a Moorish palace, abandoned and destroyed after the town had been taken from the Moors, it was hard not to see parallels with the Moorish sarcophagus hidden beneath what had once been a Christian convent. A church on top of a Moorish palace. A convent on top of a Moorish sarcophagus. One thing on top of another, or one thing hiding beneath another, depending on how you looked at it.

Other than that, the display offered little more than a floor plan of the church.

There was nothing to indicate where the entrance to any crypt might lie.

Now Annja was convinced that if there was anything to be found here, it would lie beneath this Christian building, down in the ruins of the old Moorish palace, assuming the builders had built upon the foundations of that place as they had with the theater on the other side of the city.

It didn't take long to find an area that had been sectioned off by red velvet rope. It wasn't exactly high security. A priest was busy placing fresh candles in sconces close by. She would have to wait for him to finish what he was doing before she could slip under the rope and disappear down into the crypts. In the meantime, she decided to take a proper look around, just in case there was something she'd missed.

The transept displayed two paintings by Bartolomé de Cárdenas. According to a small plaque on the wall, he had died in Valladolid in 1628. No direct link with either of the Torquemadas, but what *was* interesting was the fact that one of the paintings depicted the Conversion of Saint Paul. Cardinal Torquemada was a defender of the conversos in Valladolid—Jews who had adopted the Christian faith rather than be forced to leave Spain. Paul of Tarsus was a Jew who converted. More connections, more hints and clues. Her gut instinct was that she was looking in all the right places, but it was hard to know what was actually relevant and what was a case of her making connections where none existed.

The church included several side chapels, according to the floor plan. One was the funerary chapel of Alonso de Burgos, who had died in 1499. The date was so close to the death of the inquisitor that it had to be worth investigating while she waited for the priest to finish with his candles. It offered no immediate revelations from the outside. She stepped through the arch into the chapel proper. Although there were no doors between it and the body of the church, it was markedly quieter. The archway was obviously acting as some kind of baffle, which meant sound would almost certainly not travel out of here, either. That could prove useful if she had to hide.

There didn't seem to be anything of great interest inside the chapel, so Annja took a moment to check out the picture Roux had sent.

The sketch certainly looked as if it could be the mask they were looking for. The additional detail of the ribbon suggested that the artist might actually have seen the artifact. Of course, it was possible he had just used his imagination in deciding how the mask might be fastened around the Grand Inquisitor's head. There was no way of knowing if Goya had in fact seen the mask, or even confronted a figure wearing it, during his studies. But if he had, that meant she was looking at as near-perfect a rendition of it as she could possibly have hoped. That made it feel more *real* to her.

She pocketed the phone again.

The moment of peace gave her the opportunity to examine the key properly, as well. She held it in one hand and rubbed the ancient metal between the thumb and forefinger of the other. A few flakes of rust fell away, but no more than that. It was in incredible condition, almost perfectly preserved. It was hard to imagine it could be as much as five hundred years old. She could feel the weight of history in it as the key stretched across her palm, extending beyond the width of her hand. It was sturdy, not delicate, but it was also beautifully crafted. Judging from its size and weight, the key was designed to fit a heavy-duty lock. What did that lock protect? Something valuable, surely? Something the world wasn't intended to discover by chance. The key represented a secret. There would have been a few who protected that secret through the years, but they must all be dead now. What was that secret? The Mask of Torquemada? She wasn't sure that artifact, no matter how compelling a treasure for someone like her, was actually valuable enough to warrant such extreme measures—a Moorish grave in a Christian crypt, a Moorish palace beneath a Christian church? That had to be about more than just a mask. But if that was true, then she was just wasting time chasing it, wasn't she? This was all about the mask. It had to be.

Annja was about to leave the chapel when she noticed an inconsistency in the design on the wall. She would have dismissed it, but she realized that the repeated pattern in the mosaic matched that of the bow of the key—latticework entwined around a crucifix. And then it struck her: it was a combination of Moorish and Christian design. She was in the right place. It wasn't a design she'd encountered elsewhere.

It tied the key and the chapel together.

She ran her fingers over the distortion.

The crucifix in one repetition of the pattern was missing, replaced by something that looked, on closer inspection, like an arched doorway. There was a chance it was a flaw in the design, maybe a problem in the manufacture or a mistake made by whoever had assembled the mosaic, but that changed nothing. The pattern on the key *was* the pattern in the floor.

She ran her eyes around the room, searching for a repetition of the error somewhere in case it had been deliberately mirrored. There was nothing.

Annja squatted down, putting the distorted design at eye level.

She placed the tip of a fingernail against the arch. The surface was softer than she'd expected. She had mistakenly assumed that the image had been part of the tile, but as she teased away at the arch, she discovered that it was the accumulated dirt and grime of centuries that had built up in a hollow, perhaps even a hole inside the tile.

That got her heart pumping.

Annja brushed at the dirt, scraping it away until it became an obvious indentation in the ceramic. She felt in her pocket, searching for something thin and sharp that she could use to dig it out. She found her bike's ignition keys; they'd do the trick. After a minute of careful work, scraping away at the grime around the hole, it was obvious that it was actually large enough to allow the old key she'd found in the Moorish coffin to slide inside.

She took a deep breath and turned the key slowly, gently, trying not to force the mechanism, which had rusted with age.

The key turned.

She heard a click from behind the wall.

A panel of the wall had been released. It had widened a crack. Annja worked it open carefully. Finally, the crack was large enough for her to walk through, though she had to stoop.

She turned on her flashlight, shining the beam into the darkness beyond.

8

Mateo didn't break pattern. He turned through a series of lefts, circling around his original position, just to be sure that the car behind them really was on their tail.

The old man noticed a tattoo on the back of Mateo's hand.

He hadn't noticed it before, but now that he had, he couldn't help but be intrigued by it.

His instinct was to ask what it meant, but given the fact they were being followed, and escaping their pursuers was very much dependent upon Mateo's concentration and driving skills, distracting him with questions didn't feel particularly smart. It wasn't as if a remark about his tattoo couldn't wait a few moments, after all.

Instead, he watched the driver through the rearview mirror, well aware that his eyes kept darting up to meet the old man's gaze.

Roux didn't like being followed.

He decided to force a confrontation, rather than risk his pursuer tagging along to whatever discovery was next. Of course, the easiest option was just to give them the slip, but easier wasn't anywhere near as effective. Or permanent. "We're going to make an unscheduled stop, Mateo."

"You're the boss."

"Indeed I am. Things could get a little interesting if I'm right about our tail."

"I like interesting."

"Me, too."

"Turn in here," Roux said, directing Mateo into a dead end. The driver did as he was told, no questions asked.

Roux looked behind them again. The other car had followed them. *So much for the benefit of the doubt,* Roux thought bitterly. Roux checked for the reassuring shape of the gun inside his jacket. It was always a last resort, but when options were quickly whittled down by circumstance, it was always better to have the choice than not.

"This will be fine," he said. "Stay in the car. You don't have to get involved in this." Mateo nodded and pulled over. On cue, the other car stopped, riding their tailgate.

Roux climbed out of the car.

He started to walk toward the other vehicle as four men emerged, their eyes firmly fixed on him. They were keyed up, on edge, ready for action. Not a good sign. He stood his ground, not moving beyond the length of his own car.

The man who'd been driving started toward him, swinging a semiautomatic by his side.

There was no pointing, no shouting. No grandstanding. These men were professional, organized, disciplined. Roux's first thought was ex-paramilitary. They were a team. A death squad.

He'd been willing to think things weren't as bad as they could be when he noticed the tattoo on the back of the man's gun hand. It was the same tattoo Mateo had.

The old man didn't believe in coincidences.

He turned slightly and in the corner of his eye saw that Mateo had climbed out of the car. So, five of them instead of four, not that it made a massive difference. The odds were stacked against him. The only thing in his favor was that he was Roux. They'd never encountered anyone as resourceful or stubbornly determined to stay alive as he was.

"This isn't for you. You're not wanted, understood?" the man with the gun said.

"Not wanted by who?" Roux asked. It was a straightforward question. He was buying time. Trying to think. Had he seen that tattoo before? What did it mean?

"Doesn't matter," said the man.

"I think it does. I think it goes right to the heart of the matter."

"You talk too much, old man. Don't make me hurt you. Just turn around and go home."

"I can't do that."

"You can. Mateo will drive you back to the airport.

All you need to do is get back on your plane and we can all go on with our lives."

Roux shook his head. "There's someone counting on me."

"And now *I'm* counting on you. Mateo's counting on you. My friends here are counting on you. We don't want this to become messy."

"And if I refuse?"

"Then it becomes messy. Go back to Paris." The man was obviously well-informed, Roux realized. "Live out the rest of your life in peace. That sounds like a good deal to me."

"I'm sure it does," Roux said. He thought about going along with their request. It had a lot going for it, truth be told. Garin was a big boy. He had Annja working hard to save his life. Roux had pretty much exhausted all avenues of inquiry here in Seville and, more importantly, got his findings out to Annja. She'd find the mask if it was here to be found. All things considered, it wouldn't have been difficult to walk away. But the simple fact that these people wanted him to do that meant he wouldn't. He wasn't that kind of man. Garin always said he was an ornery bastard. He wasn't wrong. That they didn't want him here meant this was exactly where he wanted to be.

"You want me gone, tell me what you're so afraid of me finding. Then I'll think about your offer."

"I'm not afraid at all, my friend, because there is nothing for you to find."

"Really?"

"Really. We don't like foreigners coming here and poking their noses in our business. Get back in the car and we'll say no more about it. That is my final word."

Five against one.

He could improve on those odds pretty quickly.

Roux nodded and climbed back into the car without saying another word. He waited for Mateo to ease himself in behind the wheel.

Before the driver could start the engine, though, Roux had the muzzle of his gun pressed against the back of his head. That was the joy of private jets, small private airports and lax security. He'd revised his opinion on the team he was facing—they weren't professionals. They were fanatics. They were still dangerous, obviously, but the fact that they hadn't patted him down was a dead giveaway that their history of violence was short, if it existed at all.

"All right, Mateo, you are going to tell me what this is about, or I am going to put a bullet in your brain. It'll be quick, it'll be painless—you'll be dead before your body realizes it. Then I'll go after your friends. I am not a man to give second chances. This is a one-shot deal. I highly encourage you to take it."

The man tried to turn his head, but Roux pressed the gun harder, making sure he knew exactly what would happen if he continued to try to turn around. "Don't." He saw the fear in the man's eyes through the rearview mirror. "All you need to do is tell me what this is all about."

"I can't," Mateo said.

Roux drew in a sharp breath. "Can't or won't?" It didn't really matter which it was. Even if the driver was afraid of him, he was more afraid of the men out there. Mateo didn't say anything. "Okay, get us out of here."

"Where to?"

"It doesn't matter. Just turn the car around and get out. I'll decide where we're going when I know myself."

Mateo didn't need telling twice. He started the engine and pulled the car away from the curb. There were three other cars and a delivery van parked inside the dead-end alleyway. He swung the car into the parking space for an apartment block. As he did, he leaned forward and reached for something under his seat. "Idiot," Roux grumbled and hit him hard on the back of the head with the butt of his pistol. "I said no second chances." He shook his head as the driver slumped forward on the wheel, his foot still pressed down on the gas.

The car lurched forward, hitting the back of the delivery van hard enough to deploy the air bag as the horn blared.

Moving fast, Roux slid out of the far side of the car and hit the ground hard as gunfire strafed the Mercedes's bodywork. The sound of bullets punching into metal was torturous. The fact he was still alive to hear it was wonderful.

He rolled across the asphalt.

Four against one.

Twenty percent improvement in less than a minute. He intended to improve on that substantially in the next sixty seconds.

Bullets rained down, ripping into the passenger door, shredding the metal as if it were cardboard. Glass shattered. A million tiny fragments rained down across the backseat and the street around the car. Roux had made it out by the skin of his teeth. In that moment, coming up on his elbows and knees, the years peeled away and he felt *young*.

He felt *alive*.

And he was going to stay that way.

Unseen by the other gunmen—all of whom were out of their car again, looking for him—Roux scrambled behind the van, taking full advantage of the cover it offered. He watched as the leader barked out orders in Spanish, sending one man around the two cars to try to flank him while the others laid down covering fire. It was a basic maneuver. They had no idea where he was. That uncertainty bought him a few precious seconds. He used them to release a single shot of his own. The bullet caught the scout in the knee, taking him out. He went down screaming. Three against one. He had to admit, things were looking brighter all the time.

Until a woman appeared at an upstairs window overlooking the scene. She let out a scream and hastily backed away. He didn't need any superpowers to know what was going to happen now. She was going to call the police. It would only be a matter of minutes, and not very many of them at that, before the sirens would signal that the authorities were on their way.

He needed to work fast. He needed a way out of this. He couldn't be caught here.

He heard sirens in the distance.

It had taken less than twenty seconds for a response—which meant the first call couldn't have come from the woman. Too soon even for a rapid-response unit.

The leader of the gunmen ushered his team back to the car, abandoning their fallen comrades to their own fate. So much for no man left behind.

Roux watched them run.

Before the sixty seconds was out, he was the last man standing. Their car was surging out onto the main street, clipping the rear of the van as it fishtailed away and sending a trash can flying as it took the corner too tightly.

The van rocked with the impact, pushing Roux back.

Mateo hadn't moved. He was still slumped behind the wheel of the Mercedes and showed no signs of coming around soon. Roux had seen the same kind of absolute stillness several times before. He knew what it meant. He *hoped* the driver wasn't dead because of him, but the signs weren't good. He hadn't intended to hit him so hard. Everything had happened so quickly. He couldn't dwell on it. Mateo had made his own metaphorical bed, choosing to go for his gun rather than get them out of there as Roux had told him.

The fallen gunman gave out another groan.

He clutched at his knee, stubbornly trying to get to his feet. He wasn't going anywhere. His kneecap was absolutely destroyed and his leg wouldn't hold his weight. He was bleeding and in agony. It was only shock that had him half-standing, supporting himself against the bullet-riddled car.

Roux ran to the Mercedes and started to pull Mateo from the driver's seat. His body was heavy and it took Roux longer than he would have liked to heave the man out of the car. He didn't so much as groan as Roux dumped him into the road.

Roux gunned the engine, stepping hard on the gas. He wasn't quick enough. Sirens screamed. Tires shrieked. Cars slewed across the alleyway, blocking him in. There wasn't enough distance for him to get up to speed and ram his way through.

Armed police officers moved into place behind the makeshift car barricade, their weapons trained on him. The odds had turned very much against him. He was good, but he wasn't *that* good.

He climbed out of the Mercedes, keeping his hands high above his head.

"Hit the ground! Now! On your knees! Down!"

He did as he was told.

There was nothing else he could do.

9

The flashlight's beam, as intense as it was, barely penetrated the darkness.

It was as if the blackness swallowed the light whole, and no matter how brightly it burned, the darkness was desperate to keep its secrets safe. Below her, a steep stairway led down into the crypts beneath the church. She couldn't make out the bottom step from where she was. It didn't make sense that this would be a hidden passage, yet still feed into the same crypt-space the cordoned-off staircase led to.

Annja placed a foot on the first stone step—a step that almost certainly hadn't been trodden on since the door was locked and hidden away behind the new chapel's facade.

She descended into history.

With every step she took deeper down into the cold and damp, she became more certain that she'd found the remains of the Moorish palace.

Much of the stonework was crumbling, the integrity

of the stone itself fighting a losing battle against the all-pervading damp. When she reached the bottom, Annja allowed herself a little time to shine the light around her. She didn't have long. Someone—most likely a tourist—would discover the panel she'd left open up there. She'd tried to ease it closed, but there was no obvious way of closing or locking it from the inside. The keyhole hadn't been constructed with that intention.

She was standing in a place where the Inquisition and the Moors had come together, just as they had in the intertwined pattern around the crucifix—two cultures existing one on top of the other. It was obvious that this space had been used long after the Moors had abandoned it. The beam of her flashlight illuminated intricate mosaics and plasterwork that had long decayed beyond the point of restoration, but as she worked her way around the room, she spotted more and more compelling evidence of Christians having been there before her. Crosses had been daubed on the walls to claim the place for the Church, as if ritual were enough to banish the religion of the foreigners, superimposing one belief system on top of the other.

She caught her breath when the light finally reached the far end of the room.

Hanging on the wall, trapped in the middle of the beam, was a life-size statue with its arms held wide.

It was a sculpture of the crucifixion. The look of suffering on Christ's carved face perfectly captured the agony of the moment. It was a work of art. Of all the images and iconography, this was the one object that claimed these remains for the Church above all else, just as the Church had claimed the ground above her head. She moved toward the statue. Most of the evidence from the first faith that had been observed here had long since been defiled, destroyed or simply left to disintegrate.

Even the statue was showing signs of damage; a crack cut through one of Christ's outstretched arms.

Annja shone her flashlight around the rest of the room once more before she noticed that there was something off about the statue. She moved closer, running the light slowly over every inch of the Son of God's body, not sure what it was about it that had called her back. She took another step toward it, raising the light to the crack that ran through the Savior's arm. It was *perfectly* straight, which was peculiar enough, but it continued as a fissure through the background fresco.

Sometimes a crack was just a crack. But it just felt too straight, too perfect.

She placed her hands on one of Christ's knees and pushed.

The statue swung back a fraction, the split growing wider, leaving behind one arm still attached to the wall. A hidden space within a hidden space, perfect for keeping secrets from the world.

Stone ground against stone.

A shower of dust fell from the wall as the darkness opened up.

Annja's heart was thumping, excitement surging through her system. This was what she lived for, the thrill of discovery, that moment when she opened something that hadn't been opened in centuries, bringing it back to life; that moment when it was just her and the past; that moment when she bridged the now and the then, bringing them together with her bare hands.

Could this be where the Mask of Torquemada had lain hidden for so long?

It had to be, didn't it?

She couldn't believe it had only taken her a few hours to find something that had been lost for centuries.

Doubt niggled at the back of her mind.

It all seemed too *easy*.

She pressed herself close to the narrow opening and directed the flashlight's beam while she reached inside with her free hand.

10

"I'm going to ask you again—who were they?" Roux's interrogator asked.

It wouldn't be the last time the detective across the table asked it, either.

Roux had been taken to a police station and bundled forcefully into an interview room. He'd taken a number of carefully disguised blows in the process—they'd delivered a couple rabbit punches to his kidneys, cracked his head against the doorframe of the car as they'd pushed him into the backseat and shoved him across the polished floor of the interview room, cuffed, so he couldn't reach out to break his fall. It was all fair game as far as they were concerned. He had been left there to stew, the clock in the room ticking on. He assumed they were gathering information for the interrogation, but they weren't going to learn anything useful from traditional sources. He'd always been careful about what information made it out into the public domain, even on back channels. They'd stumble into a Roux-shaped wall of silence. That in itself wouldn't help much today. It'd just make him look guilty, where for once he was actually innocent. There was an irony to the whole thing he would have appreciated if it had been someone else taking the beating.

So they asked their questions, and it was soon obvious they were on a fishing expedition. They didn't have a clue who he was, who the gunmen were or how the two parties had ended up on a collision course. So he told the truth.

"I have no idea."

It wasn't what they wanted to hear.

Roux could stall them here for as long as he wanted. It wasn't as if the traditional interrogation techniques of the Inquisition were available to the men on the other side of the table, after all. But as much fun as a game of cat-and-mouse might have been, it was just wasting more time, and even if he wasn't particularly worried about Garin, he was worried about Annja. He should be out there helping her, not in here staring at a Spanish cop with a bad complexion, feigning ignorance whenever they got close to asking something interesting.

"So, what you are trying to say is your attackers came out of nowhere, started shooting at you for no reason and then ran away?"

"More or less, yes."

"Which is it, more or less?"

"I noticed that we were being followed. I instructed my driver to stop so that I could address whoever it was and square away whatever perceived problem they had.

Then they started shooting. From that moment on, I was only interested in getting away from a potentially lethal situation." Again, the truth. Unnuanced, perhaps, lacking context, but still the kind of thing that would pass a polygraph.

"Why are you here? What is your business in Seville?"

"Sightseeing," he said. No point telling the *whole* truth. It wouldn't help matters. "It truly is a beautiful city. So much history. Amazing architecture. Sometimes it's good to just slow down for a minute and take a look at the world around you. Visit the galleries and monuments and experience all that a city like yours has to offer."

"And one of the men who tried to kill you was your driver?"

"Yes. We'd never met before today. My people arranged for a car to pick me up from the airport, and he came as part of the package. I couldn't even tell you which company provided the service. I have people for that. Still, he seemed like a good man."

"Tell me, do you hire a chauffeur wherever you go?"

"I can afford it," Roux said. "Wealth isn't something I'm ashamed of." He knew he was in danger of antagonizing the policemen, but his patience wasn't limitless. Roux checked his watch against the clock on the wall, emphasizing how much time he was wasting. "Is this going to take much longer?"

"It is going to take as long as it takes. I don't think you realize just how serious your situation is. Let me spell it out for you, just in case something has been lost in translation between us. I've got two dead bodies and I have you. There is a definite connection between you and one of the victims. Let me tell you what will happen next—ballistics will match your gun with the bullets we've pulled from the bodies, and you'll be going to jail."

"Interesting theory, but for the fact that the only bullet of mine you'll find is in the kneecap of the man who was lying in the street."

The interrogator raised an eyebrow. "And what about the one in his head?"

"He didn't have a bullet in the head when I last saw him."

"You're saying that he was shot by his own men? Or maybe it was one of my men? Is that what you're saying?"

Roux struggled to keep the smile off his face. "More like his own people, but it isn't inconceivable that one of them is also one of you. It's about loose ends. He was a loose end. Leaving him behind alive meant leaving a living, breathing link back to them in your hands. Why would they do that? In their position, I wouldn't. Would you?"

The policeman leaned back in his chair and gave Roux a long, cold stare.

"How about my phone call?" the old man asked.

"Phone call? What do you think this is? You have no rights here. You are not the victim, no matter what you want me to believe, so you will get a phone call if and when I say you do. That won't be for a long time yet."

"How about an attorney?"

"You will be given court-approved representation when the time comes."

"I'd rather use my own, if it's all the same. I find you get what you pay for, and as we've already established, I'm not averse to paying for the very best."

The policeman opened a manila folder and spilled out a collection of photographs across the table between them. Some were the dead men's faces, others were of their hands.

"What can you tell me about this?" the interrogator asked, jabbing a finger at a picture of the tattoo on the back of what he assumed was Mateo's hand. Roux picked up the photograph to take a closer look.

"Very little. I've never seen it before today. And now it's on the back of two men's hands."

"And you don't think it's strange that two dead men have the same tattoo?"

"Oh, very much so, but thinking it is peculiar sadly doesn't mean I know anything about its origins. I assume it is some kind of gang mark?" It was a reasonable conclusion. He had nothing else to offer. It meant nothing to him.

"What do you know about the Fraternidad de la Quema?"

"Ferdinand what?"

"The Brotherhood of the Burning." The interrogator spoke slowly, enunciating each word very precisely.

Roux made a moue. Shook his head. "Sorry. Nothing. Alas, I am not up on the gang culture of Spain."

The policeman said nothing for a moment, weighing his next words. He obviously knew something about the tattoo's origins but wasn't sure he wanted to reveal it. Finally, he said, "They have been behind a series of hate crimes both here and in other cities across the country."

"Hate crimes?" That was unexpected. Roux leaned forward in his chair, interested now.

"They've been targeting Muslims. It started with little more than graffiti and threats, but has escalated recently to a number of severe beatings. Now, it would appear, they have managed to get their hands on weapons and escalated to attempted murder. Am I correct in thinking that you are not a Muslim?" Roux nodded. "Then that would be a flaw in my understanding. I do not like making mistakes or working on misunderstandings."

Roux could hazard a few reasonable guesses that might connect the men with his visit to the museum, but he wasn't about to share them. It wasn't his job to solve the policeman's puzzle. Right now, he needed to get out of here before the detective started asking better questions.

"And your understanding would be what? That this Brotherhood is drawing some kind of inspiration from the Inquisition?"

"I didn't say that, but it's interesting that you did. Why would that be your first conclusion?"

"Pure luck. Now how about my phone call?"

"There is something I don't like about you, something that doesn't ring true. I will find out how you are involved in this, because I don't for a minute believe you are as innocent as you'd have me think." The interrogator slipped the photos back into the folder, then took a cell phone from his pocket and handed it across to Roux.

It looked as if he was going to get his call, though he knew the detective had given him his own phone so that the number would be stored in its memory.

"It's an international call," he said. "Sorry. I don't suppose I could have a little privacy?"

The interrogator shook his head. "I don't think so. But that's fine, isn't it? It's not like you have anything to hide."

"Nothing at all," Roux said, punching in the number.

The call was answered on the second ring.

There was no need to exchange names. Roux was the only one who called this number, and the man on the other end the only one who answered.

"I'm in a police station in Seville," Roux began, giving the address to make sure there was no confusion about which one. The voice on the other end read it back to confirm its accuracy. "I need you to get me out of here," Roux continued. "I don't care how much it costs, do you understand?"

"Understood," the man on the other end said, killing the call.

All he could do now was wait and trust his man to do what needed to be done.

"This isn't Rome, you know," the interrogator said,

shaking his head. "You can't just buy your way out of a murder charge."

"Oh, I know that, but my lawyer is quite…creative."

11

Of course it had been too much to hope for. Life wasn't like that. It didn't just give you what you needed when you needed it. It made you work for it.

There was no mask hidden in the secret compartment.

But it wasn't empty.

Annja's fingers closed on something. She fished it out carefully, fingertips brushing against what felt like oilskin. Slowly, not wanting to risk damaging whatever lay inside, she unwrapped the skin. The ribbon that had secured it all those years crumbled into decay and fell away as she tried to release the bow. The only thing that didn't simply turn to powder was the red wax seal. The wrapping itself was in better condition. It creaked and strained as she peeled it back, but it had done its job protecting the contents. She held a book in her hands. It appeared to be in excellent condition, but she wasn't about to take any risks with it.

Carefully, the flashlight between her teeth, Annja

opened the heavy boards of the cover and turned over the first few pages one at a time.

The script wasn't easy to decipher, but even so, it didn't take Annja long to realize she had to be looking at some kind of ledger. On the left-hand side of the page there was what seemed to be a list of items, and on the right a column of numbers. But that was as deep as her understanding went. Even without knowing what the ledger contained, someone had thought it was important enough to keep it so well hidden. This was not the place to try to examine it, though. Not with the secret chapel door still ajar upstairs. Still, she couldn't resist taking a look at a few more of the pages in case something leaped out at her.

Somewhere in those fragile pages was a clue to the whereabouts of the mask.

She needed to believe that.

But it didn't help if she couldn't read it.

At first glance, she'd thought that the details in the ledger were in some sort of medieval Spanish, but they weren't. The unusual hand the script had been written in was deceptive, she realized, recognizing a few words of Latin as she skimmed over the page. The names set above the list of items were not. She could have been mistaken, but her gut instinct was that the ledger contained a list of Moorish names and Latinized notations, but what did any of it *mean*?

She ran a finger down one page after another, looking for words she might recognize.

All she wanted was a single red thread she could unpick in search of the truth, whatever that might be.

She found her answer in the date that ran along the far left-hand side. The first was shortly after Torquemada's rise to power and the last entry was made months before his death.

Annja knew that more than a million Moors and Jews had been driven out of the Iberian Peninsula or put to death during the course of the Inquisition. A million people. Did this ledger represent a fraction of those? She thought about the treasures that had been seized by the Nazis during the Second World War, only to be rediscovered more than a generation later, hidden in the vaults of Swiss banks. The Germans had kept meticulous records about many things. It was a shot in the dark, but Annja began to wonder if there were similarities, if this ledger contained a list of assets seized by the Inquisition. If it was, it was unlikely the Mask of Torquemada would be recorded as such an asset. And right now, as tempting as this treasure and the truth it represented were, she didn't have time for distractions. When this was over, though, she promised the dead men listed in the ledger, she would solve the riddle she held in her hands. But until then, she could only think about one thing. The mask.

She carefully wrapped the book back in the oilskin, then slipped it and the fragments of decayed ribbon into her pocket before closing the compartment and easing the statue of Christ back into place.

If the ledger was a record of a vast amount of confiscated treasure—probably only the tiniest fraction of the amount collected over the years—it could be one of the most important finds of her career. The book had been kept safe all of these years... Did that mean the treasure was hidden somewhere? It was possible, wasn't it? She was getting ahead of herself, but it was hard not to. If any such horde had been discovered, even centuries ago, she would have heard about it.

With that in mind, she retraced her steps back up to the church.

She needed to get out of there.

Ticktock. Ticktock.

The one nagging thought she had was that everything had pointed to the mask being hidden here, and yet she had found the book instead.

The two had to be connected somehow.

This couldn't just be some random discovery; she was still on the right track; her Grail Quest was progressing, even if it didn't feel like it right now. She was one step closer to finding the mask. One step closer to saving Garin Braden.

12

"Okay, time to face the music," the interrogator said. Roux still didn't know his name. He hadn't announced himself for the recording in the interview room and hadn't repeated it since he introduced his team in mumbling Spanish deliberately intended to mask their names. He'd been given a cup of weak coffee and left alone for a while to think about what would happen next. It was a fairly basic technique—rather than keep hammering away at an intractable object, sometimes it was more effective to just let the sea of doubts lap up around it, chipping away at the edges until something worried free.

"You taking me to the ball?"

"Sorry, Cinderella, we're off to the courthouse."

That caught Roux by surprise. So much for due process. "My attorney hasn't arrived yet." He glanced at his watch, for the first time that day worried that too little time had passed.

The interrogator shrugged. "There'll be plenty of

time for that later. Think of it this way—it just gives you longer to make up a convincing cover story. We're not in the habit of holding suspects in custody without charging them. Maybe that's how they do it in France, but here we believe in the rule of law. So, we can do this nice and quietly, or we can make a big song and dance out of it. I would say your choice, but it's not. It's mine. Look lively. The magistrate doesn't like to be kept waiting."

"I'm not going anywhere until I've spoken to my attorney," Roux said.

"You're going to make this as difficult as possible, aren't you? If your legal representative is unavailable, the court will supply you with one. Now, I have had to pull a number of strings to make sure that a magistrate will be ready for us, and to keep you off the front page. Best not make this any more uncomfortable than it already is."

Reluctantly, Roux rose. He was cuffed hand and foot, so any ideas of making a break for it had to be kept on hold for now. The opportunity would arise, though; he was sure of that.

"Fine, let's get this over with, then, shall we?"

"That's the spirit."

"I am going to take great pleasure in suing your ass off when you realize just how badly you've screwed this up."

"I'd expect no less." The interrogator smiled and led him out by the rear of the station house.

An armed escort was waiting for them.

Roux hadn't expected such blatant heavy-handedness; it was a declaration from the police that they'd got their man and he was *dangerous*. It was grandstanding. Despite what the detective had said, he had almost certainly tipped off the media and intended to try Roux in the most public way possible. Maybe he was trying to shake the tree and see what came spilling out. It wasn't how Roux would have done it, but there was always more than one way to win a battle of wits.

The drive was only a matter of a few minutes. He should have been grateful they hadn't decided to frogmarch him through the streets.

His lawyer still hadn't arrived by the time the entourage reached the courthouse steps. He was bundled out of the car and led inside. He didn't struggle against them. That wasn't how he'd win this. He needed to be sharp and to know his surroundings, so as they pushed him toward the courtroom, he took the time to look around and fix key geography points in his mind—staircases, doorways, windows, areas of ingress and egress, the balcony that swept around the foyer, giving the armed court officers above a panoramic view of the marble floor, the security scanners and X-ray machine that wouldn't have looked out of place at Homeland Security, and the cameras. Roux was always interested in the cameras. Someone who lived an unreasonable span of years needed to be. It didn't do him any favors to turn up at crime scenes decades apart looking exactly the same. Someone always noticed, then came looking and needed to be taken care of.

The bailiff led him into the courtroom, releasing his cuffs. Roux stretched, working the tight, aching muscles in his back, then turned to face the front. There were no spectators in the gallery. The magistrate's chair was empty, and there was no sign of his representative, though the state prosecutor was already shuffling paper earnestly at his desk. The bailiff knocked twice and called "All rise" as a side door opened and the magistrate entered the room.

He motioned for those assembled to sit. "Do we have a list of charges?"

"Your Honor," the bailiff said, reciting a list of charges grievous enough to see Roux locked up for several lifetimes at least. Before the final counts of murder in the first degree had been read out, his attorney came barreling into the courtroom, face flushed and panting as he struggled to catch his breath. He set his briefcase down beside the wall, beneath the room's only window, and mopped at his brow with a dirty white handkerchief before addressing the bench.

"This is outrageous." He shook his head as if he couldn't quite believe what was happening. "What kind of kangaroo court is this? You have no evidence to link my client to any of the events today. You have a list of spurious charges and are looking to bury him rather than risk justice being done. He is the victim here."

"This isn't the time for opening arguments, counsel. How does your client plead?"

"He doesn't." He took a sip of water from a glass that stood on the table in front of him.

The magistrate wasn't amused. "Your client must enter a plea. Am I to assume it will be one of 'not guilty'?"

"No, Your Honor. My client will not be offering any such plea. I move that the case against him be dismissed." He looked at the clock on the wall, then back to the magistrate. Roux watched him, wondering what the man had in mind. "This entire thing is a sham. An outrage. My client's detention is unlawful, lacking in sufficient cause or evidence."

"Be careful, counsel. I do not know how you do things where you come from, but in my city, we adhere absolutely to the letter of the law."

"I object, Your Honor!"

That made Roux smile. He was impressed how convincing his man had been up until that moment. The magistrate, however, was far from impressed. He slammed his gavel down, about to demand order, when all hell broke loose.

The first explosion shook the building savagely, bringing down a rain of plaster on the proceedings. There was a moment of shocked silence before the air filled with shouts and screams. Beyond the doors, people struggled to stay calm in the midst of the whirlwind, fear overwhelming them as the foundations of the building shook again and it became obvious they were under attack.

Roux remained motionless, letting it happen.

His attorney was the only other man in the room not to betray his fear. He looked at Roux and nodded. This was what the old man would pay so handsomely for. A third explosion rocked the place. The quality of the screams changed. People were hurting out there. Smoke and debris filled the air as more plaster came raining down. The bailiff moved to secure Roux's chains. The old man wasn't about to let that happen. He planted an elbow in the man's throat. He went down hard, gagging. Roux looked around the courtroom as doors burst open. Guards came streaming in, bringing with them the stench of explosives and a wave of dust. Roux identified the window at the far end of the room as the weak point. The guards moved toward him, but before they were halfway across the floor, another explosion shook the room, this one much closer to home.

Roux crouched down, covering his ears a moment too late for it to make any difference. His ears rang. Daylight streamed in where the window had been seconds before, and two men dressed in black stood in the opening. He had a choice to make and he had to make it fast. He let the two men raise hell and hurled himself over the railing, rolling and scrambling across the floor as the smoke and dust thickened. Chaos was his friend. He ran toward the main doors while the guards yelled behind him. By the window the men in black opened fire, shooting not to kill but to add to the confusion.

Roux's attorney came charging after him.

Together, they emerged from the courtroom into the foyer. The security gates had been abandoned, guards trying desperately to help with the wounded and fallen.

Roux walked straight out of the courthouse, his attorney two steps behind him.

An unmarked van was parked at the bottom of the steps, the side panel open and waiting for them. Both men clambered inside. The doors slammed behind them, plunging them into darkness. The engine gunned, and the van peeled away from the curbside.

"This is it, old man, quits," the attorney said. "As far as I'm concerned, we're even now. Agreed?"

"I'm not sure it'll ever be even, my friend. But for now, if there's a debt, I think it's from me to you. I expect you to call it in at some point. I'm grateful."

"Whatever you say," his companion said.

For the next minute they sat in silence, the van slowing, stopping, accelerating with the traffic lights, turning quickly through the city streets. They could hear sirens seemingly in every direction, but the driver didn't increase his speed. There was no need to. It would be a while before the law-enforcement guys coordinated resources and even figured out what kind of vehicle they were looking for. Right now, he doubted they even realized he was gone. The courthouse had been transformed into a bloody war zone in a matter of seconds, and those two gunmen had made it seem like a terror attack. It would take considerably longer for anyone to find out his attorney wasn't qualified to do much except blow things up.

The man held out a hand and Roux reached out to shake it, before seeing he was being offered his watch, wallet and phone.

"I thought you might want these."

"I owe you."

"You do. I'll send you the bill."

It wasn't easy to hold back the smile. Roux returned his wallet to his jacket pocket and slipped the watch back onto his wrist. The timepiece held sentimental value. It had been a gift from the inventor of the seconds chronograph, Nicolas Mathieu Rieussec, watchmaker to the king of France, what felt like a long, long time ago. He hadn't felt dressed without it. He was glad to have it back. Roux turned the phone on and waited for it to connect to the network.

He needed to get out of the city—and ideally, the country—as quickly as possible, but right now he was at the mercy of the man who had extricated him from that courtroom drama. Roux could only trust he'd thought of everything.

The van kept turning left, left and left, and Roux could sense they were climbing an incline. Not mountains, he realized. A high-rise parking lot. They came to a halt. He heard the driver's-side door open and close. A hand thumped on the side of the van before the doors were flung open to let in the light and a familiar, unmistakable, sound.

The driver held a hand out to help him out of the van.

"We ready to roll?"

Roux stepped out into the light, appreciating his man's thoroughness. A helicopter waited for him, blades turning slowly in readiness. All things considered, he couldn't have hoped for much more. "All set," Roux said.

"Then we'll leave you to it. Good luck."

Even before he was in the air, the white van had started its descent toward street level.

By the end of the day it would be resprayed, fitted with new plates or burned somewhere out of town. Either-or, didn't matter. There would be no evidence left to tie him to the van or the bombing. That was what *did* matter.

"Where to, boss?" the pilot asked as the helicopter rose steadily into the air.

"As far away from here as possible. I need to make a call, so don't go too high. Don't want to risk losing cell reception." The phone displayed four bars. That was more than enough. It didn't seem to be the wisest course of action to call someone in the police when he was on the run from them, but he'd never been one for playing it safe. There was someone in Europol he needed to talk to. She answered on the second ring.

"Roux? It's been a while."

"Too long, Elise."

"Are you in town?"

"Alas, no. I'm not even in the same country."

"That's a shame," she said. "For a minute I thought you were going to try to make it up to me." He didn't need to ask what he was supposed to be making amends for. No doubt she'd written him up on her list of heartbreakers.

"Next time," he promised.

"So if it's not my body you want me for, it's got to be my connections."

She knew him too well.

"The Brotherhood of the Burning, what can you tell me about them?"

He heard a sharp intake of breath down the long-distance line. "Nasty, racist bunch, Spanish neo-Fascists, anti-Muslim, anti-Jewish. Until a couple years ago, they were contained within two or three cities, but their influence is starting to spread. They're attracting the worst elements of society, giving them something to focus their anger on."

"And the name? Mean anything?"

"Most certainly does. They identify with the Spanish Inquisition like it's something to be proud of. They think that the Jews and the Muslims should be driven out of their country or, better still, burned alive."

Roux said nothing for a moment. He should have seen the connection himself; it had been staring him in the face. But for some reason, he hadn't joined the dots. "So they're interested in some kind of ethnic cleansing?"

"That's all that most of them are interested in, yes. It's what attracts most of their membership to the cause."

"Most? But not all of them? What motivates the rest, any ideas?" He knew she was holding back on something, a piece of the jigsaw that he still wasn't seeing.

"There are a few who are just as interested in the Inquisition itself as they are in the violence."

"I don't suppose you've got a watch list? Names? Something that might give me somewhere to start?"

"You really are pushing your luck, aren't you, sweet-heart? Is there something you should be telling me?"

"I would if I could."

"Everything I've told you so far has come off the top of my head. If you want more than that, I'm going to have to go into the system. Going into the system is going to leave a trail. So I'd want to know what I'm getting myself into."

"I'm sorry, Elise. Really. But I can't say."

"Sounds ominous."

"Quite."

"There's a guy who seems to be one of those who calls the shots. We've never been able to pin anything on him, but he's guilty. We know that absolutely. The guy is scum. Dangerous scum."

"Who?"

"His name is Enrique Martínez."

"Okay. Martínez. Got it. Last known whereabouts?"

"He's not an easy man to keep tabs on, but there's no report of him having left the country, so he should be there somewhere."

"Thanks," Roux said. "I owe you."

"Yes, you do," she said. "And I won't let you forget about it."

She gave the briefest of goodbyes, then hung up.

He had another call to make.

The pilot kept looking across at him, waiting for instructions. He still didn't have a destination. "Don't worry, whatever they're paying you, I'll double it, just keep circling the city for now."

"You're the boss."

He called up another number and listened to it ring.

"Hey, Roux," Oscar said, picking up.

"What have you got for me?" No small talk.

"Well, I'm not sure I've got anything... It's a dead zone. Nothing from any scans, no infrared, nothing."

"Then maybe that's our boy. Where?"

"The Alhambra."

He repeated the name to the pilot, who adjusted his heading, banking low over the rooftops of the city before speeding away.

"Anything else?"

"Not a lot. I've got a list of the places around the world where the feed was being rerouted, but that's not important. I'm still looking for the source."

"There's one more thing," Roux said. "A favor."

"Another one?" The hacker laughed.

"I need you to find out whatever you can about an outfit called the Brotherhood of the Burning."

"Never heard of them."

Roux filled him in, realizing how little he actually knew about them. With luck, Oscar would be able to dig up a lot more.

"Sounds like a fun little club," the man said.

"I've got a name, too," Roux said. "Enrique Martínez. It might be nothing, but maybe it's a case of find him, find the source of the signal."

"Leave it with me."

Roux hung up and pressed himself back into his seat, content to take in the view for a few hours.

Next stop, the Alhambra.

13

Annja clutched the oilskin-wrapped book as she re-emerged into the chapel.

The panel had remained tantalizingly open while she'd undertaken the search for secrets beneath its ancient protection. She pushed it back into place now and used the key to lock it. Within a few seconds, it was as though she'd never been there. The only difference between the old chapel an hour ago and now was that there was nothing she could do to disguise the keyhole. Someone would discover it, sooner rather than later, but now there was nothing remarkable down there waiting to be found, save for a statue of the Savior.

By that time, though, she would be long gone.

In the meantime, she didn't want to draw any unnecessary attention to herself.

She dusted herself down, brushing away dirt and cobwebs, before making her way back into the body of the great church.

The cleric who had been standing near the roped-off

entrance to the crypt gave her the briefest of glances, without seeming to register the book in her hand. He offered her a slight smile. Annja inclined her head in acknowledgment. It was a dance of silent communication. Anything else would have been memorable, but a smile and a nod between strangers? Was there anything more everyday than that?

A child who had escaped from her mother and grandmother tested the acoustics of the great ceiling by squealing with laughter. It drew every eye in the place to her and was more than enough of a distraction for the priest, who sent the mother a disapproving look that suggested a dozen Hail Marys wouldn't square it away with the Boss.

Annja left them to it.

Outside, in the sunlight, she breathed deeply, sucking in the air and relishing its freshness. Ticktock. Ticktock. She wanted a look at the book in the light, so she set it down on the bike's seat and unwrapped it. It truly was a thing of exquisite beauty. A real treasure. But she didn't know how to decode its secrets. She fished out her phone. It was time she touched base with Roux.

"Where are you?" Roux asked.

"Valladolid," Annja said.

"What have you got?"

"A book. A ledger, actually. I found it in a chamber behind a Morisco mosaic in the church. The key opened the way."

"A ledger?"

"I'm convinced that it's a record of confiscated wealth."

"Interesting. And it would make sense," Roux said. "If I were a gambling man, I'd say it was a pointer toward the Alhambra. Or rather another one."

"Why do you say that?"

"That video file you were sent seems to be streaming from there."

"You think Garin is there?"

"It's possible, but at the very least, the people I suspect are behind his kidnapping are located there."

"You've made inroads?"

"Butted heads might be closer to the truth. They call themselves the Brotherhood of the Burning. The police think they're a bunch of dangerous racists, while Europol suspect they're more extreme than that. Given my run-in with them, I'm inclined to side with Europol on this one. They draw some kind of inspiration from the Inquisition. It's all about religious and racial purity, keeping Spain for the Spanish and all that. No Jews or Muslims allowed."

"Sound like a charming bunch."

"Indeed. Thankfully, they're arrogant enough to ink themselves with their precious gang tattoo. Keep your eyes peeled for anyone with a tattoo of flames on the back of their hand."

"Roger that. And you think these are the people who have Garin."

"I'm not at the point of staking my life on it, but I'd risk Garin's." She heard the grin in the old man's voice.

"Well, that almost sounds positive," Annja said, trying to work out how far away she was and how long a journey to the Alhambra was likely to be. Time was being eaten up quickly, and running from one end of the country to the other wasn't an option. Or at least not a good one. "So what makes you think the ledger is pointing that way, too?"

"The Alhambra was one of the last strongholds of the Moors in Spain, and yet, curiously, it was given up without the fortress and palace coming under attack. The last Moorish sultan of Granada was driven out in 1492, so we are talking about the right kind of date again. How much of the sultan's wealth remained when his family fled is impossible to say," Roux continued, "but if the Inquisition were holding on to some Moorish treasures, then his would have been their greatest cache. Much of his palace was vandalized, of course, rubbing defeat in his face. Another case of destruction in the name of religion. It may lead us to the mask. It may not. If I'm wrong and it doesn't, but Garin is there, then finding the mask is no longer imperative."

It was logical, of course. Annja felt a pang of guilt. For a moment, she'd completely forgotten that Garin was the reason they had been caught up in this. In her head, finding the Mask of Torquemada had started to become an end in itself. But now, reminded of its position in the scheme of things, she was painfully reminded of the stakes.

"Okay, let's think about this. Is there *anything* that

links this Brotherhood of the Burning to the Alhambra?" she asked.

"As I said, some of their leadership appears to be obsessed with the Inquisition. Remember more Moors were executed at the Alhambra than at any other single place."

"Which would make it interesting in and of itself to people like that. Especially if they were looking to re-create something like the Inquisition. Where better to stage a modern-day auto-da-fé?"

"Now you're using your head, girl," Roux said approvingly.

"It will take me a few hours to get there," Annja said.

"I can be there sooner. Be sure you've explored absolutely every avenue there before you head south. We don't have time to turn back once we're committed to a course of action."

"Will do."

"I'll call you if I find anything that points to a different destination."

Annja slipped the phone back into her pocket as a car drove past. The turbulent air turned over a couple of the ledger's pages. The script seemed to dance as the pages moved. She spotted something she hadn't noticed before. Nine or ten pages of entries clearly related to wealthy men, and the list of items beneath each name was long and detailed, some going over more than one page. She carefully counted the number of people this covered. Six men. Even though she had no idea what the items meant, there was no doubt that each of the six had been worth a substantial amount. It wasn't the wealth that drew her attention, though, but rather the fact that all six men came from the same place: Calahorra.

Now she had a decision to make. Roux had basically said to leave no stone unturned, but even a few minutes' delay could be the minutes that cost Garin his life. Was Calahorra the answer or just another question? She needed to consider and reassess. That was better than charging on blindly, hoping she was going to miraculously find the answers she needed. Roux was going to get to the Alhambra long before she would. If it was a bust, they were both in the same place, whether she was with him or not. If all he found there was another clue that pointed elsewhere, then it was better she was mobile.

She looked at the list of names again.

One entry stood out from the others: Abdul bin Soor. There were far fewer entries beneath his name than the other five. The three words that sent a shiver up her spine were printed beneath his name: *Faber Argentarius Persona*. The first two were words she had come across before, meaning *silversmith*. The third stumped her for a moment, but then her pulse sped up as she realized that it referred to a mask, not the modern-day persona. Surely that meant she'd found the man who had made Torquemada's mask.

In the absence of anything else, it was always a good move to follow the money.

Or in this case, the silver.

There was nothing to say she'd find any record of

Abdul bin Soor outside of the ledger, but that didn't matter; this felt like the first bit of proof of the mask's existence, and it was linked to a physical place. Calahorra.

That was where she was going next.

Ticktock. Ticktock.

14

"Ticktock. Ticktock," the voice at the other end of the line mocked. "Half your time has gone and the clock ticks mercilessly on."

"You're a poet and you don't know it," Annja snapped back. She wasn't in the mood for games. "I want proof of life, simple as that. Prove Garin is still alive. If you can't do that, I'm going to find you and I'm going to kill you," Annja said.

She had been on the outskirts of Calahorra when her cell phone vibrated in her jacket pocket. She'd been expecting Roux.

"You want proof of life? My, my, I'm *almost* insulted. You don't believe me? My word isn't good enough for the famous Annja Creed?" The man let out a cruel laugh and the line went dead. He'd hung up on her. Annja's skin crawled. Was that it? Was it over?

She was shaking when she felt another vibration from her phone. It was a video file, only a few seconds long. She opened the file and any doubts that they were prepared to kill Garin were washed away.

At first it was impossible to be sure who the body lying on the ground was.

Then a boot came into view, kicking the man in the ribs, forcing a groan from his bloody lips.

Hands reached down and pulled him from the ground, hauling him up into a chair.

There was no mistaking that it was Garin despite the severe swelling and dark bruises that altered his features. One bloodshot eye managed to open slowly. A trickle of blood oozed from the cut above his brow.

"Hope this is proof enough for you, Miss Creed," the voice said as the image zoomed in on Garin's face, which was etched with pain. His eye had been blinking furiously. She could only imagine the torment they'd inflicted on him to break his will. Garin was tough, but even he couldn't withstand relentless torture.

"What the hell have you got yourself involved in?" she asked the picture of her friend. It didn't matter that he couldn't answer her.

The screen went blank.

She held the phone in her hand, waiting for the kidnapper to call back and continue mocking her. The call never came.

There was no point trying to reach Roux; he'd still be airborne, on route to the Alhambra. Would Oscar be able to confirm anything she didn't already know? It seemed like a stretch. He had already identified the source of the broadcast as somewhere inside the Alhambra. She wasn't sure what he'd be able to glean from this new video, and anything he could find out would probably come too late to be of any use.

She called him anyway.

"It's Annja."

"Ah, to what do I owe this pleasure? I've already given Roux everything I've got."

"I've been sent another video."

"You want to send it to me?"

"You willing to risk another laptop?"

"Forewarned is forearmed," he said. "Send it over. I'll get right on it."

Annja hung up and emailed the file to him.

Her first stop was Calahorra's tiny tourist information office, though she didn't expect to find anything about the silversmith there. A middle-aged woman behind the counter spoke to her in Spanish, but seeing her confusion, instantly switched to English. Annja smiled her thanks. The woman had a pair of tortoiseshell glasses hanging around her neck from a thin gold chain. She toyed with them as she talked.

"Good afternoon," she said, reminding Annja that the time was ticking away. "How can I help you?"

"I'm doing some research," she said, fishing out a business card for the station, along with the network's corporate logo and *Chasing History's Monsters* on it. She handed it to the woman. "For a possible television program." It wasn't *exactly* the truth, but given the way the search was developing, it wasn't exactly a lie, either. The woman's smile widened, but Annja caught the momentary panic in her eyes as she glanced around to be sure there wasn't a camera filming them.

"How can I help?"

"Well, I'm hoping to get some information as to where some of the victims of the Inquisition were buried," she began. The smile on the woman's face began to slip. No doubt the majority of her visitors asked the same or similar questions.

"I'm afraid that there's very little to see here," she began. "It's true that the Inquisition held its court here, but only for a very short time before it moved thirty miles down the road to Logroño." She slipped the pair of glasses on, pushing them up the bridge of her nose, and opened the drawer of a small filing cabinet. She retrieved a well-worn folder from inside.

"Here we go," she said, running a finger down the top sheet. "The Inquisition only held a court here from 1521 to 1570. Very little evidence of it remains, I'm afraid. Were you hoping to find something in particular?"

Annja pulled a piece of paper from her pocket.

She had written the names of the six men onto it to avoid having to remove the ledger from the bike's panniers. The woman frowned as she tried to read Annja's hasty scrawl.

"Sorry," Annja said, suspecting that it was the handwriting that was giving her trouble. "I think I was a doctor in another life. This is the man I'm hoping to find out more about." She pointed at Abdul bin Soor.

The woman pursed her lips. "I can't say I recognize the name. Was he important?" She slipped off her glasses again and looked up at her.

"Probably not in the grand scheme of things. I know very little about him," Annja admitted. "I think he either lived or was executed here. The same goes for the rest of them. I understand that they were all probably quite wealthy men."

"And all Moors," the woman added.

"There is that. I don't suppose you'd have any idea where they might have been buried, assuming they were killed here?"

The woman shook her head. "Victims were usually placed in unmarked graves," she said. "It is not a period of our history that we celebrate."

So, no easy solutions here, either. But was it a brick wall? It wouldn't be the first time she'd been led to believe something was a dead end because people were reluctant to bring bad publicity to a town. As the woman had said, the execution of innocent people wasn't something Calahorra celebrated, but was it something they'd sweep under the rug? Maybe a little coaxing would help.

"Perhaps they'd know at the church?"

"They wouldn't be buried there," the woman said, just a little too quickly. "Things have changed a lot since those times. Back then, there's no way they would have buried Moors in a Christian cemetery." That made sense. But Annja was reminded that, so far, every major find she'd made on this hunt had been a case of a Moorish relic hidden away in a Christian shrine.

If what Roux had told her about the Brotherhood

of the Burning was right, a growing number of people wanted those darker days to return, even if their motivations were racial rather than religious. Of course, the irony was that if the Inquisition actually made a comeback, a great many of those right-wing racists would no doubt find themselves on the receiving end of persecution for their own lifestyles. In a society driven by religious fervor, having no faith could be just as dangerous as having the wrong one.

"I know it's naive of me, but I'd been hoping there would be some kind of evidence that might prove these six men had lived here. Never mind, I'm sure we can use some footage of the church, a few of the older buildings that would have been here at the time, that kind of thing. They'll set the tone we're looking for."

"Did you say six?" the woman asked, her interest suddenly piqued.

Annja nodded. She turned the piece of paper so the woman could see it again.

"I'm sorry, dear. The names mean nothing to me, but there is a story…"

"Yes?"

"When the Inquisition moved from here to Logroño, the Church took more than just their documents and—" she paused for a moment, obviously searching for a word that wasn't part of her usual vocabulary "—equipment."

Annja waited.

"They took some of their victims with them," she added.

"You mean the people that were awaiting trial?"

She shook her head. "No, they took the remains of some of the men who had been executed. The bones of six men were supposed to have been taken from the ground and moved to a new resting place."

Six men? Annja could hear Roux's voice in the back of her mind: there's no such thing as coincidence.

She felt a shiver up her spine. It was more than just the air-conditioning. This was the thrill of the hunt. She was on the right track. The mystery was unraveling for her. So much history, so many secrets and ultimately a new truth that no one else had discovered in five centuries. This was why she did her job. This was what she'd fallen in love with, this connection between the past and the present, this single moment when everything crystalized and became one single, compelling story.

"They wanted to keep their treasures close to them," the woman continued.

"Treasures? That's a curious choice of words to describe six dead men."

"The six gave their confession freely. That set them apart from the other victims here. They didn't suffer torture. They willingly gave the statement that condemned them. Even when others around them were claiming their innocence, even up on the scaffold, these six men did not. They would not deny their God."

"So the remains of the truly guilty were important to the Inquisition," Annja said, thinking aloud.

"The court moved to the cathedral there. If there are records pertaining to the six, they should have them."

"You've been really helpful, thank you," Annja said.

She could only hope that they were talking about the same six men.

Ticktock. Ticktock.

There's no such thing as coincidence.

The woman's smile returned. She had been happy enough to see Annja arrive, but seemed much happier to see her leave.

15

The bike roared into life again, like a caged beast finally released.

The road to Logroño was barely thirty miles, and the traffic was light. The temptation to really open up the throttle and unleash the power of the Roadster was impossible to resist.

Annja adjusted her grip and felt the surge of acceleration as the tires gripped the tarmac. She pulled out from the slipstream of a delivery truck and shifted up through the gears. The rush of speed, the adrenaline coursing through her, reminded her of what it meant to be alive. It was primal. The Roadster flew through the curves and switchbacks.

From somewhere behind her, she heard a siren.

She gave a silent curse.

She couldn't afford to be pulled over by the police— or worse, be taken to some backwater police station and forced to waste a couple of hours explaining herself. Even somewhere like this, there was the remote chance the officer might recognize her and let her off with a slap on the wrist, but she couldn't risk the chance that this wasn't her audience. Not while Garin's life hung in the balance. She was close. Getting closer. She couldn't afford to blow it.

As far as Annja could tell, she had two choices. She could either stop and hope she could talk herself out of a ticket, or trust to the fact that the Roadster was an ungodly machine and try to outrun the cops. What would Garin do? Without question, ride...ride like the wind. She dropped a gear again and twisted the throttle hard, finding power even the Roadster itself hadn't known it possessed. The engine complained desperately. A car horn blared as she pulled back in front of it in order to overtake the next vehicle on the inside. She wove in and out of traffic without a second thought for her safety, relying on her reflexes. She focused on the road, shutting out everything else, even as the siren grew louder. It was just her and the road. The cars ahead of her began to slow in response. She didn't. She pushed the Roadster harder.

And then she was at the point of no return. A glance at the speedometer, and the dial was already nudging toward the hundred-miles-per-hour mark. It was too late to play dumb and pretend she was getting her miles and kilometers mixed up. A car had slowed, its blinker indicating it was about to pull over, but the traffic had already built up around it, trapping it in the fast lane. That meant the police car wouldn't be able to get through. That was all Annja needed. She seized the moment and pulled into the middle of the road, squeezing between the slowing car and the line of seemingly stationary traffic.

She clipped the car's side mirror, snapping it off and sending it clattering and spinning to the ground. The impact caused the bike to wobble, but she was strong enough to steady it. As an angry horn shrieked, Annja unleashed every remaining ounce of power in the bike's engine and leaned forward to cut down the drag.

The Roadster continued to pick up speed and she fought to keep it under control as she rode along in the slipstream of a semi. Then she was out, in the middle of the lane divider and flying past the truck while the turbulence battled her.

She pulled in front of the semi and eased off the throttle, out onto clear road, but she didn't relax her grip.

The trucker sounded his horn, venting a short, sharp blast.

She checked her mirror to see that the cop car was, impossibly, closing the gap.

The driver was stubborn, she'd give him that. That, or he had a death wish. She wasn't about to slow down now.

She made out the sound of brakes and the squeal of rubber as wheels locked.

Annja risked another glance in the mirror to see what was happening behind her.

The semi completely blocked the road, tipping onto its side.

Now there was no way the cop could follow her.

The sign ahead proclaimed that she'd just breached the city limits of Logroño.

She followed the road into the city, slowing but not too much, knowing she needed to get off the road as soon as possible if she didn't want more of the local law enforcement coming after her. Her description was out on the wire, for sure.

It didn't take her long to find what she was looking for—the Cathedral of Santa María de la Redonda. The name of the place had been nagging at the back of her brain all the way here. She knew it should mean something to her, but it wasn't until she stood in front of the cathedral itself that she started to remember why it was significant.

When the Inquisition had turned its attention away from the Jews and the Moors, it had turned its attention toward women accused of witchcraft.

So many innocent women had been dragged before the court to answer charges.

It had been male-dominated oppression, an easy way to silence the rising female voices of the day.

Another town, another visitors' center standing opposite the cathedral, another middle-aged woman sitting behind another desk.

This one didn't have the same smile, though. She didn't have a smile at all. Her attention was taken by a magazine spread open in front of her. The array of brochures on display showed that Logroño wasn't afraid to play on its connections with the Inquisition. Geographically, it may have only been thirty miles from

Calahorra, but it was half a world away in terms of attitude. Logroño was making the most of its history. Annja pulled an English leaflet from the rack and smiled at the woman behind the desk. She didn't respond. On the television behind her, a news report was showing footage of a courtroom explosion in Seville where a number of civilians had been badly injured. Miraculously, it didn't appear that anyone had died. The ticker across the bottom said that Spanish police were looking for an old Frenchman in connection with the events. Roux. She shouldn't have been surprised. The man had an unnerving ability to get into the kind of trouble that wound up on the national news.

"Hi," Annja said, producing the list of names from her pocket again and placing it on the desk.

"Hola," the woman said.

Annja ran through the same introduction she had given earlier, adding that the woman's colleague in Calahorra had suggested that the remains of the six men might have been moved to Logroño.

"Ah, yes, María telephoned me and said you might come in, but I was not expecting you to get here so quickly."

"I had a bit of luck with the traffic," Annja offered.

"As I am sure she told you, people were brought here from all over the region," the woman said. She reeled off a list of places, many of which meant nothing to Annja, but she listened intently in case the woman said anything that would provide some obvious missing connections. Even a single piece of the puzzle, an extra link in the chain, would move her closer to solving the mystery of the mask, and in turn secure Garin's freedom.

"Navarre, Álava, Guipúzcoa, Biscay…" The list seemed to go on and on. The woman didn't even draw a breath. Annja wondered how many times she'd reeled off these towns and cities, like a waitress running down the day's specials. Annja resisted the temptation to tell her to cut to the chase.

"It was not only women, of course. There were many men and children, too, including priests."

"Priests?"

"Yes. There were thirty-one priests who faced the Inquisition on charges of using *nóminas*, amulets with the names of saints engraved upon them."

"I had no idea," Annja said.

"Oh, yes, even the holy men were not immune as the Inquisition progressed. It spread its net far and wide," she said. "And it didn't matter which God you worshipped."

"I'm trying to find out about one particular victim."

"There were thousands of people who died here, tens of thousands, and almost all were buried in unconsecrated ground. Mass nameless graves. Many were transferred from other places. May I see your list?"

Annja gave it to her, and for the first time since she'd walked into the tourist center, the woman began to look excited. Her head bobbed up and down as she read.

"I recognize these names. These were not common victims of the Inquisition. Far from it. These were powerful men, in their own way."

"Do you know where I would find their graves?"

"Heretic's Yard, but I'm afraid you have made a wasted journey. The yard is closed to the public." Before Annja could ask why, the woman explained, "The walls are being repaired. After the storms last summer, the entire yard has been under threat from subsidence. They could collapse at any time, bringing half the cathedral down on top of anyone in there. It has taken the workmen forever to shore up the foundations."

She gave Annja directions that would take her behind the cathedral. Annja's thanks fell on deaf ears, as the woman had already returned to her seat and the magazine that had been captivating her when Annja had arrived.

Leaving the information center, Annja peered around the corner to where she'd parked her bike. A police car had pulled up next to it, and an officer was speaking into a radio, reading out the license-plate number. The ledger and her change of clothes were locked in the panniers. She'd have to recover them later, but for now she had a grave to find. She had less than twelve hours to find the mask and turn it over to Garin's kidnappers. She could worry about the Roadster and the ledger and squaring away the incident with the authorities after that, once Garin was safe.

If...

16

A signpost shaped into the unconvincing likeness of a finger pointed the way. One of the knuckles had been broken, another was chipped and peeling paint. The letters were long faded.

Annja followed the narrow path between overgrown trees and encroaching bramble hedges that hid the sun. As the woman had promised, the path took her beyond the cathedral proper and around to an enclosed cemetery garden. The high stone wall was dwarfed by the scaffolding rising on the other side of it. There was no sign of any workers on the site.

"Hello?" she called out tentatively, in case there was someone on the other side she couldn't see. "Anyone there?"

There was no response.

Annja followed the wall. If she stretched up, she could just about reach the top with her fingertips. She approached a heavy wooden door set with iron studs. There was a notice on the wall beside it, an historic-interest plaque giving details about the number of people who had been executed and buried in Heretic's Yard as part of the Inquisition.

Annja tried the door handle. It wouldn't budge. She had no idea if the workers were on siesta or just not on the site at all, meaning she had no idea how long she'd have in there undisturbed if she broke in. She walked a little farther along the wall until she reached the corner and turned right, out of sight of the main thoroughfare in front of the cathedral, and continued following the perimeter. This section of wall edged onto the back-yards of other buildings, and she risked being seen if she hung around too long. People tended to notice things that didn't belong. Had the workers been there, her presence might not have been so remarkable, but alone she stood out like a sore thumb.

There was no sign of another entrance.

She doubled back along the path until she reached the most sheltered stretch of wall, and took one last glance in either direction before taking a couple quick steps back, then running and leaping at the wall, planting her foot as high as she could and boosting herself up. Annja's fingers clawed at the old stone, scratching against loose grit as she scrambled up. She kicked out, one toe finding enough purchase to push herself up until she folded across the top of the wall. She lay flat for a second, adjusting her balance before swinging her legs up and over one at a time and dropping down on the other side.

She stumbled as she landed, because of a buildup of

dirt beside the wall that she hadn't expected, but she caught her balance and looked around.

Somehow she had expected more.

Once the scaffolding and the builders' equipment were removed, there'd be nothing here but a patch of well-tended grass and the stone walls that surrounded it. It didn't feel like a particularly fateful spot. Unsurprisingly, there was nothing marking any individual graves. But it was obvious that there weren't thousands of dead in the Heretic's Yard, even if they were buried ten deep.

She looked up to the skies, but it wasn't as if a lucky break was just going to land in her lap.

She scoured the ground, not sure what she was hoping to spot…some kind of stone or plaque that might denote a grave, maybe. But even if she examined every single blade of glass, there was no guarantee she'd find any indication of who was buried where.

She started to pace, one hand brushing against the stone, watching where she put her feet. There was nothing here; she was only wasting more time. She was beginning to doubt herself. Why had she ever thought this mission could lead to anything but a dead end?

To find the mask, if it was even here, she'd need a powerful metal detector. The chances of finding one lying around in a place like this were slim to none. A minute later, she was scrambling up the scaffold, hoping the improved view would make a difference.

Her eyes were drawn to the farthest corner, where the grass seemed to stop short of the wall.

She scanned the rest of the space from her perch, but saw nothing particularly out of the ordinary.

If there was any sort of marker stone in the grass, it was there.

She clambered down and made her way quickly to investigate, hoping that she'd just made her own luck.

By the time she was within a dozen paces of the corner, she was sure that the gray patch of ground where grass wasn't growing was a slab of stone. It could just be builder's rubble, of course, but the way the grass had receded around it made her think it hadn't been moved for years.

Grass grew close to the great stone slab and licked over its edges, while moss and lichen maintained a grip on its surface.

She dropped to her knees.

The stone appeared unmarked, nothing to indicate what it might be commemorating or covering. But this corner was the farthest part of the Heretic's Yard from the cathedral proper, possibly even distant enough to not be considered part of the holy ground. If she had to guess what lay beneath, she'd say it was something that the Church was afraid of and yet wanted to keep in its sight.

She couldn't pry the stone up with her bare hands; she needed something she could use as a lever. The builders had left plenty of equipment lying around. Something ought to work. As she started to walk toward the blue-topped work huts, she heard the sound of voices on the cathedral side of the wall. She felt a sharp stab of panic, sure it was the builders returning, but as she listened to the soft tones, she realized that they weren't the usual gruff tradesmen on the other side. Clergy, then, come to inspect the builders' handiwork, or young lovers looking to consecrate the age-old sex-in-a-graveyard rite of passage. She hoped for the latter, expecting the former. If she made any noise, the clergy would be drawn to investigate, while the young couple would likely be scared off.

She walked softly, glad that she only had grass beneath her feet. She had to be quick and quiet. She couldn't risk the first alternative.

She ransacked the builders' hut, coming away with a long iron bar, most likely used for breaking up the ground. If she could work the bar beneath the slab, then maybe she could pry it up. Assuming the six men had been buried deep, at least six feet under, she grabbed a spade, too. She might not have time to dig, but it was always better to be prepared.

She was about to head back to the slab when she heard what could only be feet scrabbling against the other side of the wall.

Fellow trespassers, then.

Great.

Annja dropped to the ground, pressing herself up against the wall, hoping they'd just go away. She held her breath and waited, still clutching the metal bar. She heard gasping, then the scrabbling stopped and whoever it was dropped heavily to the ground, still on the outside of the yard. For what seemed like an eternity, the couple—it was two people, now Annja was sure—attempted to climb up, kicking and cursing before bursting into laughter and walking away.

She noticed a crate of tools pushed against the wall.

Annja didn't dare touch anything until she was sure the would-be lovers, or whoever they were, had moved on, but in among the hammers, chisels and screwdrivers she spotted something that might be of use. As the voices receded, she reached into the crate, her fingers closing around a black oblong box. She slid it out from its resting place. Just as she'd hoped, it was a pipe and cable detector, a small metal detector designed for locating and avoiding electrical wiring and plumbing that ran within walls to prevent them from being drilled into inadvertently. It was unlikely to work at any great depth, but surely it would be enough to tell her if there was something in the ground—if she could get the slab lifted.

She went back over to the stone and punched the end of the bar into the ground, forcing it beneath the stone until it was deep enough to provide leverage when she pushed her weight down on the other end. It took all of Annja's considerable strength to work the stone free, with the earth fighting her every inch of the way, not wanting to give up the prize it had spent centuries absorbing. But once the slab was up a couple of inches, it was easier to deal with.

She leaned on the bar, forcing the gap another couple of precious inches wider, then slid the spade in, jamming the blade into the earth to prop up the stone and give her a moment to catch her breath. Then she took a grip on the edge of the slab.

Annja strained every muscle, feeling her temples bulge and her face burn red as she lifted. It was a back-breaking effort. She felt like Sisyphus, but she couldn't imagine having to move this massive hunk of rock more than a few feet before collapsing, never mind up a hill. And once she had her weight under it, she couldn't let it fall. She braced the stone with her legs, then heaved up, straightening, her feet threatening to slip on the grass, until the stone was upright. One last push sent it falling into the wall so hard she thought it or the wall would crack.

The densely compacted earth crawled with bugs and worms scurrying to find shelter from the burning sun. After a lifetime in the dark, this must have been a rude awakening for them. Amid the insects, Annja noticed a strange raised pattern in the soil. It took her a moment to realize it was an imprint from something carved into the stone. She brushed the slab with one hand, delicately removing the dust and dirt to read two letters. Those two letters were enough to convince her she was on the right track. *V* and *I*, the roman numerals for the number six. It was a simple acknowledgment of what was in the soil beneath the stone, wasn't it? No names, nothing so personal, just a number to mark six bodies. The six men who'd been moved from Calahorra to this place.

She wiped her forehead with the back of her hand, grateful as ever that she spent so much time in the gym building core muscle strength. Even so, the combination of the physical effort and the high sun was punishing.

Annja unboxed the cable detector, then powered it up, moving the head close to the iron bar to make sure that it actually worked. A red light blinked on as soon as the head came within a few inches of it. As she suspected, the detector was far too precise to alert her to anything buried well below the surface, but it was all she had, and if it meant she didn't have to waste an hour digging, then it was a godsend.

She ran the detector over the earth. Despite the constant motion of the insects, or maybe because of it, the light blinked on and off.

It was all the promise she needed.

Annja tossed the cable detector aside and grabbed the spade.

As she forced the blade into the compacted earth, Annja had to remind herself that just because there was something metallic down there didn't mean that it was the mask.

But it *could* be…

She scraped away a thin sliver of dirt that held together like a slice of clay, then another and another.

Gradually, she peeled back the surface layer by layer, aware that digging too deep too quickly could damage whatever was hidden in the ground. As she struck the earth again, the corner of the blade nicked something. She stopped digging immediately. It could have been a stone, but it she wasn't about to risk it. She cast the spade aside and knelt on the edge of the shallow hole to better see what her digging had revealed.

Carefully, Annja brushed aside the dirt with her fingers, flicking away the soil and a bloated earthworm to reveal a few fibers of old sacking. She teased at it, unsure whether it could be the remains of the wrapping that would have been used to keep the bones together during transportation, or whether it was protecting something else entirely. She kept brushing. The sack had long since rotted away, leaving barely a few fragments, and those were more dirt than burlap. She peeled the last few fragments away, heart in mouth.

Pushed into the earth, a little bent and flattened by the pressure of five hundred years' worth of weight resting on it, robbed of any luster, was the thing she had been looking for. She'd found it, she was absolutely sure. She lifted the Mask of Torquemada out of the silversmith's unmarked grave.

As Annja gently held the mask in her hands, she heard the sound of men's voices moving closer—deep jovial voices, the sound of working men returning. Siesta was over. She had to move fast. Annja set the mask to one side and with one colossal effort heaved the slab back into place. It hit the ground with a dull thud. She realized too late that she hadn't replaced the earth she'd removed from the hole. She didn't have time to worry about it. She just had to hope they weren't paying attention. She snatched up the tools and ran back to the hut, trusting that it wouldn't matter if she put them back exactly where she'd found them. She doubted the workmen would notice that any tools were out of place. She was banking on the fact that by the time anyone realized the burial plot had been disturbed she'd be long gone.

Annja heard the men cursing at the door to the yard, struggling with the old lock, then she took the first step up onto the scaffolding.

With the mask tucked into her leathers, she hauled herself up, climbing hand over hand, legs swinging beneath her as she rose, the entire scaffolding rocking with her movement. She reached the top as the door in the wall swung open.

Annja lay flat on the wooden platform, sliding slowly onto the wall. The motion worried the mask loose from her leathers. It fell, clattering against the outside of the wall before hitting the ground below. She dropped down after it, the toes of her boots scraping against the stone as she did.

Annja rolled as she landed, springing to her feet and snatching up the mask.

She couldn't believe she'd found it. The mask of the Grand Inquisitor. She could feel the contours of his face in her hand. She was so close to saving Garin, and with time on her side. It was a miracle. She needed to make contact with the kidnappers, to arrange the handover and release.

First, though, she needed to make sure she still had transport.

She jogged alongside the wall, going the long way around the cathedral to avoid the door to the Heretic's Yard. She didn't want to risk stumbling into any workers who were too curious for their own good and had followed the sound of the mask hitting the wall. When she was far enough away to be sure she wasn't being watched, she looked at the mask in her hand.

She rubbed the silver with her thumbs, feeling that familiar tingle of history thrill through her veins. This was a true treasure, something both ancient and irreplaceable in her hands.

So this was what you looked like, she thought, taking in the features described in the soft metal. She had seen an engraving of Torquemada's profile, and while this was similar, the twist in the metal gave the Grand Inquisitor an air of cruelty that couldn't be denied. It was easy to study this sexless, emotionless, alien rendition of the man's face and imagine he must have enjoyed his work. She turned it over. The inside of the mask wasn't what she had expected; instead of being smooth metal that fit against the skin, it was scoured with signs and sigils, swirls and symbols. She had no idea what they meant, but this wasn't simply tarnishing at work. There was a grand design here. It was a deliberate pattern.

She pulled out her phone and made the call.

Oscar might have identified what he thought was the source of the video feed as the Alhambra, but she wasn't convinced that wasn't just another layer of subterfuge. It was just as likely the kidnappers were still in Madrid, close to Garin's offices. If they were clever enough to hide their tracks, they were clever enough to send a hacker on a wild-goose chase if they wanted to.

"I've got it," she said.

"Indeed. Interesting that it was in Logroño all along," the voice said.

"I don't appreciate being spied on, however you're doing it," Annja said, resenting the intrusion. The idea that they were watching her every move, even if it was from a distance, was disturbing to say the least.

The only response was laughter.

"You look quite pretty when you're angry, Miss Creed," the man said.

"Do you want the mask or not?"

"Of course. I suggest you make haste. Ticktock. Ticktock. It is a long way to the Alhambra," he said. "Even on that bike of yours."

"I've got the mask for you," she snapped. "Stop the clock. It's over."

"It doesn't work that way. You've got what's left of the twenty-four hours I gave you to get it into my hands if you want to see Mr. Braden alive. Otherwise, *boom*."

He hung up.

Even if she could ride out of the city without police interference, the bike would take too long to get her there. It was more than half the length of the country away. She needed to call the old man and make alternate arrangements.

"I've got it," she said as soon as Roux picked up. "You were right. They're based in the Alhambra. I have to get down there. The clock's still ticking."

"What's it like?" Roux asked.

"Remarkable," she admitted. "A little bent and battered, but all things considered, wouldn't you be, if you were that age?"

"I *am* that age, dear girl," he said, but there was no malice in his response. "We have time on our side now, so we need to work out why they want it. Tell me, is there anything unusual about the mask?"

She thought about it for a moment. She and Roux had already amassed a wealth of information that might or might not be relevant. One thing was for sure, though— the kidnappers didn't want the mask for itself. It was just part of the bigger picture. But what was that picture? Was she already looking at it without seeing it? Everything she and Roux had found so far had to be linked, didn't it?

"There are engravings on the inside. I'm not sure if they're patterns… In a few places it looks like it might be writing, but I have no idea what any of it means."

"Send me a picture."

"Will do. I'm going to need you to sort out transport. I don't have time to ride across the country. And anyway, the bike's out of action—if it hasn't been impounded already, it's only a matter of time."

"I won't ask," he said. She resisted the temptation to point out she'd seen his latest get-out-of-jail-free exploits on TV. "Get yourself to the airport. My pilot already has my plane in the air, so I'll get him to make a diversion and pick you up at the nearest airstrip. It shouldn't take him more than quarter of an hour to get there, so mush, mush."

He hung up.

She needed to recover the ledger if she could. It was unlikely she'd be able to ride the Roadster to the airport, so she'd need to flag down a taxi, too. But the ledger was the most important thing.

She worked her way back to the main square where she'd parked.

The police car was gone, but there was a clamp in the front wheel of the Roadster.

Annja felt an element of relief, glad that it was just her parking the officers had been addressing rather than the speeding, reckless endangerment and overturned semi. It could have been a lot worse. It wouldn't take long for them to put two and two together, but for now she slipped the ticket into her pocket. She'd give it to Roux, let him smooth the whole mess out later. At least the bike was still there. She unlocked the panniers and removed the ledger along with the backpack that contained her change of clothes. She put the mask into the bag and headed back to the information office.

The unsmiling woman looked up from her gossip magazine.

"Where can I get a taxi?"

The woman held up a hand and picked up the phone.

A couple of minutes later, a cab pulled up in front of the building.

17

The helicopter circled around the magnificent fortress.

Roux had never seen it from the air before. It was a sight to behold, even after centuries of misuse and abuse, civil war and hostility. He looked for obvious weaknesses in the defenses—an old habit, and those old ones really did die hard. The Moors would have been able to hold out against the Catholics for a long time before the aggressors could have forced their way in. With any kind of military mind behind the defense of the Alhambra, the Catholics would have lost far more men than the Moors in any confrontation, and attempts to starve them out would have been futile. The fortress had everything it needed to be self-sufficient.

Down there, somewhere in that ancient warren, Roux was certain he'd find the home of the Brotherhood of the Burning. They wouldn't be able to hide from him in the walled city. He'd leave no stone unturned. That Annja had been told to bring the mask here just reinforced his certainty. With luck, though, he was ahead of the game. Even if they knew he was still an active player, that didn't mean they knew where he was or even if he was on the move. He was banking on the fact that they couldn't expect him to be here already. "How long till we land?"

"Two minutes," the pilot said. He had time.

"Keep us low. I need to make another call."

"Roger that."

Roux had given Oscar as long as possible to discover everything he could about the Brotherhood of the Burning. He placed the call, imagining the hacker sitting behind an array of computer screens, headset on, probably playing dumb computer games in between working for him. He picked up.

"Well?" Roux asked.

"Interesting stuff. This Brotherhood has its roots going *way* back to the days of the Inquisition," Oscar began. "We're talking medieval cult, secret brotherhood, sworn in blood, all that fun stuff. Their sole aim seems to have been to recover treasure that was taken from them by the Church."

"Which fits with what's happening," Roux said, more to himself than the hacker.

"As far as I can see, they were never able to get any of it back. Not that any records are readily available. And what I have managed to find proves they were still active until the late 1700s, but then they went off the map. Obviously, that could just mean that later records have been destroyed. You can never be sure with this stuff. Books burn, after all."

"Well, if they were banging their heads against a brick wall, maybe each subsequent generation just lost a little more hope, and they finally gave up," Roux said, thinking out loud. After all, how many generations would it take before people stopped searching for heirlooms and treasures taken by the Nazis? "Anything else?"

"The Brotherhood was started by a group of Mudéjars. A Mudéjar was a Moor who did…"

"Yes, yes, I'm well aware what a Mudéjar was," Roux interrupted.

"Well, anyway, one of these Mudéjars was a man who had been commissioned to create the ceiling in Torquemada's tomb, another worked on frescos and the third was a silversmith. They all had skills that were sought after by the Church, even though they saw these men as heretics and wanted them banished from Spain. They were all wealthy men. They kept themselves close to the Church, making themselves indispensable. Keep your enemies close, I guess. They seemed to think that it would give them the best chance of finding out where the treasures of dispossessed Moors had been hidden."

"Indeed. You said there was a silversmith? Do you have any names?"

"Hang on a second. Let me call up the list."

Roux knew who he was going to name. There was no chance it was going to be anyone but Abdul bin Soor, the Moor who had fashioned the mask and whose remains had lain with it for five centuries.

Roux was right.

"How many names have you got?" Roux asked.

"Nine. Seems like the Church did its best to round them up, but some of them evaded capture and managed to get out of the country. The rest were taken for trial."

"Six," Roux said.

"How the hell did you know that?"

"You've just confirmed something, that's all. What about our current Brotherhood?"

"It's all a bit sketchy. I've got to admit I thought they were just a bunch of right-wing nutjobs at first—there's plenty of those sprouting up all over Europe these days, and all that made them special was that they knew a bit of their nation's history, adopting the name to hold up the Inquisition as an example for achieving their own aims. I was wrong. It's more than that. The more I dug, the more I realized it stinks. The whole thing stinks. Someone is using them as a front. For one, the most obvious link to the past is that the people seemingly behind this are Muslims from North Africa, descendants of families who were supposed to have been driven from Spain."

"That doesn't make any sense," Roux said. "They have been behind a number of racist attacks. More specifically, attacks against Muslims. Why would they do that? Why attack their own people? What about the name I gave you? You find anything on him?"

"Plenty. I'm sure it won't surprise you to know that Enrique Martínez is not his real name."

"Nothing would surprise me right now. Go on."

"Until a couple of years ago, Enrique Martínez didn't

exist. He's a brand-new man. I like this kind of stuff. It makes life interesting. That's why I like you, old man. It's like Martínez sprang into life fully formed, complete with bank account, tax identification, passport, the works."

"Interesting." What Roux found even more interesting was that his contact at Europol didn't seem to be aware of Martínez's spontaneous incarnation, or had chosen not to tell him. "And his real name?"

"That's all I've got at the moment."

"Find out what his name is."

"I will. Trust me. This guy's got my attention now. Oh, and just a heads-up—that latest video Annja sent me, it came through a different route, but all roads lead back to the same dead zone."

"The Alhambra," Roux said, looking down on the fortress as they began their descent.

Less than five minutes later, Roux was on the ground, watching the helicopter take off.

The pilot was going to the airport at Granada to refuel and wait for Annja.

Even if they had the mask, the clock was still ticking.

18

There were security cameras everywhere.

It was impossible to tell if they were merely for show, if the fortress's security and maintenance crew had access, or if the Brotherhood of the Burning had tapped into the feeds and was using them as an early-warning system. He figured it was best to assume a worst-case scenario, given the sophistication with which they'd rerouted the video stream and covered their tracks. They were tech-savvy. And realistically, if there was this much security on the outside, what was he going to be up against once he got inside?

The complex was made up of a maze of buildings behind the defensive walls. It could take forever to find where the Brotherhood was situated, even after Roux had breached the front wall.

A number of the buildings within the public area bore signs that explained they were closed to the public for repairs and renovations, but there were still plenty of visitors milling around. They were convenient. He didn't want to stand out from the crowd, so he followed the flow of bodies and listened to a guide who was leading the party through the complex. As exotic as the ancient palace was, it was a much more mundane set of buildings that interested Roux.

Scaffolding had been erected along the outside of one such building. There was no sign of any workmen, but Roux heard hammering coming from another building not too far away. Men were back at work, but not here. Why? Sometimes it wasn't what was there that was wrong, but what wasn't there. Scaffolding without workers? A false front? Cover for something behind the wall? Almost certainly.

"Here is the altar of the open-air chapel," the guide said, waving her arms as if to accentuate the fact that there was no roof. A few of the tourists took the opportunity to turn their cameras to where she was pointing and grab a few extra shots. It never ceased to amuse Roux—tourists living life through a lens so they could look at it all again when they got home, but forgetting to actually soak it in unfiltered when they were right there, standing in the presence of such beauty.

"And here, forming the part of the floor, we have the tombstones of King Ferdinand and Queen Isabella. But before you get excited, neither of them is actually buried here. Their bodies were laid to rest in the mausoleum in the royal chapel in Granada, which obviously we'll be visiting later during your stay here in Andalucía." There were a few nods in the crowd. Roux noticed a man in a lightweight suit and sunglasses push his way carefully through the crowd without speaking so much as a word of apology as he eased gawkers out of his way.

The guide gave him no more than a brief glance, but Roux *stared*. And for good reason. The man placed his hand on the shoulder of a tourist in front of him, and Roux saw the flame tattoo on the back of it. He had to force himself to look away before the man inevitably glanced back at him, feeling the intensity of his stare. Roux scanned the rest of the crowd for familiar faces, anyone he might have seen since his arrival in Spain, but it was difficult. The sun was high, dazzling off the sandstone walls and the mirrored shades. Any one of these people could have been at the courthouse or any step along the way from there; he wouldn't have been able to tell. No one appeared to be regarding him strangely or trying desperately not to look at him, either.

He watched the man enter the small building surrounded by scaffolding.

The guide waited until he had closed the door behind him before she pointed the building out to the group.

Curiouser and curiouser, Roux thought.

"Over there is the indoor chapel. It is very small inside and no doubt would only have been used on rare occasions, given the beautiful weather we enjoy here in Andalucía. Unfortunately, as you can see, the building is undergoing renovation, so I am unable to show you inside today."

The average age of the group, Roux figured, was probably pushing late sixties, early seventies. A fair few of them looked older than he did, which he appreciated.

The group moved on, the guide urging them toward another landmark building. Roux hung back in the shadows. He really wanted to get inside that chapel. The guy in the suit was a member of the Brotherhood. He'd gone through that door. That meant Roux was going through that door, too. Simple as that.

He fished out his phone to check in with Annja, hoping to get an idea of how far behind him she was.

No signal.

He'd forgotten what Oscar had said about this being a dead zone. The fact that the kidnappers had been able to broadcast from here—even for a moment—meant that they had to be using some kind of jamming device to keep them hidden from modern surveillance techniques.

It also meant that no one would be able to call for help if the need arose.

That suited Roux just fine.

He slipped the phone back into his pocket.

"Showtime," he muttered, but he had no intention of charging inside, gate-crashing whatever party they had going on.

Unfortunately, there was no other obvious entrance to the chapel, and no windows that offered easy line of sight from the ground.

But the scaffolding would at least give him the opportunity to look inside without being seen.

He walked past the door, resisting the temptation to ease it open, even a fraction, to peer inside. The security cameras on the chapel were much newer than any of the others he had seen. And they were trained on the door. Even from here, he could see that the black cables hadn't been bleached by the sun yet, and the plastic clips that pinned them in place were still pristine white. These cameras weren't just newer; they were brand-new. The Brotherhood had increased the level of security around the chapel. It was as if they knew he was coming. He was touched.

He glanced around again to be sure no one was paying attention to him, then took a step onto the ladder that led to the scaffold's first platform. He was already in the shadow of adjacent buildings and out of sight of tourists, but he wanted to be sure he was hidden from the many cameras in the area. He couldn't be sure, but he thought he was good. That would have to be enough.

The first window was filthy with the grime of building work. It clearly hadn't been cleaned since long before the scaffolding had been erected. Roux pulled out a handkerchief and mopped his brow before applying the cloth to the glass. There were people inside, but a balcony running along the inside of the upper floor prevented him from figuring out how many. He tried the window, but it wouldn't budge, obviously locked from the inside. He cast his gaze downward in case he'd been spotted before working his way around the scaffolding and into the sun. The second window was locked, too, but a third was more promising. As he worked at it, he realized it was loose around the latch. Not necessarily unlocked, but a bit of give allowed him to work his pocketknife into the gap and worry at the latch.

The latch slipped off easily and—most importantly—without making a sound.

Roux could hear chanting. There was a steady rhythm to it. The voices didn't skip a beat. He eased the window open slowly and climbed inside, the chanting masking any noise he made. He pulled the window closed behind him, not wanting to risk any ambient noise from the street outside to register with the men down there. He waited, not moving, just listening, a hand on the butt of his pistol in case someone tried to blindside him. Drawing it would mean escalating any confrontation. He wasn't going to do that until he absolutely had to. And then he'd be every bit as ruthless as he needed to be to make sure he walked out of there, preferably with Garin.

The tempo of the chant shifted, as did the tone, and the voices swelled to fill the dome of the ceiling.

It echoed all around him.

Roux crouched lower, moving closer to the edge of the balcony. He risked a glance down through a cutout section of the balustrade to the floor below. The chanting should have been a clue. It seemed that some kind of religious or pseudoreligious rite was taking place, but the longer he watched and listened, the more sure he became that there was something strange about it.

He couldn't make out the words, but the chant seemed to have more in common with a black-magic mass than a liturgy. There were at least a dozen armed men in the throng, but none of them looked vigilant.

They held their rifles as a medieval knight might have held his sword in a similar rite.

There was a serious amount of firepower down there.

But looking at them, their pretend-knight posturing, left Roux wondering how many of the guards were able to use their weapons. He could probably have taken out half of them from the gallery before they'd even brought their guns to bear, but that wouldn't necessarily be a good thing. Not until he knew where Garin was.

Roux weighed the odds.

If he'd had any backup he wouldn't have hesitated. He pulled out his gun as he made his decision, picked out which of the men down there was marked for death, imagining the collapses and working out what would happen as they fell, like dominos, trying to foresee all the possible consequences.

The chanting stopped. The room fell eerily silent as a curtain at the back parted. Two men joined the congregation, dragging a third man between them. There was a hood over his head.

It had to be Garin.

Fish in a barrel.

Roux took aim, drawing a deep, steadying breath, ready to fire, only to hear the telltale sound of a gun's mechanism ratchet a heartbeat before he felt the cold steel of its barrel press against the back of his head.

"Give me an excuse to pull the trigger," the voice said.

19

Annja took the chance to shower and change into clean clothes, ditching the leathers. Roux's plane was more like a flying hotel than a cramped economy shuttle, with every convenience imaginable and a bunch that weren't. She emerged refreshed and awake, more alive. The first few minutes in the plane's air-conditioning were bliss. The call from Roux came, telling her he had a helicopter waiting for her at the airport. The old man was always one step ahead of the game. But then, he'd been playing it for a very long time. She was still new to this, really, despite the incredible things she'd seen and done since her hand first closed around the sword in the otherwhere. That felt like so long ago now.

The pilot didn't emerge once from the cabin or waste his time with small talk over the intercom. He just did his job moving her from point A to point B at Roux's request.

She sat back in the supple leather armchair and pulled the mask out of her backpack. She wanted to see what she could decipher, if anything, before they landed. She was searching for an edge. If she could work out what this was all about, she'd be a step ahead of all of them, and a step closer to getting Garin out of the mess he'd gotten himself into. And she had no doubts that Garin had walked into this with his eyes wide open. Knowing something was a bad idea had never stopped him before. She was going to need help, though. The plane was equipped with a satellite phone, meaning she was still hooked up to everything that made the world tick. Annja made a couple of calls, getting a referral from an old associate in Bonn to a colleague in Bern who just happened to know exactly who she should be talking to: a history professor in Rome, an expert in the field, having spent more than twenty years researching the fate of the Moors during the Inquisition.

A couple of minutes after making the first call, she had him on the phone.

"Miss Creed," the man said in a soft voice.

"Professor Zanetti," she said. "Thank you so much for this. I can't begin to tell you how much I appreciate it."

"Nonsense," the man said. She could hear the smile in his voice. "I am always happy to talk about things that captivate me. I understand that you are interested in discussing the Moriscos?"

"Actually, I want to talk about their treasure."

"Ah." There was a moment of silence on the other end of the phone as the professor reassessed the conversation. His tone shifted slightly. "Are you a treasure

hunter, Miss Creed? I was led to believe you were a serious student of archaeology, no?"

She took a deep breath. "Today, technically, I'm a
treasure hunter, I guess. But every other day of my life
I'm a serious student of history and archaeology. And
yes, I can well imagine that a lot of people would be interested in finding the Morisco treasure if they knew it
existed, but honestly, I'm not one of them."

"Then what are you trying to accomplish here, Miss
Creed?"

"I'm purely helping out a friend."

"Well, I'll tell you this much—advice, if you like, so
take it or leave it as you will. Even if this treasure still
exists, no matter that it would make the finder as rich
as Croesus, rich beyond the dreams of avarice, it's not
a road you want to be following. And you are the second person I have said the same to in as many months."

"The second?"

"Yes. Perhaps it was someone else associated with
your television program? I must admit, I suddenly feel
like one of the cool kids. I don't think I've been this
popular since I was in high school."

"I'll check with my producer," she said, wondering
who Zanetti had been talking to. She could already hear
Roux's voice in her ear banging on about there being
no coincidences. "Can I ask you, Professor Zanetti, do
you have a personal theory on what happened to the
confiscated wealth?"

"I do indeed. Of course, a lot depends on the nature
of this wealth. The Moors held a tremendous amount

of riches, and while those who fled the country often retained theirs—or at least what they could carry with them—as did the Moors who converted to the Christian faith, some treasures were confiscated by the Church. These weren't obvious treasures. Many wouldn't even see value in them. They seized thousands of books—of course, many of them had jeweled bindings that were of value in themselves—but of even greater value was the information inside them. Many of them were religious tracts, but perhaps surprisingly, others contained a vast amount of scientific knowledge. We are talking about a tremendous wealth of learning, destroyed and denied to scholars. Certain books on medicine were retained, though others likewise were considered to be heresy and destroyed. You could draw parallels with today, when even some enlightened people believe that the words in the Bible carry more weight than the discoveries of generations of scientists. If it doesn't come from the mouth of some God via a burning bush, they don't want to know."

"No actual money, then? No jewels? These were wealthy people, weren't they? What happened to their belongings once they were executed?"

"Ah, now we are back into the world of the treasure hunter, Miss Creed. And there we are confronted on all sides by supposition, presumption and, to be honest, make-believe. Yes, material wealth was certainly lost, particularly when the Moors abandoned the Alhambra. But was there ever enough to make up a great horde like something out of *Ali Baba and the Forty Thieves*?

Would it have been gathered, or would light-fingered enforcers have made off with it? Lots of variables we have no answers for. Tell me, have you heard of the Moor's Last Sigh?"

"The book?"

"No, though Rushdie's novel is in some small part inspired by the events of the time. When Muhammad XII, the last sultan of Granada, led his people from the Alhambra and through the Puerto del Suspiro del Moro—the Pass of the Moor's Sigh—he was supposed to have looked back at what he was leaving behind and wept. It is my belief they abandoned far more than books. But is that your missing treasure? I do not claim to know."

"Can you remember the name of the man who contacted you?"

"Not off the top of my head, I'm afraid. Something Hispanic. Perhaps unsurprisingly, given the subject matter. He had an American accent, though, I think. Hernandez?"

Annja felt the chill certainty that she was following in the Brotherhood's footsteps. "Martínez? Enrique Martínez?"

"It could well have been. Like I said, it was a couple months ago, and names aren't really my thing."

"Do you remember what you talked about?"

"The same as you. The treasure. He was most interested in the Alhambra itself, but—and I found this interesting, given that its existence isn't well-known—he asked a lot of questions about the Mask of Torquemada."

The words sent a shiver up her spine.

The Brotherhood already knew she had the mask. Likewise, they knew she was on her way to Granada. She had a choice to make. And not long to make it. This professor could be one of them, testing her. She decided to play a game of you-show-me-yours-and-I'll-show-you-mine.

"Professor, I know this might be one of the strangest requests you've ever had, but would you mind showing me the backs of your hands?"

"On the telephone?"

"Take a photograph of your hands, with your face in the shot, then send it to my email. I'll wait for it to arrive, then we'll talk."

"How very mysterious, Miss Creed. Very well, I'll play along."

A moment later, she was looking at a photograph of his face and his hands, sleeves pulled back to reveal his forearms. There was no sign of the telltale tattoo Roux had warned her about. She decided to trust him.

"Would you mind telling me what that was all about?" he asked. "Worried that I might have something up my sleeve?"

"Not at all," she said. "I'd like to show you something, and I just needed to know I could trust you. Let's take this conversation over to video chat."

"You really are quite…different…Miss Creed. Again, I'll humor you, mainly because I'm curious now."

It took a couple of minutes for them to connect over video, but they were face-to-pixelated-face soon enough.

"I want to show you something, Professor, but this stays between us, understand?"

"Pinky swear," the Italian said, smiling. He saw just how serious Annja's expression was and added, "You have my word."

She said nothing. She reached for the mask and held it up in front of her face.

She watched the professor's expression through Torquemada's eyes.

He gasped. "Is that...? Are you telling me...? Is that thing...*genuine*?"

"Very much so."

"Where on earth did you find it? How...? Do you have any idea what this means?" The questions came tumbling out in an avalanche of words.

"I'd rather not say just yet," she said. "I intend to get it tested properly so we know exactly what we're dealing with before we make it public, but basically, from what you can see here, do you think it could be the real thing?"

"Impossible to say without examining it properly, but look at it... You can't rule it out, can you? The likeness— even though it's clearly been damaged over the years— is remarkable."

She turned the mask around to reveal the inside, the swirls and signs engraved in the discolored silver. "And my second question." She moved it closer to the webcam. "Do you have any idea what this might be?"

The professor made a face as he inclined his head. He licked his lips, then chewed on the bottom one, but didn't say anything for the longest time. So protracted was the silence that Annja thought for a moment the video chat had frozen. Eventually, he said, "Could you send me pictures of this?"

"Does it mean anything to you?"

"Possibly. Part of it looks like it could be Mozarabic."

"Mozarabic?"

"A dead language. It was spoken among Muslims until the fourteenth century."

"But if this is the Mask of Torquemada, surely the language would already have been dead for a century by the time of its manufacture?"

"It wouldn't have been in common usage, I agree, but that doesn't mean that it was lost completely at that point in time. Indeed, it could even have become a way for like-minded people to pass messages without the Church interpreting them. Send the pictures to me as soon as you can, and assuming the script is Mozarabic, I'll get them translated for you."

He ended the call, leaving Annja staring at the screen.

This changed things.

Not everything, but enough.

She had thought that the treasure had been taken and hidden by the Inquisition, but what if she'd been coming at this from the wrong angle? What if the Moors had been hiding their secrets from the Church before the Inquisition could lay their hands on them?

She was still lost in her thoughts when she heard

the warning sound and saw the fasten-seat-belts light come on.

"We'll be starting to descend in a moment," the pilot said over the intercom. "Landing in ten minutes."

She felt the plane start to bank and turn, losing altitude slowly.

She stashed everything away, ready to move on to the next leg of her journey.

She tried to reach Roux, but his phone went straight to voice mail. Maybe he was already in that dead zone. She left a message, telling him she was touching down, then settled in for the landing.

Fifteen minutes later, she disembarked. The afternoon heat hit her, almost making it impossible to breathe after the cool comfort of the plane. There was a large plane sitting on the tarmac along with a cluster of smaller private jets, including one not unlike Roux's. She'd flown on his Gulfstream often enough to recognize the shape of it. That was one expensive toy some billionaire playboy had parked up by the hangars.

Across the hardstand she saw the helicopter waiting for her. It was a fair distance away, nestled on the far side of the solitary terminal building. She started walking toward it when her phone rang.

She answered it without even looking at the screen.

"Annja."

20

Roux knelt with his hands held up in surrender.

The man kicked his pistol out of reach as Roux interlaced his fingers behind his head. There was nothing he could do but go along with it. Even if, by some freakish gymnastic feat, he could have thrown himself out of the window, he would have been cut down before he reached the ground. So he surrendered. He was where he'd wanted to be, in the belly of the beast. Assuming they didn't kill him straightaway, he'd just have to wait and seize whatever opportunity presented itself. They hadn't killed Garin, after all, so the odds were on his side. It would be too much to hope they didn't know who he was, though. The Brotherhood was organized. They'd done their due diligence. And he knew that because they'd tried to take him out once before. They wanted Annja, though. Not him. Their interest in him started and ended with not letting him help her. She was the one they'd sent on the treasure hunt. They'd put Garin's life in her hands, not his.

"On your feet."

Roux reached for the edge of the balcony, no sudden moves, and started to pull himself up, rubbing his knee with his free hand as he rose. He winced, playing up the old-bones angle without making it obvious that he was faking it. He *had* just scaled a scaffold and climbed through a window, so he could hardly be a frail pensioner. But maybe the man with the gun would underestimate an old man.

"Move it," the gunman said, prodding him in the base of the spine with his weapon. The gunman bent down to retrieve Roux's gun. The moment the cold steel wavered, Roux struck.

He swiveled and kicked out at the man's hand, knocking the gun from it. The semiautomatic clattered toward the window. Even before his foot had landed, Roux whipped his other leg out, taking his assailant's legs out from under him. The man sprawled backward, flailing out at Roux. Roux drove the heel of his hand into the man's nose, then rolled him over the gallery railing. The gunman fell. All element of surprise was gone by the time he hit the ground, dead. That put the cat amid the pigeons.

They were coming for Roux, but he was ready.

Heavy footsteps sounded on the stairs.

Roux snatched up his gun and, in the silence between heartbeats, took in his surroundings. That was all the time he needed. A door burst open along the balcony. A heavily armed man filled the opening. The gunman saw him and swung around to take aim: shoot first and ask questions later—or never. Hesitation killed better men than him. Roux didn't hesitate. He fired a single shot at the man in the doorway, taking him square in the chest. The impact of the bullet slammed him back into the men coming behind him.

It bought Roux a moment.

He sprung onto the top of the balcony railing, a sitting target for those below, and took three sure-footed steps before they could gather their wits and send the first volley of gunfire toward him. Bullets strafed through the air, embedding themselves in the wall behind him, the ancient stone spitting dust. Those same walls had survived five hundred years of conflict unscathed. They didn't withstand more than a few minutes of the old Frenchman. He didn't smile. He ran along the gallery with perfect balance, oblivious to the danger of the drop.

He needed to cut down on the number of guns trained on him.

There were eight bullets left in his weapon.

There were more than eight men who wanted him dead.

He needed to improvise.

A chandelier hung below the level of the balcony.

It was an inviting means of evading at least the closest of the gunmen.

He leaped from the rail like a gymnast, arcing his body and grasping the chain that supported the gilt construction. The metal links strained and stretched under the sudden pull of his weight, threatening to send him crashing to the ground. A shower of plaster fell, raining down on his head. Below him, two of the men dragged Garin out of the room while another offered covering fire. His aim was poor. Two rapid shots from Roux saw him crumple to the ground, a pool of blood slowly spreading out around him.

Six bullets.

Another shooter appeared on a lower balcony, directly in Roux's path as he swung.

That was unlucky for him.

Roux fired again, still one-handed, swinging on the huge chandelier. This time his shot took the man low in the gut. His screams as he crumpled up and fell were brutal. His weapon tumbled over the balcony rail, going off as it hit the floor.

There was no respite. More bullets whizzed by, too close for comfort, coming from above. One struck the chain supporting the chandelier. The link opened where the bullet clipped it, and Roux felt the change in the chain's integrity. The only way was down. And he wasn't in control of his descent.

One of the gunmen on the upper gallery looked over the barrier, letting off two shots in quick succession— not at Roux. Both hit the chandelier.

He felt the link finally sheer, and as it did he launched himself into the air, kicking out, arms windmilling frantically as he fell.

It was a long way down.

Roux reached out with his free hand and grabbed

for the rail of the balcony where the gunman had been standing a moment before.

Wood and plaster splintered again as a bullet thudded into the balustrade. Another brother leaned over the gallery behind Roux as he tried to pull himself up with one hand. His feet flailed wildly trying to snag on to anything to stop him from falling. He kicked hard, arcing his back—once, twice, three times—and then his toes connected with something solid.

Roux leaned back, one hand on the balcony railing, one foot on the stanchion supporting it, and released two shots back in the direction of the gunman. Two shots. That left him with three more. Far from ideal, but better than dead.

The chandelier crashed to the ground, cracking the tiled floor as it hit. That mosaic had survived a diaspora—generations of worshippers driven out of their homeland—and the Christians who had come after them. It didn't survive the chandelier. The man Roux had shot at followed it to the ground a heartbeat later.

The odds were evening up.

He almost felt sorry for them.

Roux hauled himself up with one hand, using the support of the stanchion to take his weight, and rolled over the railing. The man he'd shot in the gut was on his back. He wasn't dead, but he was in a bad way. His face was ashen, sweat peppering his forehead. He was panting hard, struggling to suck in a breath. He wasn't about to get up and fight. Roux stepped over him, looking for a door and a flight of stairs that would take him down to the ground level. He had to focus on what was important: getting Garin out of here. He found the door. It had a bolt, which he slid. He wasn't sure how long it would buy him, but any extra second was one he wanted.

The stairwell was noticeably cooler than the gallery. There were no windows in here. Nothing to stir the air save the echoes of his feet as Roux ran down the stairs.

From somewhere he heard the sound of an engine starting. It was followed by the heavy metallic slam of a vehicle's doors. They were trying to get Garin out of there. He charged down the stairs, but before he'd reached the bottom he heard the shriek of rubber spinning on stone. They were gone. So close. But they'd gotten Garin out while he'd been fighting for his life. Roux punched the wall in frustration. So close. So damn close.

He could only hope that meant they were taking him to the rendezvous with Annja, ready to trade for the mask, not out into a dusty field to put a bullet in the back of his head and drop his body into a shallow grave they made Garin dig himself.

Roux went back up to the gallery and the bleeding man.

He stood over him, not saying a word, letting panic seep in as the blood seeped out.

The man looked up at him with fear in his eyes. His gaze darted from Roux's face to the gun in his hand and back again. Roux raised the pistol, allowing himself a moment to smile as if this was a part of the proceedings that he enjoyed. The man looked as though he was about to cry.

"Please," he begged, the word coming between wet, sucking breaths.

"You're asking me to spare you? I could," Roux said agreeably. "But you weren't going to give *me* the chance to beg, were you? You wouldn't have spared me. Given the chance, you'd have put me down like a rabid dog. So give me a reason *not* to pull the trigger."

"I'm…"

"What, sorry? That hardly feels adequate, certainly not enough to spare your life."

The man squirmed. He knew he was about to die. He was frightened. That surprised Roux. Normally, zealots welcomed the chance to be martyred. Roux wanted to make that pay. And if it didn't, then he'd pull the trigger and put the man out of his misery.

"What can I say?"

"You can tell me who is behind all this."

"I can't," the man sobbed.

"Well, that is disappointing," Roux said, crouching down beside him. He put his face no more than a few inches from the other man's, and the barrel of the gun closer. "But let me check something, because words are important. Is that *can't* or *won't*?"

"Can't," the brother said, his eye fixed on the black hole of the barrel. Roux pressed the gun against the man's cheek.

The last dregs of color drained from his face.

"Want to try again?" Roux asked.

"El Zogoybi," the man said through clenched teeth.

"El Zogoybi?"

He nodded desperately. "Yes...that's...the name... he uses."

"What else?"

The man shook his head wildly. "It's all I know. Please."

Roux dropped the gun to his side. He had a name. El Zogoybi, the unfortunate. It was the name given to the last sultan of Granada. Boabdil, better known as Muhammad XII. El Zogoybi was the man who had been driven out of the Alhambra by the Inquisition.

"What else?" Roux repeated.

"That's all I know."

"Can I believe you?"

"I'm begging you."

"Mercenary?"

The man nodded, grimacing against the pain.

"Stomach wounds are bad. Chances are you're not going to make it through this. I can put you out of your misery if you want, make the pain go away?"

"I want to live."

There was a hammering on the door—whoever was left standing coming to clean up the mess—and then a shot was fired, followed by another.

They were shooting at the lock as if that was what was keeping the door closed, not the body of their fallen brother.

"Looks like it's your lucky day," Roux said.

He sent a shot of his own back through the door and they stopped firing. Two bullets.

He started to make good his own escape.

21

"Annja here," she said into the phone.

It wasn't Roux. It was the kidnappers.

"Welcome to Granada," the voice said. "I trust you had an enjoyable flight?"

"What next?" she asked. "Where are we meeting? I've got the mask. You've got my friend. Let's get this over with and get out of each other's lives."

"Tetchy, aren't we? There's a car in the parking lot," the voice said, ignoring her question just as she had ignored his. "A red Alfa Romeo. The keys are tucked in the sun visor. Take the road to the Alhambra. I'll give you instructions as you drive."

"I want to know where I'm going," she said.

"And you will. In time. Now get in the car and start driving. Ticktock. Ticktock."

Annja headed out into the parking lot. Part of her was surprised that the man hadn't mentioned the helicopter, but she took that as a sign that she had at least a few secrets from the kidnappers. She didn't know if she'd be able to use that to her advantage, but it was always good to have an ace in the hole.

The bright red car was easy enough to find.

From the outside, it appeared to be in near-pristine condition. As she slid inside, she was hit by the new-leather smell. The dash still carried that sheen of show-room-fresh polish. The keys fell into her lap as she pulled the sun visor down. Annja put them in the ignition and felt as much as heard the roar as the engine burst into life. The odometer registered less than a thousand miles.

She pulled out of the parking lot, onto the airport-centric ring of roads that eventually pointed the way to the Alhambra. She kept the phone beside her on the seat, ready to answer the moment it rang.

She didn't have to wait long.

"Next left," the voice said, then hung up without waiting for her acknowledgment. She did as she was told. A few miles later, another call came, instructing her to take the next left to leave the main road and drive a few miles on another. This time the kidnapper didn't kill the call. He directed her through a series of turns until she found herself in the middle of nowhere. In the distance she could make out the fortress city of the Alhambra bathed in the final rays of the setting sun, the light picking out some of the gilt-laden decorations.

"Look for the sign—it's a parking lot. Pull in there and wait. Kill the engine." She followed his directions and then waited.

Trees lined one side of the parking lot, making it feel like a viewing platform. She could hear the man's breathing through the phone. It prevented her from enjoying the view that the Moors had left behind.

The light faded far faster than she had expected, shifting from gloom to near-darkness in what seemed like a matter of minutes.

She heard the approaching vehicle long before she saw it as it swept into the deserted parking lot. A black van, headlights off.

"Now get out of the car," the voice on the phone said. She'd almost forgotten the call was still live.

She climbed out, leaving the mask on the passenger seat with the window down so she would be able to reach inside for it when she needed it. The van's lights turned on, blinding her for a moment. The glare forced her to shield her eyes. She heard men getting out of the back of the van; a panel door slammed and feet crunched on gravel as the men moved toward her.

"Where is he?" she said, not sure which of the shapes belonged to the man who had been calling her.

"In good time," one of the silhouettes said. Two figures moved forward, dragging a third between them. His feet dragged in the gravel. They dropped him. He fell forward, not even reaching out to break his fall.

Garin—it had to be him—was stripped to the waist with his hands tied behind his back. Even with the sack on his head, stained with dark patches of blood, it was obvious that he was in a bad way.

"Garin!" she cried, unable to stop herself.

She started to move toward him.

"Not so fast, Miss Creed."

She stopped, fighting every instinct to run to his side. She could hear the ragged flare of his breathing, so she knew he was alive, but that was it. The two men who had dragged him out of the van stood in her way.

She faced them down.

The van's headlights lowered from the dazzling high beams, revealing a little more than just the silhouettes of the men. They were like something fresh out of a nightmare, all of them dressed in black, all of them wearing silver masks.

They looked inhuman in the hazy glare of the headlights.

The silver masks were obviously intended to serve duel purposes—to intimidate and to hide their identities. Annja was face-to-face with the Brotherhood of the Burning.

She considered her options for a moment.

There had to be at least eight or nine men standing in front of her, all of them armed to the teeth with too much firepower—Steyr TMPs. Even in the bad light, the shape of the handheld machine pistols was distinctive. Joan of Arc's sword was only an arm's length away, and with it Annja was more than a match for the masked men, but all it took was one stray bullet, no matter how good she was or how unlucky they were. One bullet. That was how much a human life weighed at a time like this. She flexed her fingers, picturing the hilt of the sword, but stopped short of drawing it back from the otherwhere. It wasn't worth taking the risk when she was this close to securing Garin's freedom. They could stop the Brotherhood after he was safe.

"The mask," one of the men said. His voice was muffled, but Annja recognized it as the one from the phone calls.

"It's in the car," she said.

"Get it."

"Take that thing off his head first."

"Very well. Do it," the voice told one of his cronies.

One of the masked men bent down and pulled the sack from Garin's head.

"There you go. See, no tricks."

In the harsh blaze of the van's headlights, Garin looked even worse than he had on the video stream. Shadows played on the cuts and bruises, distorting his features even more, making them almost monstrous. But there was no doubting that it was him. He coughed once, doubling up in pain, and spat blood. He didn't try to struggle to his feet. He just lay there on the ground, breathing hard, blinking. He was alive. That was all that mattered.

Annja backed toward the car. Without turning her back on the masked men, she reached in through the window to retrieve the Mask of Torquemada and held it up for all to see.

"Is this what it's all been about?" she asked.

What they didn't know—couldn't know—was that she'd photographed the relic from every possible angle, recording as much of it as she could. She and her colleagues could render those photographs and use them together with a 3-D printer to reconstruct the mask. It wouldn't be the same, but if the mask itself was lost to the world here, a replica would be better than nothing. Still, losing the mask would be a pretty dramatic failure on her part, and she wasn't in the habit of failing. She'd hand it over, yes, but Zanetti was already working on the mysterious swirls and text, trying to decipher them, and she'd do her damnedest to get the real thing back.

Contrary to what the kidnappers might think, it didn't end here.

One of the brothers walked toward her. The others kept their Steyrs trained on her.

There was no going back.

Like it or not, she had to hand the mask over. Even then, she couldn't be sure they intended to let her and Garin walk away from this little showdown. She looked down at him. He was in bad shape. He wouldn't be able to do anything fast.

The man, the apparent leader, held his hand out. "The mask. Give it to me."

She held on to it for a moment longer than necessary, mentally connecting with the sword in the otherwhere. A mistake now could be fatal for more than one of them. Right now it was all about staying alive.

He took the mask from her.

She could sense him smiling behind his own mask.

Before the night was out, she'd wipe that smile from his face. She promised herself that.

He turned the mask over in his hands, running his fingers over the curious swirls and symbols and debossed letters, then turned his back on her and started to walk toward the van.

And for a fraction of a second—less—she thought he'd given her the moment she wanted. It was too early, though. If she reached into the otherwhere now and struck him down, it wouldn't end well. Different scenarios flashed through her mind. She could cut him down in a single slash, then grab him as he fell and turn his body into a shield. It would absorb a lot of the damage from the Steyrs, but at such close proximity, with so many of them trained on her, it wouldn't be enough. This wasn't her moment.

She watched him walk away, feeling lost and hopeless, as the other men climbed back inside the black van behind him. The door slammed, and seconds later, the tires spat gravel as it drove away, leaving Garin on the ground and Annja staring at their taillights, red spots disappearing down the road.

Annja ran to Garin's side.

"Sight...sore...eyes." He tried to grin.

"Shh, save your breath. We've got to get out of here." She knelt down beside him and untied the cord binding his wrists. Without the headlights to show the complexities of the knot, it took a few seconds longer than it might have. "Then we'll get you to a hospital. Get you checked out."

"No hospital," he mumbled.

"Yes, hospital. You're a mess."

"No..."

"We'll argue about it in the car," she said, not exactly conceding the point as she helped him to his feet. He leaned on her every step of the way as they walked gingerly back to the waiting Alfa Romeo. It wasn't the ideal car for transporting the weak and the wounded, but it was better than trying to walk the miles back to civilization.

"Not so fast," a voice called from the darkness.

She felt her heart sink.

The Brotherhood had no intention of letting them walk away from here, after all.

She took a deep breath, steadying herself.

She was never comfortable around death, unlike Roux and Garin. She hoped she never would be, either. If there was another way, she'd always seek it out, even if the sword was only ever a thought away, waiting for her to draw it from the ether. It was a last resort, never a first option.

"You don't have to do this," she said. But of course they did. They were acting under orders. The boss had the mask, and now it was time to tidy up the loose ends. And that was exactly what Annja and Garin had always been to the Brotherhood.

And that meant she had no choice. Not everyone was going to walk away from this ambush.

"Step away from the car."

She did as she was told. One step, and another, holding her hands out away from her body. It looked like a sign of meek surrender. It wasn't. She was doing what was needed to be ready to defend herself. She could al-

most feel the familiar weight of the sword in her hand.
Her breathing quickened.

She stared into the darkness.

She could make out three distinct shapes.

They were spread out a few feet from one another.

This was only going to happen one way, and there
was no use pretending she'd be able to talk her way out
of it. Her hand closed around the hilt of her mystical
blade, and in an instant it was there, forging a connection between Annja and the saint, blazing white in her
hand as her would-be assassins unleashed the first burst
of bullets. The sword was a weapon of justice as well
as death. And for as long as she could, she'd use it to
stay alive, not to kill. Metal ricocheted against metal as
the blade intercepted the shots, deflecting them harmlessly away. The bullets, more than a dozen, clattered
onto the hood of the Alfa Romeo in a chorus of steel
rain. More shots. Her muscles burned. She went with
instinct over sight, picking each one harmlessly out of
the air as she stepped forward to meet the deadly hail
of bullets. One of the Steyrs stuttered.

Annja hurled herself to the ground, hitting it hard
with her right shoulder, rolling out of the dive and rising in front of them. The maneuver had taken her out
of the line of sight with the Alfa, minimizing the risk
that a stray bullet would puncture the shell and hit Garin
while he was unable to defend himself.

"Do you really want to die out here, boys?" she
called, hoping to strike a chord of fear inside them. It
came down to who they feared the most—her with the

otherworldly blade in her hand, the devil they didn't know, or their leader, the devil they most definitely did.

She was answered by a spray of bullets.

"You're slow learners, aren't you?"

More gunfire.

She moved fast, scrambling across the gravel. Bullets tore up the ground around her feet. Shots plunged into a tree beside her, splintering the bark.

Too close for comfort.

She moved between the trees, using them to conceal her as she ran along the side of the parking lot. Muzzle flare and the bark of gunfire filled the night. She didn't slow down. Bullets ripped chunks out of the trees on either side of her. Annja took one on the length of the blade, sending the bullet high and wide in a shower of sparks.

She burst out of cover, running head-on at the gunmen. Three guns became two as one of the Steyrs fell silent. The brother lost his nerve and dropped his gun, realizing that the bullets weren't up to the task.

He turned and ran.

Annja closed the gap between her and the remaining men, her blade still slicing through the night in a deathly arc of silver. One bullet ricocheted against its length, spinning away in the direction of the shooter. It took the brother in the shoulder. His cry of pain had barely left his lips when the man beside him fell to his knees, blood leaking from a gaping wound in the middle of his chest. He pitched forward, his breathing almost nonexistent. He wasn't going to be long for this world, and he knew it.

Another hail of bullets almost caught her unaware. The last gunman was a stubborn one.

"Okay, sunshine, you had your chance," Annja said, dropping to her knees as a bullet took the dying man in the back of the head and put him out of his misery. She heard another staccato burst of gunfire. Then a grunt and the sound of stumbling feet followed by collapse.

In that moment, the gunman with the bullet in his shoulder turned and ran.

And he moved like a jackrabbit, bolting for the anonymity of the dark.

She had to move quickly, while she could still make out the fleeing gunman's position. He wasn't getting away from here. She needed the Brotherhood to think these men were dead.

Another shot came in her direction, wide of its intended target.

Muzzle flash gave her something to aim for, and the briefest glimpse of the man behind the trigger. He was firing blindly.

She started after him. She was faster. Fitter. He stumbled, sensing her behind him, fired wildly again, high over Annja's right shoulder. She was no more than a couple yards from him when he realized how close she was. The brother was caught half-turned, and he went down in an ungainly tangle of legs. He landed on his back, the Steyr pointing up at her face, so close he could not possibly miss.

In that second, Annja Creed felt regret for the things she hadn't done far more than for the things she had as she thrust the sword into his chest. His death was accompanied by the unmistakable sound of the Steyr clicking on an empty chamber.

Annja sank to her knees, breathing heavily, her heart racing.

She couldn't have known that the gun was empty, and the man beside her, whose life was draining into the parking lot's gravel, couldn't have known, either. Annja stood up and began to make her way back toward Garin and the car when she heard the crack of another gunshot.

"Garin!"

She ran, cursing herself for leaving him alone and not suspecting there would be a fourth gunman. The sword was light in her hand. It gave her strength. Power from that ancient connection to the maid flowed through her veins, filling her body and soul. She was ready to cleave the gunman's head from his shoulders and end this here, praying every step of the way that Garin was still alive.

She reached the car. Garin stood above one of the masked brothers. He leaned on the car to support himself. The brother was dead, a bullet hole in the middle of his silver mask.

"He came back for more," Garin said simply.

She stepped in close, taking his weight. He was rank, reeking of stale sweat.

"Did he say anything?"

"Only that El Zogoybi will kill us for this."

"El Zogoybi?"

"Their leader," Garin said. "Damn, it's good to see you, Annja. About time you saved me for once."

She laughed at that, relief flooding through her system. She could feel herself shaking as the adrenaline abandoned her.

"I heard them say his name a few times, like he was some sort of divine master, one of these holier-than-holy nutjobs. I never saw him. At least I don't think I did. It was hard to tell who was who behind those creepy masks."

Annja bent down and pulled the masks off the dead men, but she'd never seen any of them before. She'd hoped one of them might have seemed familiar, a face she'd seen tailing her and reporting back about her movements over the past day. But they were strangers. Each of the dead men had the tattoo of flames on the backs of their hands.

"The Brotherhood of the Burning," Annja said as she got back to her feet.

"I'm not with you?"

"Let's get in the car," she said. "We can talk while I drive. Sticking around here's not good for our health. I'll tell you what's been going on while you've been out of action."

"Sure, where's Roux?"

"Taking care of business," Annja said. "We'll catch up with him and work out where we go from here. But first, let's get you patched up."

"I'm good. I just need to sleep. I could kill for a hot bath."

He clambered into the back and was asleep within minutes of his battered body sinking down onto the leather seats. She drove in the direction of the airport.

It was a lonely road.

22

As Roux left the tiny chapel, his phone lit up with notifications of missed calls and voice mails.

The dead-zone effect.

The vast majority of the messages were increasingly frantic calls from Oscar demanding that he call him back. He'd found something, but he wasn't going to just leave it on Roux's answering service—which meant it was something important. Roux walked through the streets, hurrying away from the chapel. The surviving brothers would come after him soon enough; his best hope was to lose himself among the tourists. Safety in numbers.

Not that he'd recognize the men when they came, unless he could spot the distinctive tattoo on their hands. So, from that moment on, everyone was a prospective threat. Thinking that way made staying alive easier. Trust no one. The man beside him in the crowd could have been one of them. The man leaning against the wall smoking a thin licorice-paper cigarette and seemingly admiring the female tourists could have been one of them. Or neither of them. Or both.

Roux looked left and right, knowing his own fur-
tiveness marked him out as suspicious, but there was
nothing he could do about it.

He needed to get away from there.

The clock was ticking, but Garin was still alive, and
he wasn't here anymore. That made Roux's role in this
less urgent. That could change at the drop of a hat, but
for now he had to move about unseen. It didn't help that
his face was all over the national news, wanted in connection with the bombing of the courthouse in Seville.
They'd released his name, too. Of course, it wasn't his
real name, though it did mean that that identity was
dead to him now, which was inconvenient.

But Oscar sounded desperate for him to call back.
That much was obvious, but it didn't change the fact
that it was going to have to wait. Annja was on her way
to secure Garin's release and Roux was a rat in a maze
with a bunch of trigger-happy men on his tail. Nothing
the hacker had turned up would alter the outcome of
the meet or the chase.

At the moment, it was all about priorities. He'd get
out of there, find somewhere safe and then make contact. It came down to trust. He trusted Annja. He trusted
Oscar. They would do what they had to. If the kid's info
was that vital to the outcome, he'd reach out to Annja—
he wasn't dumb. Besides, given the number of missed
calls, he'd probably try Roux again before he was halfway out of the complex.

He moved quickly, following the last of the visitors.

Only a handful of staff remained, cleaning up before they closed the site for the day.

His phone rang again.

He took it out of his pocket, turning the corner and moving quickly down a narrow set of steps, taking them two and three at a time as he answered.

It was Oscar.

Roux slipped into a narrow passageway between buildings and emerged into a courtyard.

"What is it?" he rasped, still moving.

"Finally. I thought you were dead."

"Not yet. So something's got you wound up?"

"You've been in that dead zone, haven't you?"

"Yes."

"You're one crazy SOB, you know that, old man? Do you have any idea how much trouble you might have been walking into?"

Roux drew in a sharp breath. "I do now, put it that way. You were desperate to talk—I assume that wasn't because you wanted to berate me on my lack of caution?"

The hacker grunted. "Now I know you're safe, it's not so urgent."

"Tell me, anyway. Let me be the judge."

"I've been monitoring the dead zone, like you asked. I might have missed it if I hadn't been looking for it."

"For *what*?"

"It's not always dead. I mean, it bursts into life, only for a few seconds at a time, never at set intervals, never for the same length of time, but never longer than a minute. I set up a lurker in case they came on again."

"A lurker? In English, please?"

"It's a Trojan that just hangs around, waiting for the system to go online, then it embeds itself."

"Let's pretend that means something to me."

"The code gathers information and creates images of the entire drive when the system is online. Even if the network is shut down and restarted, the Trojan will pick up again where it left off. It's much easier than trying to hack into the network in the bursts when it's online. It also means I get to dig around properly without fear of setting off any security. Score one for the good guys. I haven't managed to get everything yet, but I've found something very interesting. Actually, it's more than just interesting—it's *weird*."

"I'm not paying you by the word. Spit it out," Roux said.

"How's this—while I was waiting to download stuff, I decided to take a look at the CCTV footage from the kidnapping at Garin Braden's offices. Some of it was missing."

"What do you mean? The kidnap footage?"

"No. That's all there. Every second of it. It's the twenty minutes or so immediately before the kidnappers crashed through the window. It's been erased."

"Okay, strange, I'll give you that. How does it help? What are you thinking?" Roux couldn't see how footage from *before* the kidnapping was going to reveal a great deal, but he humored the man. "Maybe he was in there with a client? Some of the people he deals with are very private. Maybe they didn't want any record of their meeting."

"I thought of that. Big-business, late-night clandestine meetings, all very cloak-and-dagger. Not worth losing sleep over. Until I found it."

"Mystery solved, then?"

"Very much not. The footage wasn't on the company servers. I found it stored on the system in the Alhambra. It was in the first burst of data that came through from my lurker. The Trojan is designed to send me the most recent files first. And there it was."

"I'm not getting it. Why would the Brotherhood have footage from Garin's office that wasn't on his own system?" Roux was thinking on his feet. "Okay…maybe they were on there? One of them wasn't wearing his mask? So they wanted to wipe out anything linking them to the kidnapping? But then why keep a copy of their own?"

"Weird, isn't it? I know you like weird, so I figured I'd let you know."

"I appreciate it," Roux said, his mind racing. This was important. Somehow. "Send it to me."

"Will do. Watch it. Tell me if you see what I see. I had to watch it a few times before I worked out what it was that someone was trying to hide, but I figured it out. I'm a smart guy, and I didn't see it straightaway. But you…well, you just might. I don't want to color your reaction, though, so I'm saying nothing. Take a look, then tell me what you see."

Roux hung up and waited for the video clip to arrive. He could hear people in the distance, but no one was approaching, so he stayed where he was, in the deepest of the courtyard's shadows.

The phone vibrated and he opened the video file.

Looking at the image, Roux realized that he had never been inside the office in Madrid. But he'd been in a dozen like it across the world. Garin was predictable in his taste. The room was well-appointed, the furniture comfortable and functional, but very definitely fashionable. It was a classic case of style at considerable cost, the kind of comfort that could only be achieved when money was no object. It was ostentatiously chic.

There were a couple of men in the room with him, behaving as if they were at home. That marked them as bodyguards. They were relaxed. A little too relaxed, but that was unsurprising, given the seeming impregnability of the office. It was essentially a fortress hundreds of feet above the city. Any threat of danger there was minimal.

Garin said something to one of the guards and got to his feet. There was no sound on the footage and Roux couldn't read his lips. The man stood, as well, and slid the sofa he'd been sitting on forward a couple of feet.

Garin stepped behind it and removed a picture from the wall.

Roux had seen the style before. He was reasonably sure it was a Mark Rothko, and knowing Garin, it was an original, meaning it was valuable. Like everything else in the room.

Garin studied the painting for a moment, holding it out to the light.

He spoke again, then left the room, taking the picture with him.

The two remaining men continued to chat, clearly relaxing even more now that their employer was out of the room.

Garin returned a few minutes later, still carrying the canvas.

He replaced it on the wall.

The sofa was pushed back into position and drinks were poured for everyone.

Garin checked his watch a couple of times while they drank.

Then the clip ended. Roux wasn't quite sure what he'd just seen.

Thoughts ran through his minds like cogs and wheels in a gradually accelerating machine. He weighed everything in the clip. There was something important in that short piece of security footage. Something fundamental to everything that had happened in the past twenty-four hours.

It made him uneasy.

The uneasiness quickly changed to anger as things started to fall into place.

It took a moment to piece it all together, but when he did, that changed his perception of *everything* he'd just witnessed and everything that had happened since.

He'd caught the look on Garin's face as he sat there sharing a drink with those two men. Two men who

would soon be dead. He had checked his watch because
he knew what was coming.

He had known to the minute when the kidnappers
would shatter the huge bulletproof window and come
rappelling in. There was no surprise. He had known
he'd be the only one of the three leaving the room alive.
That was what the drink was about. It was a toast. A
send-off. It was the Rothko original that gave it away,
though. He hadn't just taken it out and then returned to
rehang it. Garin had known what was coming. He knew
there would be gunfire. He'd known it would get messy.
He had switched the picture, replacing it with a print of
the same image so no one studying the security footage
would notice anything amiss. That was Garin's weak-
ness. He loved beautiful things. Roux stared at the small
screen, feeling sick. Betrayed. He should have *known*.
He was well aware how venal his friend was. He'd always known how duplicitous the little snake could be—
after all, he'd spent centuries avoiding Garin's elaborate
attempts at murder. Even so, the sight of him taking
his seat and waiting for the kidnappers to arrive sent
a shiver down the old man's spine one bone at a time.

Garin wasn't the victim here.

Roux needed to warn Annja before she walked into
the cross fire.

23

The hotel was almost full.

Annja had passed it on the way from the airport. It was business-class, not a tourist trap, which meant an added layer of anonymity, plus decent food. She was starving. She headed straight for the hotel rather than waste time looking for something else. They needed to freshen up, regroup, think. They needed to get that mask back.

Garin stood beside her, the only colors in his face the red-brown of the cuts and grazes and the blue-black of the bruises that bore testament to the beating he'd taken. He wasn't his usual talkative self. He didn't try to flirt with the woman behind the reception desk. There was no dazzling smile. That, more than anything else, convinced Annja that he was in worse shape than he was letting on.

So Annja pasted the smile on her face and leaned across the desk. "Two rooms, please. As close to each other as possible if you can manage that?"

The receptionist looked down her nose at Garin. Annja had to admit the only fashion statement he was making in his bloody jeans and torn T-shirt was how drugs still screwed you up. He had Annja's leather jacket draped over his shoulders and was shivering. Either shock or cold. Or both.

"Certainly, madam. Unfortunately, the only rooms we have available are on different floors."

"That's fine," Annja said. She likely wouldn't get to use hers for a few hours, anyway. She'd be fretting over Garin, making sure he was settled and resting properly. Then she'd have to track down Roux, wherever he was. The old man had been out of contact for longer than she would have liked, but that was him all over—not exactly selfish, but easily preoccupied with his own thing. He'd be in touch when he needed something, and now that they'd made the handover and Garin was safe... Well, for the first time since she'd woken up in Valencia, there wasn't a little voice in her head going "Ticktock."

She handed over her credit card. The receptionist ran it and handed it back along with two sets of keys. If the numbers were any indication, their rooms were almost one above the other. She waved away the bellhop. They didn't have any bags to carry.

Annja took Garin to the lower of the two rooms and helped him inside, leading him across to the bed, where he sprawled out. The room was like any one of a hundred hotel rooms she'd stayed in around the world. They weren't designed for visits of more than a couple days. That was just fine. They wouldn't be staying that long. Garin wasn't in any condition to complain. He rested on the bed for ten minutes. She thought he'd fallen asleep but he was just staring at the ceiling. Finally, he said, "I need a shower. I stink."

She couldn't argue with that.

"Do that. You want anything from room service? I'm so hungry I could eat a horse." She picked up the menu.

"Anything bloody," he said, pushing himself up from the mattress. He hobbled toward the bathroom. "Not that I can promise to stay awake long enough to eat it."

She ordered a steak and fries for each of them, making sure hers would be sent to her room. They promised to have it with her in twenty minutes. She listened to the water run, trying not to imagine Garin's bruised and battered body standing under it.

"Make sure you eat something," she called to him. "And then get yourself into bed. I'm going to go freshen up. Give me a call when you're awake. I'll go out and get you a change of clothes. I can't imagine there'll be much available in the gift shop apart from a nice touristy T-shirt. I'll leave my spare key on the nightstand."

He laughed at that. Maybe there was a little bit of Garin Braden that hadn't been battered out of him. She smiled and headed up to her own room.

It had the same layout as Garin's, the same decor, the same pictures on the wall, identical down to the smallest detail. That was part of the appeal to the traveling businessmen. All she wanted to do was kick off her boots and stretch out on the bed, but she knew if she did that she wouldn't be moving until the sun rose. Besides, room service would be knocking on her door in a few minutes. She punched in Roux's number. The call went straight to voice mail.

"Roux, it's Annja. I'm at the…" She glanced at the key, realizing she didn't even know the name of the hotel. "The Alhambra Sol Hotel. It's near the airport. Garin is here. He's safe. Call me when you get this. We need to put our heads together. They've got the mask. They tried to take us out, so right now the Brotherhood is probably working under the misapprehension that we're dead. That buys us a bit of time, but someone will find their bodies soon enough. I'm not leaving here without the mask, so call me. Doesn't matter what time you get this, okay?"

She hung up.

She knew that the Alhambra, or at least the part of it they were interested in, was a dead zone. Roux had warned her he'd be incommunicado. She wasn't worried about him. He'd check in when he could. She looked at her watch. It was late. They were only a few hours from the imposed deadline the kidnappers had set, meaning she'd been running on adrenaline for one long, seemingly endless day. Now the reality of the situation was beginning to sink in and exhaustion was catching up with her fast. The Brotherhood didn't have Garin. She was off the clock. She could afford to relax for a few hours. But she'd eat first. And shower. Then she'd worry about what was going to happen in the morning.

Her phone rang.

She snatched it up from the bed. "Roux?"

"This is Aldo Zanetti. We talked earlier today? About the mask?"

"Sorry, yes, of course, Professor," Annja said, pulling herself together. "I was expecting someone else."

"No need to apologize. I shouldn't be calling at such an ungodly hour, but I thought you would want to hear as soon as I finished the translation."

"Absolutely. What have you got for me?"

"It's a map," he said.

"A map? I didn't see any... How...?"

"Actually, to be more precise, it's a treasure map. Yes, you heard me correctly. Assuming I'm not mistaken, what you have in your possession is a map that purports to lead to the Moorish wealth hidden from the Inquisition and kept safe until such time as the Moors—or their descendants—would be able to return to recover it."

"Okay," Annja said slowly. "But how can that be? The map was engraved on the inside of the Mask of Torquemada? He *was* the Inquisition. It doesn't make sense. Surely he was the one they were hiding it from?"

"Ah, but there's the ingenuity of a dead language guarding your secrets. The man who engraved the mask, Abdul bin Soor, was one of the men who hid the treasure. Part of it was his. It belonged to him and the five men from Calahorra who died with him. They knew that the Inquisition would never find out where or what it led to, and they were sure that by hiding the truth amid complex patterns and Mozarabic script, their enemies would never be able to translate it. A wonderful irony, don't you think? The treasure the Church sought hidden right in front of the Grand Inquisitor's eyes. Wonderful. Just wonderful."

"Devious," Annja said appreciatively. "And you're certain?"

"Absolutely."

"Incredible…" A thought struck her. "Was there any reference to something called the Brotherhood of the Burning?" She tried to remember what Roux had called it the first time he'd mentioned it. "I think it would be something like Fraternidad de la Quema in Spanish? That won't help you at all, will it?"

"Well, there were several symbols engraved on the interior of the mask that I haven't been able to decipher, ones I took to be somewhat elemental in nature—earth, air, water and, yes, a flame. But there was no specific mention of a brotherhood."

There was one obvious question she hadn't asked. She couldn't help herself. "I have to ask," she said. It was obvious he knew what was coming. He didn't try to hurry her along. "The map itself…were you able to work out where the Moors hid their treasure?"

"Oh, yes, and this is where the strangest of coincidences arises. You recall we talked about Boabdil's regret, looking back from the Pass of the Moor's Sigh on everything he had abandoned?"

"Yes."

"As far as I can tell, that's where the treasure is. I haven't been able to decipher a precise location, but I suspect it is hidden within the iconography rather than the Mozarabic text. I'll work it out, I have no doubt about that. For now, if you were a treasure hunter, I think the Pass of the Moor's Sigh would be the best place to start looking."

"You are an absolute legend, Professor. Thank you," she said.

"My pleasure, Miss Creed. Just one thing, a small request. If you ever find yourself this way, I would dearly love to see the mask for myself. To touch something that has sat against the Grand Inquisitor's face, to look through its eyes as he must have done so many times... Perhaps we could even arrange for it to be exhibited here in Rome?"

"Of course," she said warmly. She hoped she could make good on that promise.

Annja's medium-well steak arrived, along with a healthy selection of dips and sauces to accompany the fries. She took a soda from the minibar to wash it down and watched the news while she ate. There were no stories about the bodies she'd left behind. That was something. There was, however, plenty about the suspected act of terrorism in Seville that had seen the courthouse bombed earlier in the day. The police were looking for a man whose photofit was a perfectly grainy likeness of the old man. Roux would be delighted that they'd burned one of his identities. That was what they were for, she supposed.

Annja decided she would give him another twenty minutes, taking it up to the hour, and then she hit the shower.

She emerged feeling half-human again.

She dressed and decided to check in on Garin.

The tray of food she'd ordered for him was sitting outside his door.

She assumed he'd crashed out and tapped gently on the door, then used her copy of the room key to enter. The room was dark, the thick curtains drawn, but in the dim light from the hall she could see that the bed hadn't been slept in. Something felt wrong.

"Garin," she called softly as the door swung shut behind her. "Garin," she called again, a little louder this time. There was nowhere he could hide in the room. She felt the stir of a breeze. He'd opened the window. She went to check the bathroom, terrified he'd blacked out in the shower and that she'd find him slumped against the ceramic wall tiles.

Damp towels were strewn over the floor but there was no sign of Garin.

He was gone.

24

Annja took the stairs two at a time.

The lobby was only a couple of floors down, and the elevators were clogged with new arrivals from a late flight. She reached the ground floor much quicker than she would have if she'd waited. The receptionist who'd checked them in was still on duty. She glanced up as Annja approached, still half running, and pasted a too-friendly smile on her face.

"Excuse me," Annja said. "Have you seen my friend? The man I checked in with?"

She nodded. "*Sí*. He left a little while ago."

That didn't make any sense. "Left?"

"*Sí*. He met a man here in reception. They left together."

"Did you see which way they went?"

"No, madam. Once people step out our front doors, I have no idea what they do." She shrugged.

Annja looked toward the huge glass doors. There was no sign of Garin out on the curb.

"Perhaps when he returns you could suggest he change his clothes?" The receptionist paused for a moment as if she was searching for the right word. "It is a little unsettling for the other guests, you understand."

The same bellhop that had offered to carry their bags up to the rooms emerged from the elevator as Annja was digesting what the receptionist had just said.

"The man who came for him gave him a sweater," the receptionist continued, lifting her nose a fraction. "But he still had no shoes."

"What did this man look like?"

Her first thought was that it was Roux. That the old man had come to collect Garin and whisked him off with some harebrained scheme to get the mask back by themselves. Would they have returned to the Alhambra? But then why hadn't Roux phoned her?

"Tall, dark, late thirties, early forties, maybe. He was Spanish."

Definitely not Roux, then. The bellhop spoke rapidly in Spanish. Annja thought she caught some of it, but his accent was too strong for her to understand more than the occasional snippet. The receptionist responded more slowly, only to get another rapid response. Annja could pick out individual words, but not enough to make sense of what they were saying.

"It seems that you are in luck. Franco saw your friend leave with this other man."

The boy nodded rapidly. "*Sí, sí*, I saw him get into a car."

"Do you know which way they went?"

The boy's expression became puzzled and the receptionist intervened on their behalf. "He says that he thinks they were heading toward the Alhambra."

"*Sí, sí*, Alhambra," the boy repeated.

Annja reached into her pocket and pulled out a twenty-euro note. It was less than the information was worth, but the bellhop smiled gratefully and pocketed it without a word.

"Thank you, both of you," Annja said.

"We are here to serve you," the receptionist said, that same fake smile in place.

She'd left the keys to the Alfa Romeo in her room. She cursed the lost minutes, even though she knew they were unlikely to make any significant difference. She was behind Garin now, playing catch-up. She really didn't like playing catch-up.

She rode up in the elevator and was sliding the key card into the lock of her door when she heard her phone ringing on the other side. By the time she reached it, the call had gone to voice mail.

One missed call: Roux.

She called him back as she grabbed her jacket and keys, and was already halfway out of the door when he picked up.

"Have you made the exchange yet?"

"Yes, nearly an hour ago."

"Damn. You've already handed the mask over?"

"How else was I supposed to get Garin released?"

The old man sighed in her ear. "There's no easy way to say this, my dear, but we've been played. Garin is part of it."

"What?"

"It was a charade, smoke and mirrors. A scam. Whatever the hell you want to call it, he was part of it. A willing accomplice. Who knows, maybe the bastard was even the brains behind the whole thing."

"But his injuries? His bodyguards?"

"Collateral damage. And he obviously thought more of his damned paintings than he did of them."

"What? I don't understand what you're saying, Roux. This doesn't make sense. Garin couldn't have been part of it. He wouldn't do that. Innocent people died!"

"Trust me, Annja. I'm not wrong about this. I've seen the evidence with my own eyes."

"What evidence?"

"Security footage from the Madrid office. Minutes before the kidnappers stormed the conference room and killed Garin's bodyguards, he had the foresight to exchange a priceless work of art hanging on the wall and replace it with a worthless print. He knew what was going to happen in there. He took steps to protect the only thing he has ever cared about. His beautiful possessions."

She couldn't believe it. "You're kidding me. This has to be some kind of mistake. Surely?"

"I only wish it was. That selfish piece of shit is as much to blame for the deaths of those men as the men who fired the shots. He's always been a magpie, attracted to shiny things, but I never thought he'd do something like this—use us…put you at risk."

"But why would he do it?" Even before the question

had left her lips, Annja knew the answer. This was all about the mask—not as a treasure itself, but as a key to a bigger haul. Garin had figured out that the mask was the one thing he needed to get to the Moorish wealth. As always with Garin, this was about greed.

"Do you need me to spell it out for you?" Roux asked.

"No, I get it. He's a scorpion. It's in his nature. I'd just forgotten who he really is."

"So where is he?"

"On his way back to the Alhambra," she said, though she wasn't completely sure. There were other places he could have turned off the main road. Theoretically, he could be anywhere by now, but her money was on him going back there, especially given what Zanetti had said about the Pass of the Moor's Sigh being at the heart of the mystery. "Where are you?"

"I'm already here," he said. "Our hacker friend was right about this being the Brotherhood's base. They set up their operations in a tiny chapel here. There's scaffolding up against the outside wall, but it's the only building not being worked on. It's the center of the dead zone. You'll be alone, no cell phone, no gadgets. There's some sort of dampening field in operation. You'll know it when you see it. I'm going to take a quick peek around before he gets here. See what I can find now that I'm looking with a different set of eyes. Knowing he's not the victim means I'm looking for completely different stuff."

"True. How on earth did you find that footage?"

"I didn't. Oscar did. He found it on the Brotherhood's computer network. We got lucky."

"I still can't believe it," Annja said.

"He's played us, Annja, and that sticks in my craw. We're going to get that mask back one way or another. I would rather destroy it than have it become yet another one of his beautiful treasures hidden away in his offices, lost to the world."

"It's not the mask he's interested in," Annja said. "It's never been about some wonderful artifact from the past. It's all about greed. Those engravings on the inside of the mask are basically a treasure map. It's not even riches that the Church took from the Moors, like I thought at first. This leads to the real treasures of the Moors, the objects so precious to them they couldn't risk them ever falling into the Inquisitors' hands."

"So the ledger was their own record of what they had hidden away for safekeeping," Roux said, piecing it together. He didn't sound the least bit surprised by the revelation.

"Okay, but it doesn't explain why the ledger was recorded in Latin," Annja said.

"Unless there was someone in the Church who was helping them."

"Would they have done that?"

"There were enough people, good people, who didn't approve of what was happening, even though they were part of the Church. Remember, Torquemada's uncle was unhappy about the way the Moors were being treated. He was not alone."

Sometimes it was easy to forget just how long the old man had been around. He delivered that last statement with absolute certainty. She knew he'd been alive during the Inquisition, but he'd brushed over it. Suddenly, she was struck by all the things he must have seen—and all the things he must have done in order to stay alive. She'd never considered the possibility that he might have known some of the people caught up in it.

If there was someone in the Church helping the Mudéjars smuggle belongings away, making sure that their wealth was preserved for the next generation, that would have demanded absolute trust, absolute faith.

"Who could they have trusted that completely? Given everything that was happening all around them. Who could they have believed in?"

"I don't know," Roux admitted. "All I know is that I'm not having that son of a bitch Braden undo their sacrifice. He's not getting his hands on a penny of their treasure. Come here. I need you to help me stop him."

"I've got a car," Annja said, turning the keys in her hand as she made her way back to the door. "I'll be with you as soon as I can."

She hung up, still not quite believing that Garin could sink so low.

Yes, he had caused enough problems in the past that now she didn't trust him, not completely, and that went all the way back to their first meeting, when Garin and Roux had been at each other's throats, Garin trying to kill him before he could find the last piece of Joan of Arc's shattered sword and put it together again. That had been about staying alive. That had been Garin's fear that once the blade was re-formed, it would undo whatever curse it was that had kept them breathing for six hundred years. Self-preservation was a powerful instinct.

This was different.

This felt like a step too far, even for Garin Braden.

25

Roux didn't have much time.

Garin was already on his way back—and he wasn't alone—and there was a good chance that he only had minutes to spare.

He needed to be ready for them.

Roux checked his gun. One shot wasn't going to get him far.

He was already regretting not taking one of the fallen brother's weapons. Of course, it was unlikely anyone had been into the chapel to clean up, so realistically there was a wealth of firepower just lying around waiting for him to pick it up. The problem was he didn't know how many men might still be in there.

Roux could handle himself—that wasn't what he was worried about. The chapel was the heart of the Brotherhood's operations. If Garin came back to the Alhambra, he'd be headed to the chapel for sure. Roux would be in there, waiting for him. It was crazy enough that the Brotherhood had been able to take over a part of the Alhambra and remain undetected under the cover of building work. It was unthinkable that they could have occupied two sites. If Garin wanted somewhere private to examine the Mask of Torquemada and decipher the map it contained, then the chapel was the perfect place for him and his accomplice to work in peace.

What Garin wouldn't suspect was that Roux had breached the Brotherhood's security and that he knew he wasn't an innocent victim in all of this.

Garin wouldn't be expecting Roux.

The sound of boots running on cobbles made him glance back over his shoulder. The Brotherhood was still looking for him. They had no idea where he was, though. They seemed to be conducting a grid search of the streets, running from one block to the next, keeping to the pattern. All he had to do was get behind their lines and they'd never find him. The Alhambra was full of shadows and empty buildings to hide inside, though many would be locked once the staff had finished their cleanup.

He slid back into the alley, pressing himself close to the brickwork as he saw one man running past the outside of the building.

The brothers were panicking. They wanted to track him down and deal with him before their paymaster returned.

They'd never think of looking for him in their chapel. So that was where he needed to be. It was as simple as that.

Staying tight to the sides of buildings, moving only in shadow, Roux made his way back toward the chapel.

The lights were still blazing in there while almost every other building was shrouded in darkness.

Security lights illuminated the cobbles, spearing through the gaps between buildings. Even so, there was more shadow than light on the narrow streets.

Footsteps rang out, echoing against stone, making it hard to know which direction they were coming from.

Roux had to be careful.

He crept along, running when he needed to, hiding in the recesses when it sounded as if the search cordon was drawing in.

The final few yards would put him out in the open. There was nothing he could do but step out of the shadows. He paused before making the dash, drawing his gun. One shot was better than none. He rushed across the stones, sprinting lightly on his toes and barely making a sound. Almost too late, he saw the door to the chapel open. Roux changed his direction and reached the side of the chapel before the guard saw him. He hit the wall hard and hugged it, not moving, calming himself before he did anything else.

He edged forward and peered around the corner.

The door had been closed behind the man who was more intent on enjoying his cigarette than keeping an eye out for Roux. The brother was lax, assuming Roux was long gone. He should have been on high alert, but instead he was lighting up a cigarette. Roux was going to use that to his advantage. There were times for brute force, and there were times for stealth.

He was four strides from the door. Five at most.

The man leaned back, one shoulder against the wall. He had his back to Roux. His Steyr submachine pistol was slung over his shoulder. Even if he heard Roux approaching, he wouldn't have enough time to turn, slip the shoulder strap from its resting place, bring the Steyr to bear *and* shoot. That certainty was all Roux needed. That was his edge. He wouldn't even need to waste his one shot.

He reversed his grip, feeling the weight of the butt in his palm.

Accuracy was more important than force. He needed to do this as silently as possible.

He watched as the man took another draw on the cigarette. Then he flicked it away, sending the glowing tip end over end. Now. The man had no idea Roux was there until the butt of the pistol was swinging toward his head. A fraction of a second sooner and he might have missed, might have cracked the butt off the guard's temple or cheek instead of behind the ear. He crumpled. Roux caught him with one arm as he fell, the handgun still in his grip. He reached around with his free hand, took hold of the brother's head and gave it a single sharp twist.

Roux supported the dead man's weight, knowing that if he let him slip to the ground it would make moving the body much more difficult.

He glanced around quickly, checking both directions to be sure that no one was watching, and backed up against the door, pushing it inward.

His entire plan rested on a single gamble: that every

other brother was out there hunting him and that the dead man in his arms had been the only one left to monitor the chapel itself.

Roux dragged the body inside, the heels scraping against the mosaic floor as he pulled the corpse into an alcove at the bottom of the stairs, hiding it from view. That would do for now, but the man was hardly well-hidden. At least he wouldn't be the first thing someone saw when they walked through the door.

The other bodies were still lying where they had fallen.

Roux didn't move them.

He didn't have the time.

He heard the sound of an engine in the night.

Right now, speed was everything.

26

The Alfa Romeo growled to life.

Annja roared out of the parking lot next to the hotel.

She'd placed her cell phone on the passenger seat, ready to snatch it up if Roux called again. She floored the gas, knowing she had no hope of catching Garin before he reached the Alhambra. It was all about making up lost ground. She was so angry with him she could have spat bullets. She couldn't believe what he'd put her through, how he'd lied to her face. And she knew how angry Roux was, too. She didn't know what would happen if the two of them came face-to-face without her in the middle. She wouldn't put anything past either of them right now. As angry as she was, she was the reasonable one of the trio—which wasn't a reassuring thought, given that she could put Garin's lights out right now.

She gripped the wheel too tightly. The muscles in her shoulders knotted. She concentrated fiercely on the road ahead, not wanting to think. She turned the music up loud. The streets became less regular, and soon she couldn't see beyond the long reach of the car's headlights. The road twisted and turned. She was taking the bends too quickly, and she knew it. Tires squealed as she yanked down on the wheel, hard.

Something ran out in front of her.

A dog? A fox?

She couldn't tell. It was small and fast.

She slammed on the brakes, sending her phone spinning off the seat and into the foot well, out of reach. She pulled up just in time for the critter to disappear into the undergrowth on the other side of the road.

Her heart was racing.

Annja took a deep breath, forcing herself to relax, slow down. There were no other cars on the road. She turned the radio down and pushed the stick shift into First again, setting off a little more cautiously.

Better to arrive a few minutes later than not at all.

The Alhambra was in near-darkness as she approached. Annja knew that her headlights would stand out like a beacon as she crested the horizon. While the Brotherhood might not be able to recognize the car from its headlights alone, anyone looking would know they had a visitor.

Hoping to retain some element of surprise, she killed the lights and slowed her speed, taking her foot off the gas as she descended silently toward the site. She was all too aware of how little she could see. A single mistimed turn could prove fatal if taken too quickly. As the shadowy outline of the palace fortress loomed larger through the windshield, she picked out a handful of lights in the darkness.

Annja pulled the car over to the side of the road. She fished her phone out of the foot well and climbed out, leaving the keys in the ignition in case she needed to make a quick getaway.

She was never truly unarmed, even if the only weapon she appeared to have was her Maglite. The sword was only a heartbeat away, so close she could almost feel it in her hand now, just because she was thinking about it.

She didn't dare use the flashlight as she made the slow trek toward the ancient buildings.

Even before she reached the gate to the ancient palace-fortress, she spotted a few lights dotted along the wall with CCTV cameras alongside them.

She was used to being watched. Someone had been monitoring her every single step of the way. But right now she was sure she was being scrutinized, the cameras tracking her every move. It couldn't be helped. Even if she backed off and tried to find a blind spot to scale the wall, it wouldn't help; it would only slow her down. Garin had to assume she'd follow him, even if she wasn't supposed to know he was a deceitful sack of garbage. If he was watching, he'd expect her to walk right through the front gate. That was her style. He'd expect a full-on, frontal assault on the Brotherhood's base of operations, so that was what she decided to give him.

She put on a show for the cameras, pulling the sword out of the otherwhere and making sure the lens picked it up.

Annja approached the gateway. She didn't duck into

the shadows, didn't break her stride. She stared straight
into one of the cameras. She wanted their attention.
The sword blazed in her hand, lighting her face as she
stepped into the Alhambra.

Garin and his accomplice knew she was coming. The
sight of the sword on their security screens would, she
hoped, distract them from the mask. If they couldn't
crack the riddle it presented, that would buy Roux time
to close in, and maybe, just maybe, they'd get the mask
back before Garin could cause more trouble.

Roux had told her to make for the chapel. There was
no guarantee that they would still be there, but Roux
was expecting her to head that way. He'd be basing his
movements on her being there. She wasn't about to hang
him out to dry. But first she had to find it, and all she
had to go on was Roux's mention of scaffolding.

She moved deeper into the dark warren of crumbling
buildings, the blade lighting the way.

There were few lights in the streets, and only the
occasional security camera. Roux had said the chapel
was well monitored. The more cameras watching her,
she felt sure, the closer she was to her goal.

She didn't bother trying to hide. Let them come.

She heard the sound of running feet.

It was impossible to tell where they were coming
from. The acoustics of the cramped ancient streets were
utterly disorienting.

It wasn't Roux. The footsteps were too heavy—boots
on cobbles, not the old man's style. Despite his appear-
ance, he was still lithe and athletic. She had seen him

run, part gymnast and part ballet dancer, barely touching the ground.

Running from building to building, shadow to shadow, she scoured the area for any signs of life.

The whole place appeared to be deserted, and yet she knew Roux was here.

So was the running man.

She would also stake everything she had on Garin and the mystery man being here, too. Five of them. There could be more. Garin wouldn't run this operation without a small army at his disposal. She remembered the first time he'd exploded into her life. He'd turned a quiet French town into a war zone in a handful of seconds. That was how he did battle, and it seemed that was how he'd set this up so far—as a battle. He'd sacrificed four men out in the deserted parking lot. Roux had almost certainly neutralized the same number when he'd gone into the dead zone. She had counted a dozen in the parking lot, give or take, including the men who had driven away.

No matter how many brothers there were, Annja realized, Garin wasn't likely to keep them around much longer, given the way he'd sacrificed the rest of his team. Garin wasn't the kind of man who left himself vulnerable to outsiders. He didn't like leaving behind anyone who knew his secrets. That would explain why he'd returned here: to tidy up loose ends before he went after the treasure.

It made sense.

In fact, given everything she knew about Garin Braden, it made *perfect* sense.

Annja put the sword away.

She had no intention of doing his dirty work for him.

27

Roux passed through the curtain behind the altar and stepped away from the remnants of medieval culture and into the brave new technological world.

An array of screens showed the video feed from the security cameras outside the building along with images from all around the complex. The images shifted every few seconds into another angle on the rotation. From where he stood, it looked as though these screens captured every inch of the Alhambra, so the Brotherhood was obviously tapping into the feeds of other cameras along with their own. One image caught his eye. It showed the road leading to the main gate. In the distance, he could just make out two pinpricks of light approaching. Headlights. It had to be Garin. It was too soon to be Annja, but she couldn't be too far behind. He just hoped he'd get some alone time with Garin. They had stuff to talk about.

He scanned the room.

A door at the far end looked as if it would lead outside. That meant the place had two exits. Good. He liked options. A heavy brass key was set in the lock. He went across and twisted it—better to be prepared.

The old man had spent the past few decades avoiding many of the technological advances, preferring to outsource his needs, but he wasn't completely ignorant. You couldn't exist in this world of Twitter and Facebook without knowing something about how it was all connected, but unlike Garin, Roux wasn't anywhere near the cutting edge. The equipment in this room was state-of-the-art. There was stuff in here that wouldn't have been out of place at NASA's Ground Control in Houston. Actually, there were machines and instruments here that NASA wouldn't even be getting for a couple of years, knowing the stranglehold Garin Braden had on certain lines of trade. Billionaire playboy, two-faced, backstabbing mercenary, uneasy friend—Garin was all of these and more. Their lives had been spent intertwined, with so much time devoted to trying to kill each other. It was almost like old times.

The old man smiled.

He recognized a couple of the labels on the bits of tech as one of Garin's shell companies. He had his fingers in so many pies it was difficult to keep track, but those little stickers reinforced everything his hacker had claimed. The evidence was stacking up. Roux had been willing to give Garin the benefit of the doubt for a while, assuming he was some sort of unwitting accomplice in this mess, that he'd gotten himself in over his head and was desperately trying to get out again. But this wasn't a case of in-too-deep. Garin was involved in this up to his neck. At best, the most innocent version of events was that someone had come to him with this plan, hoping he'd finance it. At worst, it was his own plan. Roux tried to think. Assuming Garin hadn't come up with the whole thing himself, whoever was the brains behind it knew he'd be unable to resist those shiny, unique objects like the thieving little magpie he was at heart. That meant they knew him. And Garin was careful. He didn't leave a trail. So knowing him was tough.

Roux ran his hands across the various pieces of expensive tech, trying to find something that might be functioning as a signal jammer, but truthfully, he didn't have a clue what he was looking for. A box was a box—be it hard drive, router or jammer—and they all looked the same to him. Assuming the dead zone originated in this room, the best thing he could do was take out the lot of it rather than worry about trying to pinpoint a specific piece of equipment, and the best way to do that was pull the plug. That or torch the stuff, which would be ironic, given the Brotherhood of the Burning motif. But smoke and flames would almost certainly bring attention to his presence.

Roux checked the screens again. Garin was almost at the gate. Two minutes away at best. The obvious hunter's move was to lie in wait, then spring an ambush on the duplicitous SOB. He had the guard's Steyr, which would cause some serious damage. He didn't need anything else to make Garin's life a living hell. And yes, the old man decided, that was exactly what he was going to do. Garin was going to pay for every little betrayal he'd countenanced over the years. Roux was done being his fool.

Anger dulled the senses.

He'd been so engrossed in elaborate thoughts of revenge on Garin that he hadn't heard the chapel door opening. Now footsteps echoed in the vestibule.

He checked the screen again. The car was still passing through the gate. This newcomer couldn't be Garin. Maybe one of the men he'd taken down had decided to play Lazarus.

"Javier?" a voice called.

Roux held his breath. He eased the machine pistol from his shoulder silently.

Javier was lying under the stairs. He wouldn't be answering the call any time soon.

"Javier," the voice called again, closer now.

The edge of the curtain moved.

Roux felt like the Wizard of Oz waiting to be exposed as a fraud.

He waited until he had the confirmation he needed— a hand with a flame tattoo parting the curtain—before pulling the trigger. Roux unleashed a short burst, the bullets shredding the curtain and ripping into the man behind it. The brother went down, still clutching the ruined fabric as he fell. The brass rings broke away from the rail under his weight.

There would be no hiding now.

Which, to be perfectly honest, suited Roux just fine.

He was ready for Garin to walk through the chapel door.

And he'd made up his mind. He wasn't going to let the bastard charm his way out of this one.

Roux checked the screen again. The car was gone. Almost two minutes had elapsed. He should be here any second. Roux smiled. It was all coming together.

There were no headlights on any of the screens.

Roux toggled through a few different views, using a little joystick on the console to pan the camera angles wider, but there was no sign of Garin. There should have been. He should have been pulling up outside the chapel by now. Roux ran through the feeds again, but there was absolutely no sign of Garin's car in any of them.

A vaguely familiar sound filtered through from outside. It took him a second to place it because it was so unexpected. It grew louder gradually, until the old windows seemed to vibrate in time with it.

When he realized what it was, he cursed himself for being so slow and headed outside.

28

Annja heard the noise before she saw the light in the sky.

She needed to get to a position where she could see the chopper touch down. There was no obvious landing site that she remembered. That meant she had to find higher ground. The rooftops. Plenty of buildings were fronted by scaffolding, so she ran to the nearest, eyes on the sky, trying to follow the helicopter. She climbed quickly, hand over hand, and leaped from the platform to the rooftop proper.

She kicked herself. Of course Garin had more than one reason for wanting to return to the Alhambra. It wasn't just about deciphering the mask, and it wasn't even about tying up loose ends. Garin was more than capable of walking away from carnage with a grin on his face. She'd seen it before. He had no problem avoiding responsibility for his actions. The one option she hadn't considered was that he already *knew* what was on the mask and the ancient fortress was only a rendezvous point.

She raced across the flat roof, then launched herself

into the air, catapulting across the gap between buildings, and came down in a front roll, rising again, still running, with the moon picking out her silhouette.

The helicopter was already descending.

She raced across the rooftops, leaping nimbly onto a perimeter wall that skirted a dry soil bed between houses, then scaling another high point, never once looking down.

She heard footsteps.

Two sets.

These weren't the heavy boots of the first man, either.

Garin and his accomplice? It had to be.

The helicopter made its descent and she ran toward it, covering the distance quickly. She was *fast*. But she had no idea if she was going to be fast enough. She could hear Garin running through the streets below. He made no pretense at stealth. She needed to stop him from boarding. It wasn't exactly the confrontation she wanted, but she couldn't afford to let him get on that helicopter.

Once he was in the air, there'd be no catching him, even if she knew where he was going.

The helicopter touched down in a courtyard. She stood on the tiled roof, watching helplessly as two shapes emerged from the shadows, oblivious to her presence.

There was no mistaking Garin.

She called his name.

Both men stopped for a moment, their faces illuminated by the glare of one of the security lights.

"Wait," she said, running hard, arms and legs pumping furiously as the tiles cracked beneath her feet.

Garin looked so much more *alive* than he had less than an hour ago.

His bruises had already begun to fade in the strange, harsh light. He was a fast healer, but not that fast.

But it was the other man she stared at, and the other man who stared back at her. There was a moment of recognition. Panic. Then he tugged at Garin's sleeve to urge him toward the chopper.

She'd seen him before.

Back when this nightmare day began.

She hadn't expected to ever see him again.

But there was no mistaking the easy style of Francesco Maffrici, the curator of the Monastery of Saint Thomas Aquinas in Ávila.

Here.

Now.

With Garin.

They had been tracking her the whole time. They'd known every single move she'd taken from that very first step. How many more of the people she'd met in the past twenty-four hours were up to their necks in this conspiracy? Had they been feeding her what she needed to get here drip by drip, manipulating her into thinking she was solving some ancient riddle?

Her phone rang. She couldn't take her eyes off the pair of them. And she couldn't reach them. Garin broke into a sprint, breaking the spell. He gave a cry, drawing a guard from one of the alleyways. The brother had a Steyr machine pistol in his hand, but he wasn't as quick on the draw as she was. Annja threw herself forward in a combat roll and rose with the sword already in her hand, drawn from the otherwhere in time to stop the first bullet, sending a shower of sparks flying in the dark night as metal struck metal. The brother kept his finger on the trigger until the hail of bullets stopped coming, ripping up the tiles beneath her feet. By the time the gun dry-fired it was too late for him to save himself. Annja spun on her heel and hurled the otherworldly blade, sending it scything through the air in a vicious arc.

The brother fell, his last breath caught on his lips.

His head hit the ground a moment later and rolled away across the cobbles as the sword reappeared in her hand.

Annja saw Garin duck into the waiting helicopter, Maffrici a second behind him. She was too far away to stop them. She could have hurled the sword at the rotors as the helicopter started to rise…but she didn't want to kill him. He was gone.

Unless she could catch up with the helicopter as it rose, somehow snag one of the runners before it was out of reach…

She bolted across the roof that ringed the courtyard, trying to get as close as she could before launching herself through the air, stretching with all of her will for the runner.

She caught it with one hand, clinging on for dear life as the helicopter surged upward.

She could see the horror on Garin's face as the downdraft from the rotors pummeled her.

She swung her second arm up, kicking her legs desperately. Her fingers slipped on the slick metal of the runner. There was no way she could hold on without getting her second hand around the stanchion, which meant relinquishing her grip on the blade. It didn't help. As she reached up, Maffrici leaned out of the cockpit and stamped down on her hand. Then she was falling, battered toward the ground by the fierce windstorm.

It was a long way down.

She hit the cobbles hard in what would have been a backbreaking fall for anyone else. The impact drove every ounce of breath from her body. She thought her spine was going to shatter. The pain was blinding. It sent a sunburst of agony through every nerve and fiber. The sword flickered in her grip as she clenched her hands, gritting her teeth, but she couldn't hold on to it. She stared up at the belly of the helicopter.

Garin was gone and there wasn't a damn thing she could do about it.

She tried to sit up, but the pain was unbearable, so she gave up and lay on her back, unmoving, watching the helicopter as it banked and flew away in the direction of the mountains.

Her phone rang again.

She didn't want to move.

It didn't stop ringing.

"There's a helicopter coming in to land."

"Too late," she said into the phone. "The only thing coming in to land is me…and not gracefully." She didn't elaborate.

Roux cursed, a stream of French that would have turned the air a vivid shade of sacre bleu if they'd lived in a cartoon world.

"I know where they're going. At least I think I do. But we're on the back foot now. Garin's with a guy called Francesco Maffrici."

"You know him?"

"The curator from the Torquemada tomb in Ávila."

"Strange bedfellows. Did it look like Garin was going willingly? Or did Maffrici have him at gunpoint?" Meaning, was Garin complicit. She tried to remember exactly what she'd witnessed. Could she have misinterpreted some aspect of the scene? Maffrici had been behind Garin, not leading the way. Could the curator have been running the situation? She hadn't seen a gun, but that didn't mean he didn't have one. She realized what Roux was asking. He wanted her to say definitively that Garin Braden had betrayed them, or give them an out so they could still believe he wasn't the devious, conniving, unfaithful, backstabbing, two-faced liar he was. And the truth was, she didn't know. Maybe he had been at Maffrici's mercy.

"I can't say for sure. And to be honest, I don't want to think about it right now. I hurt all over. Get to the gate. Follow the road maybe three hundred yards. You'll find a red Alfa Romeo parked by the side of the road. The keys are in the ignition."

"Right. And once I get there, where am I going? I can't read your mind, girl."

She was still on her back. She wasn't entirely sure she could sit up. She should have been dead. Any normal person would have been. But since she'd first laid hands on Joan of Arc's sacred sword, she'd been anything but normal. "Turn the car around, and head away from the Alhambra. Drive half a mile, and you should see a dirt road on the right. It'll take you up into the mountains. You're aiming for a V in the skyline. A pass. That's where he's heading. The car won't get all the way to the top. I'll see you there."

"What are you going to do?" he asked.

"Me? I guess I'm going to haul my battered ass up there the old-fashioned way."

She watched as the helicopter disappeared into the distance, its searchlights spearing ahead, pointing toward the Pass of the Moor's Sigh.

She needed to run.

Which was going to be difficult, because she could barely stand.

29

The car was exactly where Annja had promised it would be.

Roux slid behind the wheel and turned the ignition.

On another day, in another place, in a better frame of mind, he'd have loved to take the Alfa out onto a long straight road and unleash the full power of the horses under the hood, maybe hit the coast road from Saint-Tropez to Monte Carlo and onward into Italy, top down, wind in his hair, enjoying the view and looking like a walking, talking midlife crisis. Today, though, he had to find a way around the side of a mountain in the dark. At least he didn't have to do it on foot. Leave that kind of stupid exertion for the young.

He followed Annja's directions, keeping an eye out for the side road she'd mentioned, almost missing it because it wasn't lit or signposted. It looked too narrow and too steep to be a real road, but there was nothing else for miles around, so this had to be what she meant. Four-wheel drive would have been better, being a sheep or goat, perfect. But he trusted Annja.

As the road wound up the hillside, he caught sight

of the helicopter's searchlights far off to his right. They were moving faster and more directly than he could, but they gave him something to follow. It seemed as if Annja's hunch was right. So she'd solved some other part of the mystery. It would have been good to have been able to spend a few minutes with her before setting off on this wild-goose chase, but time was a luxury they didn't have right now. Still, he wished they were together. Being separate had made sense when they needed to be in different parts of the country, but now, this close, maybe two was better than one. Attack the problem head-on, face Garin down, find out if he'd played them…

It wasn't an "if," though, was it? As much as Roux wanted to believe it was, he'd seen the evidence with his own eyes. Garin was not purely a victim in all this. And Roux knew full well Annja would be too soft on him, that she'd swallow whatever sob story he put in front of her. She'd do that because she always wanted to see the good in people. Roux was old enough to know that sometimes there just wasn't any.

Roux's phone rang. He grabbed it, steering one-handed.

"Roux?"

"Kinda busy right now."

"I'm sending you some stuff," Oscar said. "You'll want to read it as soon as you can."

"Want to summarize for me?"

"No, it's best you read it."

He hung up. Roux tossed the phone aside, but not

before he'd taken a bend a little faster than intended, tires crunching on the hard dirt of the shoulder. He felt the car pull to the right and adjusted. He reached for the phone and checked the screen, one eye still on the road as he eased up on the gas.

He looked up as the headlights picked out eyes staring at him from the scrub along the roadside.

The Steyr machine pistol he'd appropriated from the brother slid off the passenger seat, hitting the side of the foot well hard and coming to rest with the muzzle pointing up at his face. Roux ignored it. He wasn't about to allow himself to be distracted—not by the gun or the local fauna or anything else around him. He had a job to do. People were counting on him. And right now that meant concentrating on the god-awful road he was trying to navigate and keeping track of the helicopter in the distance.

Anything else was just getting in the way, including the hacker's information.

He climbed higher and higher, the road becoming even more unnerving as he rose, with not so much as a guardrail to stop him from overshooting a turn and doing a Thelma and Louise off the side of the mountain.

A glance back the way he'd come revealed a handful of lights in the distance. They had to be the spotlights of the Alhambra. And looking forward, beyond the hills, the sky was starting to lighten. It was just the slightest tinge of red, but dawn couldn't be that far away, and it wouldn't be long before the fortress was teeming with visitors. And that would mean someone would discover

the bodies in the chapel. How long until that happened?
When it did, it would change everything.

They said that the only thing worse than bad publicity was no publicity, but with the Seville courthouse and
now the Alhambra murders, Roux had become a one-
man crime spree. They'd be locking him up and throwing away the key if they caught him here. He needed to
get this out of the way quickly and be back on his plane
before the police pulled their act together.

There would be rain before the day was over, but he'd
be back in the château in France long before the first fat
drops fell. He promised himself that much.

But first, before he could think about any of that, he
had to take care of Garin.

The helicopter started to descend, dropping out of
sight over the far side of the mountain.

The road began to meander off in the opposite direction, with no sign of doubling back on itself. Annja
had warned him he wouldn't be able to make it all the
way to the top in the Alfa. It was time to start walking. Long before he reached the V carved between the
peaks, it would be daylight. Garin had a decent head
start, whatever he was intending to do here. That didn't
mean he couldn't stop him, though. Roux recovered the
machine pistol and clambered out of the car. He left the
keys in the ignition, just as Annja had, although he'd
already decided he wouldn't be driving back to town.
Instead of calling Oscar back straightaway, he put in a
call to make sure they would have a ride when this was
all over, then he slung the Steyr over his shoulder and

allowed his mind to wander back to when all this had begun—a time when Garin had still been his apprentice and little more than a boy.

30

Annja ran.

She'd spent far too many of the past twenty-four hours hunched over the handlebars of the bike, in a car and—as luxurious as it was—Roux's jet. Her muscles were cramped, her joints stiff. Still, considering she'd just fallen thirty feet from the runners of a helicopter and landed on her back, she felt brilliant. Alive. She powered across the dusty desert, eyes always on the prize: the V in the mountains that marked the Pass of the Moor's Sigh.

Her phone vibrated against her side.

Annja fished it out of her pocket.

It was the professor; obviously, he was every bit as much an insomniac as she was. She didn't answer, assuming he'd leave a message. She'd check it at the top. She didn't want him to think the heavy breathing was for his benefit.

The gradient increased.

Annja had to dig a little deeper to maintain momentum as the path rose sharply.

Sheep grazing on the mountainside watched her

progress with detached interest. Their stares were disconcerting, but they didn't dip their heads in preparation to charge her, which was a plus. The absolute silence out here was eerie, but it felt good. Special. Almost magical. It was the kind of silence you could never hear in a city. But she couldn't afford to savor it. She gritted her teeth and pushed on, feeling the burn as she raced up the mountainside.

Dead earth crunched beneath her feet.

Overhead, she saw the first birds of the morning. They were big, wheeling in the sky and scattering, only to re-form into a solid, seething mass of wings and settle in the high branches of a distant tree.

Her cell phone vibrated again, one short, sharp shiver. Zanetti had left a message. She spotted a path that wound around the mountain. It was a well-worn shepherds' trail, and it promised to be the easiest route up to the pass. Annja pushed on. She wasn't slowing down.

Gradually, the going became easier as the terrain leveled out. Her stride lengthened and she began to cover the ground more quickly until she was running freely into the morning red sky.

She pulled the phone from her pocket without breaking her stride.

"Hi, Annja," the message began. "Aldo Zanetti here. You're going to want to hear this, I think. I've had a breakthrough. There was a piece of the map that I was struggling to decipher, where the metal was bent out of shape." He sounded breathless, as though he were the one running up a mountain. "I think I've managed to work out what it means. Everything I suspected about the secret being hidden in the Pass of the Moor's Sigh still stands, but the extra information from the buckled segment of the mask seems to suggest that the opening will only be revealed at the start of the day. I'm not entirely sure how this will work, but it says that you must face the doorway, then turn to face Mecca, say the prophet's name three times, then turn back to the door. I know, it's probably hokum, but do what it says. The door's supposed to open then. There are also some fairly dire warnings about traps or challenges lying beyond. The language is nowhere near as precise as modern ones, though, so I can't be sure which. You'll need to overcome these once the door opens. Okay, that's everything I've got. I don't know if that helps, but without the mask itself, it's the best I can do. I'm afraid I remain skeptical as to there being any actual treasure to find, but I'd love to be proven wrong. Maybe there still are mysteries left to be solved in this world. If so, I hope you're the woman to solve this one, at least. Give me a call sometime and tell me how it went. And if you're ever in Rome, lunch is on me. It's been a pleasure."

The message ended.

Only at the start of the day.

Annja's mind was filled with questions. How could a door be hidden? It had to be shadow, she thought, the angle of the sun at sunrise revealing the door for a brief moment. In that case, the entrance—whatever it was—faced east. That didn't help much, but every little bit of knowledge she could gain before trying to find a way into the mountain was a good thing. The sky was growing lighter. She lowered her head and leaned into the sprint.

The helicopter had dropped out of sight, but she could still hear its rotors.

Annja glanced to her left. The narrow track rose up from the main road and wound up into the highest points of the hills. In the gloom that still clung to these last few moments before dawn, Annja could see the lights of a single car. Roux. She did a quick mental calculation, trying to work out how far behind her he was and how quickly she'd have backup. Not soon enough. She'd have much rather done this next bit with the old man at her side. Still, beggars couldn't be choosers. She crested a ridge and saw two men duck low and hurry away from the blur of rotor blades. The helicopter hovered a couple of feet above the uneven ground, rocking slightly in the air before the engine sound changed and the chopper rose, peeling away from the peaks. There wasn't a good place to set down. That didn't mean that the pilot wouldn't be returning as reinforcement once he'd found a spot, though.

Always consider the worst-case scenario, expect it to happen and avoid disappointment when it does. That was one of the old man's many rules to live by. Normal people might have added: and be grateful if it doesn't. Not Roux. He expected the worst because, when he was around, the worst had a habit of happening.

But despite that, it was hard to believe Garin was

behind all of this, no matter what Roux said about him switching out the painting in the office before the kidnappers smashed through his windows. He was a jerk some of the time, sure, but he was Garin. He was one of the good guys. It had to be the curator. Maffrici. She didn't know anything about him, so it was easy to blame him. She couldn't be sure what she'd seen back in the courtyard. When she thought about it, Garin had looked...what? Scared? Had he seemed scared when he saw her up there on the roof? She wanted to believe that he did. Because that would mean the seed Roux had planted in her mind was right, that there was another explanation for what was going on. He was caught up in this; that was impossible to deny. He might even be responsible for some of it. But Annja wasn't ready to accept that he was the instigator. And she remembered his bruises. He'd taken a battering. Garin wasn't the kind of guy who'd subject his body to that type of punishment willingly. He was too vain for that. Maybe it was Stockholm syndrome? His abusers had treated him so badly he'd come to see any little kindness as a kind of salvation. Maybe that was why he'd led Francesco Maffrici into the helicopter. That would explain why he wasn't acting like a captive.

Annja heard birds chirping nearby. It would only be a matter of minutes before the sun rose above the hills. And if Zanetti was right about what was engraved on the mask, then the hiding place of the Moors' treasure would be visible, and anyone who turned to Mecca and said the prophet Muhammad's name three times would open the door. She needed to hurry. She scrambled up the loose shale, skidding as she climbed toward the V in the skyline above her. There was no catching Garin and the curator. They'd reach the doorway before her. Assuming they could find it. Zanetti's information might give her a badly needed advantage.

She slowed down as she reached the V, knowing she was completely exposed. She kept low, almost on her hands and knees, as she reached the Pass of the Moor's Sigh, trying not to be spotted from below.

The helicopter was long gone.

The ground was strewn with boulders that had fallen down the hillside over generations. There were hundreds of them, all different shapes and sizes, offering countless places to hide and throwing shadows across the terrain as the sun came up. She turned. Through the mountain pass she saw the majesty of the Alhambra as it must have been centuries ago. The first light of the sun struck the incredible gold ornamentation on the building, transmuting it into an almost molten form. It came alive in the sun. Annja understood in that single moment why the Moor had sighed when he had looked back at what he had abandoned. The loss must have been visceral.

She turned her back on the Alhambra and scanned the mountainside for Garin.

There was no sign of him or Maffrici.

Panic overtook her. They had to be close by. But she couldn't see them. If they'd found the way into the mountain, she might never find them, not in time. She

had to think. They could not have left this narrow valley
without her knowing—it was impossible. That meant
they were still here somewhere. She scoured the eastern-
facing hillside, still half-bathed in shadow, searching
for something that would show where they had gone,
some darker shadow or bare cleft in the rock. The slope
was covered in rocks and boulders, many of which were
precariously balanced and threatened to come tumbling
down at the slightest breeze. But nothing seemed even
remotely out of place.

She tried to think like Garin.

What would he have done?

If nothing was out of place, she had to look for the
obvious, something that didn't belong…but what?

Something in the shadows?

A shape?

She scanned the slopes again, shading her eyes. This
time she saw a flash of light, barely above the shadow
line. It hadn't been there a second ago. It glinted again.
The newly risen sun was reflecting off something—
or someone. Maybe it was a gun, a pair of sunglasses,
a cigarette lighter, a watch face, even a belt buckle.
It didn't matter. There was definitely someone in the
shadows between rocks, and they were moving. Could
it be Garin trying to tell her where he was being taken?
Giving her a bread-crumb trail to follow?

Or was it a goon waiting at the doorway, intent on
stopping her from getting inside the mountain?

31

Roux picked out the silhouette of a woman running along the ridge, the light of the rising sun behind her. She was vulnerable out there. A hostile sniper could have brought her down without difficulty. He didn't like it. But she was moving *fast*. She streaked across the horizon, a primal force at one with the world, her powerful stride eating up the ground much more swiftly than his could, even though she'd been running for miles already and he'd had the luxury of a sports car at his disposal. The woman was incredible. He never ceased to marvel at the sheer physical strength she possessed, or the mental fortitude that accompanied it. She didn't think twice about racing headlong into danger if it was the right thing to do. She truly was a worthy heir of Joan's sword. That made the twist of the knife that was Garin's exploitation all the more painful.

She dropped out of sight as she moved between two hills. This V carved into the peaks had to be Puerto del Suspiro del Moro. Nothing else around here fit its description. Roux had heard the story of the last emir, who had deserted his beautiful city rather than stand up to the demands of the Catholic monarchs. It was a beautiful place for a coward to come to terms with his failings. Even now, Roux couldn't help but be cowed by the natural gravitas of this spot. No man could ever compete.

The only sign of the modern world was the distant hum of the helicopter. The sound of the engine echoed through the narrow valley in the stillness of the morning.

For the second time in a few hours, Roux found himself transported back to a much simpler time, when he and Garin had been so much younger, before the bitterness between them had really had a chance to develop. Roux wanted to believe they had both been good men once, before life shaped them. But sometimes it was hard to remember what they had been, though.

The hacker had sent him an email, providing details of financial transactions. Roux studied the documents for a moment, trying to make sense of them. There were a lot of numbers, but when he stripped them away, what he held in his hands proved beyond a shadow of doubt that Garin Braden was not an innocent victim in this mess. He was linked to the activity in ways that Roux had desperately hoped he wouldn't be. These were Garin's financials, and they exposed everything he'd been doing. *Everything.* The amount of information Oscar had uncovered was overwhelming—and deeply disturbing. There was no way this had all come from the server at the Alhambra. The kid had gone to town, tearing into every company and shell corp that Garin was tied to, no matter how loosely, looking for anything incriminating. And he'd found it in spades. Most telling were a couple of documents he'd singled out for Roux's attention: details of a helicopter lease, payments for a pilot's contract, invoices for his Gulfstream for bays in Granada, shipping details, car rental. It just went on and on. He didn't have the time now to study the paper trail in detail, but he would. He'd pore over it all. He'd digest everything. And he'd act on it. For now, the important thing was that this was irrefutable proof. Garin was a self-serving son of a bitch, and he was no one's victim. That was all Roux needed to know. Garin had cost those men their lives. There would be a reckoning.

Roux shook his head. It wasn't as though he hadn't expected it. He'd known somewhere deep down since all of this began that something was rotten. But having it spelled out to him so bluntly…well, it undermined so many of the inroads he thought they'd made over the past few years. He should have known better than to trust his young apprentice. So what was the end game here? What did Garin want out of this? Surely it wasn't just money? He had accumulated enough of that over the centuries. He always had a deeper plan. That was one reason he'd always been so much more successful in modern business than Roux had. He was ruthless. He was made for this cutthroat world. It was a long time since he'd stopped being Roux's apprentice, that was for sure. He was his own man. Garin only did what Garin wanted to do. And he had grown very rich with that philosophy.

The sounds of the helicopter changed.

A moment later it was rising into the air again, cresting the hillside less than twenty feet above Roux's head and banking away. Roux caught the briefest of glances inside the cabin before he felt the force of the downdraft from the rotor blades. There was only one man inside, and that was the pilot. He'd left Garin and his coconspirator on the mountain. Roux crouched, hands flat against the dusty ground to maintain his balance while he struggled to catch his breath. *I'm getting too old for this*, he thought bitterly, tempted to take a shot at the helicopter as it passed overhead, just to put a spanner in Garin's plans. But unlike his former apprentice, he did think about the collateral damage his actions caused. It would have been different if Garin Braden had been on board, though. Then he wouldn't have hesitated.

As Roux crested the hill, he looked into the pass. They'd all come to the right place. More than that, though, he was struck by a sense of déjà vu. He'd been here before. He couldn't remember when. That was one of the drawbacks of living six centuries. They all started to blur into one another. The changes were subtle—the wind had eroded a sliver of the mountain, the rain had washed stone into dust and the valley floor had gathered more rocks and boulders. But he wasn't seeing it for the first time, he was certain. He'd been here before.

He scanned the slope, hoping to catch a sign of either Annja or Garin.

There was no sign of Garin or any of the men he likely had out here with him. He wouldn't have risked going it alone. He wasn't that kind of man. No doubt their pay stubs were in the bundle of files Oscar had sent him. They hadn't disappeared into thin air, he was damned sure of that. Garin was a lot of things, but he wasn't a magician.

Roux spotted Annja. She was climbing up the side of the narrow valley, gradually moving across his line of sight until she swung down into shadows again and disappeared. One second she was there, the next she wasn't. She'd found a way into the mountain. He resisted the urge to yell at her to wait; he didn't want to show their hand too early. Any shout loud enough for Annja to hear would be loud enough for Garin to hear, too.

Likewise, he could call her cell, but without knowing how close she was to Garin's crew, he couldn't risk betraying her presence with a ringtone. The last thing he wanted was to let Garin know just how close they were to stopping him.

Annja was smart. She would have seen the Alfa's lights as he made his approach, so she would know he wasn't too far behind her. She wouldn't do anything reckless in the meantime.

At least he hoped not.

32

Annja skirted around the crack in the rocks, doing her utmost to remain out of the sight line of the guard Garin had left at the entrance to the underworld.

Actually, it was more of a fold than a crack.

The guard stood just inside the opening, almost completely in shadow. The glint she'd seen earlier hadn't been Garin or Maffrici, but this man. Which was lucky; she never would have found the fold otherwise. It was so subtle, almost invisible to the untrained eye, that it was no wonder it had gone undetected for so many years.

The sun drifted lazily into the sky, turning night to day in its own sweet time. She edged along, keeping boulders between her and the guard. The broken stones were large enough to offer cover and break up the monotony of the landscape, meaning there was less chance of him spotting her movement as long as she kept herself out of his eye line. She'd be in trouble if he emerged from the fold, though. Then she'd be on her own, exposed. But like any good soldier, he wasn't moving from his post. Sometimes discipline could be someone's undoing.

She dashed from boulder to boulder and more than once lost sight of the fold in the rock face and ended up drawing closer to it than she had intended. The natural camouflage was incredibly effective. Stones skittered down the mountain as her boots caught on the loose ground. More than once she had to grasp scrubby clumps of grass to stop herself from sliding down after them.

In the stillness of the morning, even that soft sound of shifting scree could be enough to rouse the guard's suspicion. She worked her way closer, holding her breath when she reached a ledge above the opening. She'd managed to circle up and around the fold to a point almost directly above it without alerting the guard to her presence. She adjusted her feet, scuffing up a shower of dust and grit. Granules fell in front of the opening, a fine, dry rain.

The guard took a half step forward, craning his neck to look up, expecting to see a mountain goat grazing on the narrow ledge.

Annja seized the moment.

She dropped down, landing with a leg on each of his shoulders. His knees buckled under her. He staggered, reaching out with one hand to try to keep himself upright, but it was a losing battle. Annja had the better of him and they both knew it. She tucked her ankle behind the knee of her other leg and squeezed, clamping both hands over the man's mouth as he kicked and struggled, flailing about. He dropped his gun, a machine pistol, and clawed at her hands, but there was no dislodging her grip. He couldn't shake her off, and the more desperately he struggled, the more strength she put into her stranglehold. She tensed her thighs, choking him. The guard threw himself backward, slamming Annja against the stone wall. It was a desperate move. The impact knocked the air out of her for a second, but she clung on, her vicelike grip tightening relentlessly, until the fight began to leave him. The pressure on his vagus nerve took effect.

The man crumpled, unconscious, and fell to the ground.

He wasn't going to be moving for a while.

She checked his pulse. It was still strong.

She picked up his Steyr machine pistol and felt the weight in her hand. She'd never felt particularly comfortable around guns. They weren't her thing. But she didn't want to leave it behind. There was no telling who might follow her into the dark. Yes, Roux was out there, but how many more of the Brotherhood of the Burning were working their way toward the cave? She didn't want to risk arming them if she didn't have to.

Annja stepped deeper into the shadows, reaching out as the opening turned through ninety degrees and feeling around for a way in. She felt wood beneath her fingertips. She pulled out her flashlight and shone the beam on a door. There was a rust-pitted ring that served as a handle, but it didn't matter if she twisted or turned it; it wasn't budging. There was no sign of a lock, but there was obviously some kind of hidden mechanism securing the door. She recalled Zanetti's instructions—

face Mecca, turn back to face the door and say the name of the prophet three times. She didn't see how it could work, but as she turned to face west, she realized that the ground beneath her feet was shifting. She played the light across her feet, revealing a circle of stone set into the rock floor.

Annja smiled.

She faced the door again and took hold of the handle before making the turn again.

The circle of stone moved with her.

"Muhammad…Muhammad…Muhammad," she said, and this time when she turned the handle there was an audible click as the door was released.

The prophet's name was a timing device.

She turned the flashlight into the space as she entered, lighting up the space beyond.

She stepped inside. The door started closing behind her. Almost too late, she realized she had no idea how to get back out. Not only that, she hadn't told Roux how to get in. Thinking fast, she dropped to her knees and wedged the door open with the only thing she had to hand—the fallen brother's Steyr machine pistol. It couldn't be helped. And if Roux was unarmed, it'd level things up once he entered the mountain.

Happy she had an escape route, Annja took one final breath of fresh air and headed into the mountain.

She hadn't gone more than fifty feet before she saw the glow of a naked flame up ahead.

33

Roux tried not take his eyes off the point where Annja had disappeared, picking out enough features on the rock face to be sure he didn't lose the spot as he made his way toward it. Even so, it was difficult. With every step he took, the shadows shifted, casting an entirely new facade to the stone wall. Without knowing the precise location of this portal into the mountain, it would be virtually impossible to find. It wasn't the kind of thing a wandering tourist could just stumble upon. Then again, part of Roux really wanted to walk into that cave and find it had been picked clean. That kind of irony would serve Garin right. The look on his face would be as priceless as the treasure he'd lost.

Total humiliation might be the one thing that saved Garin from the old man's wrath.

As he inched his way through the stones and boulders, Roux kept glancing up toward the faint scar in the mountainside, making sure that he could still distinguish it from the countless shadows conjured by the rising sun.

In the last few strides, he slipped the machine pistol

from his shoulder, ready to use it if he had to. He had no qualms about pulling the trigger. The guys he was facing were being paid well to make sure he didn't interfere with their paymaster's plans. They made themselves legitimate targets by taking Garin's dime.

But that dime wasn't anywhere near enough compensation for going up against Annja Creed.

Pity they didn't know that before they cashed the checks.

Roux approached what appeared, as he drew closer, to be a fold in the rock. In the shadows in the hollow, he almost stumbled over a body propped up awkwardly against the cold stone. Even in the limited light, he recognized the unconscious man as one of the brothers from the chapel inside the Alhambra.

The man was alive, which made him luckier than he had any right to be. Had Roux been leading the charge, he wouldn't have left a single enemy combatant alive behind him. But that was the old soldier ingrained in him. Annja wasn't a soldier, and he had to admit he admired her no-nonsense approach. She hadn't wasted a bullet, nor had she felt the need to call upon the sword. The tunnel beyond the door would likely be tight, and he could see the sword being cumbersome. She was resourceful. In this case, it was obvious she'd used her body as the weapon.

Roux stepped over the fallen brother and slid through the doorway, which had been held open by a Steyr machine pistol just like the one in his hand. No doubt

Garin had ordered a bulk shipment of arms, probably from some Russian dealer with an aversion to questions.

Stepping into the darkness without the benefit of a flashlight, Roux moved slowly and stealthily, one hand trailing lightly across the rock wall to guide him. Even in the dark, the old man was light on his feet. It was impossible to tell in the dark just how sound or unsound the passage was, or what the integrity of the walls was like, especially since it likely hadn't been visited for hundreds of years. He could feel the weight of the mountain above him, though. He hated being underground. It was akin to being buried alive. Who in their right mind wanted to spend more time than they had to out of the sun and the wide-open spaces? He moved forward, careful not to kick any scattered stones, placing each foot slowly so it didn't crunch on the grit that had accumulated over all that time.

Whoever had found—or made—this vault inside the mountain had chosen the site well.

It was secure.

Up ahead, Roux saw the glow of an orange flame.

It grew brighter.

Roux stayed tight to the wall, feeling his way along it another few paces, painfully aware that the tunnel was crushing in on all sides without needing to reach out and prove it to himself. He shuddered. The ground beneath his feet sloped slightly upward, no doubt to ensure drainage rather than risk flooding out the entire subterranean complex. That slight incline meant a lot of careful thought had gone into the engineering of this place, too. He shouldn't have been surprised. The Moorish builders were among the world's premier architects in their day. This narrow path wasn't easy to walk, and deliberately so. The construction was intended to protect the treasure in the mountain's heart.

There was no way those Moorish architects would have left the protection of their greatest treasures to a door in a hidden fold of the rock, no matter how complicated it was to unlock.

They would have taken other measures to protect their wealth.

He was absolutely sure of it.

And his conviction was proven right.

The flickering flame cast shadows across the passage. Seeing what it was, Roux crept toward it: a torch burning in a sconce set into the wall.

He almost walked into a spear that had been fired from a hidden mechanism set into the tunnel's ceiling.

By the light of the torch, he saw the trap had been sprung by a careless footfall pressing down on an uneven slab set into the floor. There was a dark smear on the spear tip. Blood. Meaning that whoever sprung it hadn't come away unharmed. He hoped, grimly, that it stung more than just Garin's pride.

He peered into the darkness, feeling the heat of the flame against his face.

He couldn't hear anything ahead of him.

He should have been able to hear *something*.

The silence was almost more unnerving than the bloody spear tip.

Coming, ready or not, he thought.

34

The beam from the flashlight picked out the spear before she stumbled into it.

Annja had been moving carefully long before she reached that point, though, wary of where she put her feet. She'd been half expecting a similar trap since she stepped into the tunnel. One misstep was all it would take if there were any more weighted traps or pitfalls. Professor Zanetti's warning had been crystal clear. He'd been spot-on with everything he'd deciphered thus far, so she had no reason to doubt what he'd said about the challenges between her and the waiting treasure. It only made sense to proceed with extreme caution. The sophistication of the door's locking mechanism had suggested a level of craftsmanship that wasn't necessarily easy to figure out, either. So why risk it?

Yes, Garin and Maffrici had taken this path before her, but they could have been lucky and avoided any number of other traps. Not for the first time, she wondered how it was that Garin had first heard of this place. Had it been Maffrici who had come to him, knowing the secrets the Mask of Torquemada carried? Garin could have known the language inscribed on the mask, as he was born before it died out, but still, it was unlikely. So was it Maffrici? The curator was the variable in all of this. She just didn't know enough about him. Was he Garin's translator? Or was his role something else entirely?

She looked at the tiny black spot in the ceiling where the spear had thrust down, and then at the bloody spear tip. It had clearly done some damage—but how much? And to whom?

Someone had lit a torch and set it into a sconce on the wall, no doubt lighting the way for their return.

She shone the beam of her flashlight along the floor. She didn't expect there to be signs of another trap so close to this one, but she couldn't afford to take any chances. All she found, though, was a trail of dark splashes that couldn't have been anything other than blood.

Less than thirty paces later, Annja caught sight of two men standing close to another blazing torch. They didn't see her—or at least they acted as if they didn't. She killed the flashlight. Even without being able to see their faces, she could tell that Garin wasn't one of them. They didn't seem to be particularly on edge. Hadn't Garin warned them to expect visitors? Surely he would have if he'd set them as guards. Maybe he didn't want them knowing what the stakes were in this search, in case they got ideas of their own.

She needed to neutralize them quickly and quietly.

Annja reached out, willing the sword into her grasp

even as she closed her fingers into a fist around its hilt and drew it from the otherwhere.

The tunnel was cramped, and the blade emitted an eerie glow that made her appear to be some fatal revenant coming charging out of the darkness. Still, it was subtler than the machine pistol.

"Raul?" one of the two men called, mistaking her for the unconscious guard she'd left back in the doorway. She closed half of the gap in silence.

It was already too late when the man realized his mistake. She stepped into the circle of light cast by the flame. No matter how desperately they struggled to raise their weapons, they did not stand a chance.

Annja danced to one side and pulled the sword back behind her, wielding it like she would a golf club, its edge cutting through the air. The blade caught the first man below his belt buckle, biting through metal and leather. The sword cut clean through him, slicing deep into his flesh and through internal organs in a single stroke. The man's expression betrayed his surprise. There was no pain or fear. He glanced down at the ruination of his flesh as he sank to his knees, clutching at his stomach as if he could stem the flow of blood with his fingers and force the contents of his body back inside the gaping wound as his life spilled out onto the floor.

Annja heaved the sword away from him just as the second man leveled his machine pistol, finally grasping the threat she posed. He swung the muzzle toward her, point-blank. But before he could squeeze the trigger and riddle her flesh with steel, Annja pushed the barrel of the gun to one side, slamming it into the stone wall with dexterity and speed that defied thought or counter. His brain simply couldn't think that fast. Annja fought on pure instinct. She thrust the sword deep into his chest, ramming it all the way in, until the tip of the blade emerged blood-slicked on the other side.

Blood frothed from his mouth, his lips moving but not making a sound as he collapsed at her feet.

They were both still alive when Annja stepped over them, but they wouldn't be for long.

The torch burned on.

At least they would not die in darkness.

35

Only too aware of how close she might be to the men in front of her, Annja kept the flashlight pointed at the ground, with one hand over the beam. Ideally, she'd have done without it, but she needed to see where she was treading. The ground was uneven and any protruding edge could have been the trigger for an elaborate trap.

She crept forward, listening for the slightest sound, anything to warn her that Garin and the curator had come to a stop or that they were coming back her way.

The corridor bent ahead of her, the rock illuminated by another torch set in a sconce beyond the curve. She killed the flashlight for as far as the burning torch lit the way. As she reached the turn she paused, again straining to hear, before she risked peering out around the corner. Annja pressed herself tight to the wall. As the tunnel straightened out it widened, leading into a cavern. She could see the bright colors of the first few tiles of a floor decorated with a complicated Morisco mosaic. A genuine work of art filled the space.

The sight was engrossing, and part of her wanted to

rush forward and see exactly what it was, to revel in its simple existence after all these years. But in the center of the masterpiece, she saw Garin and Maffrici along with half a dozen heavily armed guards. One man sat propped up against a wall, his legs splayed out in front of him, to help keep him from toppling. He clutched at a dark patch in his side, his face white in the artificial light. The spear trap's victim.

The presence of the gunmen was almost enough to convince her that Garin had been brought to this place against his will. Almost. She recognized the avarice in his face. Yet Garin was part of what she did, of who she was. She couldn't imagine it any other way. Garin was as much a part of her world as Roux was, and without him and his place in it, everything would be off-kilter.

She desperately wanted to believe that Roux was wrong, that *she* was wrong.

And she almost managed it.

Garin held the mask, turning it over and over in his hands. He traced the inside of it with his fingers, feeling the silversmith's craftsmanship. He handed it to Maffrici, who had a jeweler's glass wedged to his eye. She'd guessed right; Maffrici was Garin's translator. But instead of examining the smooth face or the inside of the mask, the curator tipped it on its side, moving the edge closer to his face as he shone a penlight along it.

Annja hadn't even considered the possibility that there could be more instructions engraved into the edge of the metal. She kicked herself for being sloppy.

Maffrici knew more about what lay ahead of them than she did.

But if he had known about the spear trap, why did he let one of their men walk into it? She shuddered as she remembered what Roux's hacker had found, evidence that Garin had willingly sacrificed his bodyguards to sell the lie of his kidnapping. He had no regard for life, she realized. Or no regard for the lives of those around him. His own, he was incredibly fond of. Of course he had sent one of his guards ahead to trigger the trap. It was expedient. Set it off rather than spend time searching for it. A sprung trap couldn't hurt anyone else.

So what was on the mask's edge?

What other message could the silversmith have engraved?

Maffrici looked up, a satisfied smile spreading slowly across his torch-lit face as he took in the ceiling. He returned his gaze to the mask and nodded, then pointed to something on the ceiling and drew Garin's attention to the mask. They were partners. The man wasn't giving Garin instructions; he was seeking his approval. Annja strained, trying to make out the words that passed between them. Voices echoed around the chamber, but the strange acoustics made it impossible for her to understand what was being said. It was obvious from their body language that Garin was the one giving orders.

He counted the tiles, his gait awkward. She realized that he was stepping over certain tiles in the mosaic. No doubt they were part of the traps Zanetti had identified. Garin appeared to have a good idea of where it was and, more importantly, what was likely to trigger it. All she could do was watch and wait. Without knowing what was written on the edge of the mask, she was in the dark, both literally and metaphorically.

Two of his men tied a length of rope around the legs of the man who had been gored by the spear trap.

Annja had only taken her eyes off the injured man a minute or two. In that time, everything about him had changed. The hand that had clutched at his wound had slipped away and lay limp in his lap. His head leaned to one side. He'd lost the fight. Garin rattled off a string of instructions, pointing at the spaces where it was safe to walk, shouting warnings when one of his men veered off the path.

This time his voice carried.

"Move to the edge." The two men who had tied the rope around the dead man's legs made their way around the cavern until they stood opposite where the corpse was slumped. "Yes, yes, now! Pull!"

They did as they were told, without question, taking up the slack until the body began to move. The dead man's head hit the tiled floor with a sickening thump. Annja gritted her teeth. She'd remember this. This was wrong. This wasn't the Garin she knew. This was someone else. She knew exactly what they were doing. She couldn't bear to watch, but she couldn't look away.

The pair dragged the body slowly but surely across the mosaic.

Its movement was jerky and erratic, each handful of

rope the two men hauled drawing it a foot or so across the ground.

A smear of blood trailed in the dead man's wake, marking his passage.

When the body reached the center of the room, they stopped.

They were all waiting.

Something was supposed to happen.

She could sense the anticipation in the chamber.

All eyes were on the corpse.

She held her breath and counted silently, marking the passage of time.

She hadn't even reached five before the rumbles began deep in the belly of the mountain.

By the time she reached eleven, the floor had begun to shake.

At fifteen, dust and grit began to sprinkle from the ceiling.

Twenty, and the men in the middle of the chamber were on their knees, heads in hands as the mountain began to fall upon them.

36

The walls around Roux began to shake.

Far below, it sounded as though the world had sheered in two, two great hemispheres of stone separating. The deep basso profundo rumble told another story. The passage was collapsing. The Moorish builders had left the ultimate trap to protect their treasure, preferring it to be lost to the world rather than fall into the hands of their persecutors. He liked their style.

Fighting every instinct to get the hell out of there before the place came down around him, Roux ran *into* the collapsing tunnel. Annja was in there. He wasn't leaving her. He choked back the dust and dirt that filled the air. Another rumble, this time followed by the unmistakable sound of falling rock. He ran on, stumbling as the ground lurched beneath him. He had to get to Annja, to be sure she was all right. He heard a colossal thunder crack of stone tearing apart and was hit by a sudden, sinking dread that the mountain was robbing him of his revenge.

He saw two bodies in the passage ahead. They lay with their weapons out of reach. Even with the debris around them, it was obvious they hadn't been hurt by the rockfall. They'd been taken from this world with deadly precision. The corpses bore the hallmarks of Annja's handiwork. The men hadn't stood a chance against her ruthless ferocity. She was capable of controlled violence beyond anything Roux or Garin could ever muster— she could become a pure killing machine if it was the only way. Annja Creed, mercifully, was on the side of the angels. It was where she belonged.

He followed the tunnel deeper still, placing his feet carefully, not because he feared more traps but because a turned ankle now would be disastrous—even fatal. Everywhere he trod seemed to carry an element of danger. A light shone farther along the corridor, another torch, where the tunnel started to bend. There was another rumble. The ceiling above him shivered. The ground beneath his feet groaned. A huge cloud of dust billowed toward him, swelling to fill the passageway with choking, cloying white. The flaming torch snuffed out, stifled by the dust. He was in absolute darkness.

He couldn't breathe for the choking dust clawing its way into his lungs.

Roux held one arm across his mouth, trying desperately to keep from swallowing or inhaling too deeply. He kept his eyes closed, dragging his free hand along the wall as he moved. There was no turning back. Not now. Each step took him closer to Annja, closer to Garin. They were in there—in with the worst of the collapse, where the heart of the mountain had given out.

He needed to see them both, but for very different reasons.

Roux could not live without certainty; he needed to be sure of what had become of both of them. His apprentices. Turning around without finding out would leave him even more lost than coming across either of them in the rubble would.

37

Stone and rubble from the ceiling came crashing down all around them, jagged spurs driving into and cracking the mosaic's tiles and burying the body of the dead man they'd used to spring the trap.

Annja looked at Garin, reading his mind. It wasn't difficult to read, either: better him than me, his expression said. And he was right. If he'd been under that ceiling when it collapsed it would have taken more than the miracle of the curse to keep him breathing. He might, for all intents and purposes, be immortal, but that didn't mean he couldn't die. At least she didn't think it did, though Roux might want to put that theory to the test before they were out of this place.

The air was full of dust and grit. It billowed out to fill every expanse of the subterranean complex. She could see rather than feel the draft that drew the dust cloud toward the outside world.

As the air started to clear, Annja saw that a huge section of the floor had fallen away.

Blinking back the sting of dust, she realized she was wrong—it hadn't collapsed. Rather, it had sunk, or most of it had, with the tiles forming a spiral staircase that led down. She couldn't see where it led.

"Move," Garin called to the rest of the men. "We don't have time to waste. In and out. There are enough bodies in our wake that someone is going to alert the authorities. We don't want to be here when they do."

Annja knew that someone he was referring to had to be her, and she wanted to slap him silly. He was so conceited.

What would happen if she stepped out of the shadows and faced him down? Would he try to kill her? Could he, even if he tried? He was resourceful, but with the bit between her teeth, she'd sure as hell test his immortality. Was she expendable? He'd used her up to this point... Would he cash her in like a pile of chips in a casino now that he was done playing with her? As hard to swallow as that was, it felt like the truth.

The two men who had hauled their dead comrade across the floor were still holding on to the rope.

"I said, move!"

They jumped to attention, casting the rope aside, and started for the staircase.

There were fewer guards now, she noted. A few had perished beneath the great slabs of ceiling.

The odds were starting to even up, but it still wasn't a fight she wanted to have unless it was absolutely necessary.

Garin and Maffrici started to descend with the three remaining guards following behind them.

She needed to stay close, but did not dare move until

the last of them had disappeared from view. Even then, she took the time to be certain none of the men had stayed behind to stand guard.

Annja made her way across the floor.

She saw bodies and broken limbs in the debris. She picked a path through the devastation, one eye on the ceiling above in case there were still chunks of rock yet to fall.

Garin's voice rose up from below.

It sounded as if he were in the grip of a heated argument, but then Roux had said more than once that Garin was capable of causing an argument when he was the only person in a room. She dropped to her hands and knees and crept to the edge, peering down the spiral stairs to a floor more than thirty feet below. Garin was shoving Maffrici, the flat of his hand on the curator's chest to drive home whatever point he was making. The curator looked frightened.

The space that had been hidden below the mosaic floor almost took her breath away.

It was flooded with light as high-intensity lanterns were turned on.

The light bounced off every surface of the hidden room.

Every inch of the chamber was a testament to the incredible skills the Moors possessed. They understood the nature of beauty and were capable of harnessing it. The walls were covered with too many patterns to distinguish one from the other, some picked out in silver and others gold. It was a treasure beyond imagining, a time capsule. And yet it wasn't enough for Garin.

Was this the treasure they had left behind, this secret shrine to their God?

A place of worship rather than material possessions... That would have been in keeping with their faith, and a vast amount of wealth must have been needed to create this wondrous chapel in the mountain. Did it have to be anything more than this, a room dedicated to their God so close to the heart of the Inquisition?

Annja drank the place in.

More than five hundred years must have passed since this place of exaltation had been completed, and yet it looked as fresh as the day it had been created.

It could have been tended to every day, polished by loving hands for generations, but it hadn't been. It had been sealed from the world for all this time.

This great, great secret...

Annja's heart was racing. She couldn't have imagined a greater treasure waiting at the end of her quest. This was how Howard Carter must have felt when he broke into the tomb of Tutankhamen. This was a find for the ages. This was wealth beyond any dreams of avarice, a work of art in the glory of God. She didn't know where to look, trying to take it all in, trying to imagine how the world would react to such an incredible find.

Garin, on the other hand, looked as though someone had taken a leak in his cornflakes and expected him to eat them.

"Is this it?" Garin yelled, holding his arms out wide. "This worthless room? Is *this* it? We've moved heaven and earth...for this?"

"Don't you see the beauty of this place, the artwork, the skill and craftsmanship?" Maffrici asked with more than a touch of incredulity in his voice. "This place is a national treasure. Just standing in here makes everything we have done worthwhile."

"But where are the jewels, the gold and the silver?"

"Look all around you," Maffrici said. "It is all here. Just as I promised."

The curator picked up one of the lanterns and turned it to face the wall, pointing out individual features, tracing patterns with his fingertips. "Gold and silver, rubies and emeralds, amethyst and jade. Use your eyes. Every inch of these walls represents immense wealth. You could buy a small country with the contents of this room."

Garin pushed him aside and pulled a knife from his pocket. He slid the blade behind one of the stones and prized it from its setting in the wall, pocketing it.

"What the hell do you think you are doing?" Maffrici said, pushing Garin's knife away from the wall before he could pry a second stone free. "Vandalism. Sheer, wanton vandalism. This treasure has survived intact for centuries. I will not stand by and watch you break it up. It needs to be saved for the nation. The Brotherhood of the Burning was founded to protect this place from the Catholic Church. I'll die before I let you tear it apart."

"That can be arranged," Garin said coldly. "And give

me a break…the Brotherhood of the Burning? That's a joke. They may have stood for something once upon a time. Now they are nothing. Less than nothing. This is it, these three men. Do they look like they care what happens here?"

Garin took his knife to the wall again.

This time, Maffrici pulled his hand away more forcefully. "I said *no!*" the curator shouted, the man's aggression taking Garin by surprise. He stumbled, losing his footing, and before he could right himself he staggered backward, dropping the knife in the process. It clattered to the jeweled floor.

Annja saw the rage on his face, saw him wrestling to maintain control, and knew his grip was slipping.

Garin flung himself at the Spaniard. His fist slammed square into the middle of Maffrici's face, snapping his head backward. He stumbled back a step. As he brought his head up, Annja could see the red rose of blood that had bloomed in the harsh light of the electric lanterns. His nose was a mess.

"Do we understand each other?" Garin asked. It was a rhetorical question. The man nodded, clutching at his ruined face, no longer protesting as Garin set about the wall with a vengeance. "Get to it," he told his men. "Strip this damned place. Anything shiny, it comes out. Anything that looks like it's worth money, it comes out." The brothers set to the task with greedy abandon.

But…surely this wasn't Garin.

He wasn't simply a thief…

Was he?

Annja could almost understand him doing this for some great work of art, some incredible thing of beauty he felt he needed to possess…but just money, just jewels? That didn't feel right. It felt…cheap.

There was no doubt that Garin was the dominant man down there. Any influence the curator had possessed entering the mountain was gone, crushed by one punch. It was notable that none of the armed men had moved to intervene. They knew which side their bread was buttered. That didn't mean they worked for Garin, though, only that they respected his power in this new dynamic. What was the name Oscar had turned up during his digging into the Brotherhood…Enrique Martínez? Did they work for Martínez? Was he the power behind this particular throne or just another one being deceived by Garin Braden? All that was certain was that the guards had no allegiance to Maffrici. So that meant the curator had been used every bit as much as she had.

She edged closer to the top of the stairwell, unwilling to put even a first foot on it until she was sure of her next move.

She was still leery about charging in to confront Garin, even though she knew she should. She'd rather wait for Roux before she did that. He couldn't be more than a few minutes behind her now, assuming he hadn't been caught in the collapse.

And then there was the risk of a trigger-happy soul down there. If she was seen making her way down, even if she shouted out a warning, there was no predicting what a nervous guard could do. Yes, she could use the sword to deflect the shots, assuming she could see the bullets coming. Every bullet was a risk. Every bullet was a possible checkout.

She needed to get down onto the same level, to get close to them, if her attack was going to be effective.

As she watched, she noticed something that seemed so strange, so out of place, that she knew it had to be the key to the treasure, to the reason why the Brotherhood of the Burning had started building this chapel in the first place.

And Garin had missed it.

In almost all of the places she had visited in the past twenty-four hours, there had been things that did not belong, Moorish artifacts hidden away in Catholic shrines, Christian emblems in the heart of Islamic places of worship. This was another one of them, so utterly familiar it couldn't possibly be what she thought it was. And even when she was sure it was, she didn't understand. She'd seen it before.

And that was impossible.

It had an exquisite beauty of its own.

And if this shrine had been sealed up for as long as she thought it had, as she *knew* it had, then it couldn't be a fake.

In fact, it could be the original, carved even earlier than the one she had seen.

The marble statue sat on a plinth at the far end of the room, as though on an altar. Garin ignored it while he tried to prize every last jewel from the walls. The carving was almost identical to the *Madonna of Bruges*, the only sculpture by Michelangelo to have left Italy during his lifetime.

Was it really possible that there had been a second?

Annja had only seen the other version of the sculpture once in person, but she had studied it in countless photographs. The depiction of Mary and the child Jesus had been a radical change from all previous representations. Earlier images and statues had almost always shown the infant as still a babe-in-arms while his mother looked on him adoringly, but Michelangelo had chosen to capture Christ as a child, almost able to stand upright, ready to slide from her lap and step out on his own. Instead of smiling at the child, Mary is looking away with sadness on her face, as if she already knows what fate has in store for her son.

The statue Annja was looking at now was so similar it was virtually indistinguishable—at least from the memory she had of it—from Michelangelo's masterpiece.

In this one place, the Moors had created things of great beauty that represented the pinnacle of both Islamic and Christian art. Neither seemed out of place, as if the two religions should be able to exist side by side rather than competing for hearts and minds, forcing people into a position where they had to choose.

The statue enthralled her.

She wanted to go down there to take a closer look, to run her hands over marble that hadn't been touched since the master had carved it.

"Help me move this," Garin barked.

Annja wanted to shout down to stop him, to tell him to leave everything where it was, but even as she opened her mouth, her cry was silenced by a hand placed over it.

38

"Shh," Roux whispered into her ear. "Don't go doing anything stupid, girl."

He slowly removed his hand from her mouth.

Annja wasn't entirely sure she *would* have called out, but she was grateful to Roux that she would never know.

"For a moment, I thought you were dead. Actually, I thought you both were. Not that I'd have missed him. You, on the other hand, I'm just getting to know, and I still rather like you."

Annja grinned, sharing his relief. "Goes both ways, old man. Glad you're not flat. We're all alive and kicking," she whispered.

"For now."

They pulled back from the opening to make sure they were out of sight of the men below, not that anyone was looking up. They were utterly engrossed in the act of desecrating the shrine.

"If you need proof, I can give you proof," Roux said. "Garin is El Zogoybi. He's the head of the Brotherhood of the Burning. The hacker managed to find a hell of a lot more about the things that Garin has been getting up to than either of us could have imagined. I'm going to see about putting a spanner in a few works with his help. Someone needs to bring our boy down a peg or two."

"But how is that possible?"

"With Garin, almost anything is possible."

"But to become their leader? Why on earth would they trust an outsider?"

"Because he isn't an outsider. He didn't join an organization—he founded one. He must have found out about the name somehow and then went out of his way to recruit a few far-right fanatics. Almost all of the Brotherhood's early attacks—aimed at striking fear in the public—were on his own buildings. But the movement grew beyond him, and now it's getting so out of hand that even Europol has to commit manpower to try to bring the rampant spread of racism through this country under control."

A string of questions was starting to form inside her head, but before she could voice any of them, she was distracted by the sound of stone grinding on stone.

Annja eased her way forward again to see Garin instructing two of the guards to move the statue of the Madonna from its plinth.

Garin had realized that this was the shrine's true treasure.

The sound wasn't just coming from the movement of the statue against the base; it was coming from all around her. Survival instinct screamed that she should run, but where could she go? How could she possibly seek safety if the whole cavern came tumbling down?

And how could she leave Garin down there, no matter what he had done? He was one of them.

She had to speak up. "Garin! No! Don't move it! Don't move the statue!"

But it was too late. The two men struggled to keep hold of the Madonna, its weight too much for them. Garin shot a glare in her direction. He'd expected her. Before he had the chance to say anything else, the bottom step of the spiral stairway fell away from its position, cracking as it hit the floor. An instant later, the second step did the same, then the third and the next and the next. The whole staircase folded in on itself like a house of cards coming down, each dropping to the ground when it no longer had the support of the one below.

Garin rushed forward as they fell, trying to reach up and grab a handhold before it disappeared.

In less than half a minute, the entire miraculous construction had fallen away and lay shattered on the ground around his feet.

Garin stared at the remains, picking up two sections as if he could fit them together like an elaborate jigsaw, but there was nothing to hold them together. He was trapped down there. This was the last trap that the mask had warned them about.

Annja stood on the ledge, looking at the men stuck down there.

"Ah, good to see you again, Annja. I was counting on you to get here sooner," Garin said as if they were catching up over coffee, two friends who hadn't seen each other for a while. "I don't suppose you'd do a guy a solid? There's a rope up there. Would you mind throwing one end down so we can get out of here?"

"Difficult, old boy," Roux called down, making his presence known. "Given that it's tied around a dead man. But I'll see what I can do."

"Ah, Roux, my old friend. Even better. It's like a family reunion. Just the three of us. Though I have to admit, I'm a little disappointed in you. I thought you would have worked this all out a long time ago. Or is your memory not what it used to be?"

Roux said nothing for a moment, then walked over and grabbed the corpse by the collar and dragged him to the edge. Garin stared up at him as he pushed the dead man into the chamber, the rope tumbling after him. "You didn't say which end," the old man said, then turned to Annja. "Let's get out of here." He took hold of Annja's arm and led her away from the crumbled staircase.

"We can't just leave him here," she said.

"Oh, my dear, not only can we, that's exactly what we are going to do. We leave him here to rot along with the treasure that he used us to get his hands on. He deserves it. He can sit there and enjoy the beauty of it for the rest of his life. Which could be a very long time. We both know that he wouldn't hesitate to do the same to either of us if the positions were reversed."

He wouldn't listen to her arguments.

He led her out into daylight, where his helicopter was already circling. There was no sign of the guard she'd left slumped against the wall, but he had at least had the foresight to leave a rock jammed in place to stop the huge door from closing in case someone made it out of there alive. Roux kicked the rock away as he let the door slam behind them.

The only other thing he said all the way back to the hotel was that everything came down to greed over beauty. Had Garin simply been content to savor the beauty of Michelangelo's masterpiece, he'd be in the helicopter with them, bruised and battered but there just the same. His obsession with owning beautiful things had been his downfall.

39

Annja lay in the darkness of the hotel room, the curtains drawn against the brightness of the day.

Her body told her that she should sleep, but her mind refused to relax.

Leaving Garin behind in that tomb was eating away at her. Roux could rationalize it all he wanted, and yes, maybe the old man was correct, maybe they were only doing to him what he would have done to them. But that didn't make it right.

It just made them as bad as he was.

Now all she could do was lie on the hotel bed and turn the events over and over in her mind.

In the darkness, she heard the soft creak of her door opening.

She didn't need to look at who had entered, didn't need even the smallest amount of light to know who it was. She recognized his breathing.

"Hello, Garin," she said.

"Am I that predictable?" He laughed.

She didn't bother to answer. All she did was reach for the switch to turn the bedside lamp on.

"I suppose I should thank you," he said.

"Thank me?" That surprised her. She'd done nothing worthy of his thanks. Then again, she thought bitterly, when she'd thought his life was at risk, she'd raced halfway across Spain searching for a relic that had been lost for centuries. He *should* thank her. He should also get down on his knees and beg for her forgiveness. "Why would you want to thank me?"

"For being there. If you hadn't, I don't think Roux would have hesitated in pulling the trigger. You being there probably saved my life. Hell, even if I hadn't tried to take the Madonna, he would have found a way to trip that staircase. He's a resourceful old bastard."

"And yet you managed to get out, anyway."

"Only because you are you."

"Will you please stop talking in riddles? I've had a long day. I'm tired. Just tell me what you mean."

"You didn't kill the brother I left guarding the door. Again, if it had been Roux, he'd have been dead. You let him live. That's the kind of person you are. That's why I owe you. Compassion. He wasn't trying to kill you. None of them were. You just did what you had to do to get past him and make sure that he wasn't a threat."

Annja wondered if that was really true. She hadn't shown the two guards in the corridor any compassion. She had moved swiftly to eliminate a threat, but what if she could have found a less permanent solution to the problem they presented?

"What about Maffrici?"

Garin shook his head. "He didn't make it out."

"You killed him?"

"Not me. He fell when it was his turn to climb up the rope. There was nothing we could do for him. He wasn't exactly athletic, alas. All those years wasted hunched over books instead of hitting the gym."

Annja wasn't sure that she believed him.

She wasn't sure if she believed anything that came out of his mouth any longer.

"So you just left him there." It was a statement, not a question, and it was obvious that Garin didn't intend to grace her with an answer. He acted as if none of his actions needed defending. Maybe in his world they didn't.

"You used us, Garin. You used me and you used Roux. How many more people did you take advantage of to get what you wanted?"

"Me? I was trying to *protect* you, Annja."

"Don't make me laugh."

"You don't believe me?"

"Okay, tell me, how was anything you did supposed to protect me? I'm curious."

He shook his head. She needed to remember he was good. He was very good. She'd never met a more accomplished liar. The nuns would have said he had the gift of the gab, that one, could charm the birds from the trees. He licked his lips. Another sure sign he was stalling, working out his lies. "I made a mistake, Annja, and I was in too deep before I knew it. When I tried to pull out, they said they would kill you if I didn't follow through on my promises. You know me, always shouting my mouth off, writing checks my body can't cash.

They said if I walked, I might be able to disappear, but
you couldn't. They'd always be able to find you. I did
it for you. I did it all for you."

"Who are *they*?"

She felt sick to her stomach, listening to him as he
came out with lie after lie, each one almost plausible.
That word again—*almost*.

"Fraternidad de la Quema."

She shook her head.

"They call themselves the Brotherhood of the Burning."

"I've heard the name," she said. She was going to let
him keep digging until he could dig no deeper. Once
she could prove that he was lying, she would tell him,
put him out of his misery, and then she would remember this moment. Every time he said he needed her, she
would think of this and try to remind herself not to get
caught up in his lies. As far as she was concerned, he'd
just become the boy who cried wolf.

"The guy in charge, the real power player, he makes
Roux look like a pussycat. I couldn't let him hurt you,
Annja. You have to believe me. I was doing everything
I could to protect you."

"What was his name?"

"Name?"

"Yes, the man in charge of this Brotherhood."

"Martínez. Enrique Martínez. Why? Does it matter
what his name was? They won't bother us anymore,
Annja. We've beaten them—you, me, even the old man.

We stood up to them and we won. We should be celebrating here. Today is a good day, Annja."

"It really isn't," she said. Annja never trusted a man who kept using her name, even less so when it was out of character. Garin only ever used her name when he wanted something. In this case, it was for her to buy the lies he was selling. She wasn't having any of it. She picked up her phone and scrolled through the information that Roux had sent to her.

"I know the name," she said. "Funny, it seems like he didn't exist until two years ago. I could show you, if you want? Someone made him up and gave him a whole life story, a proper background so that Europol would have someone to go looking for."

"Are you sure?" he asked uncertainly. He didn't like the way the conversation was going, that much was clear.

"Of course I am, *Garin*." She stressed his name, wondering whether he'd pick up on the sarcasm. "I've even got a copy of his driver's license."

She held out her cell phone so he could see it. The license featured a photograph of Garin's face.

"Fair enough." He shrugged and held his hands up. "Guess I'm busted."

"You used me, Garin. I don't know if I'll ever be able to forgive you for that. I came running because I thought you were in trouble. I thought you needed me. I won't come running next time. That was your last chance, and you blew it."

"Oh, I'm sure you'll forgive me. It might take time,

but you love me, really. I'm a lovable rogue. It's just who I am. It's my nature. And the thing is, I can wait as long as it takes. I've got all the time in the world."

"Not if Roux has his way," Annja said. Garin inclined his head slightly, acknowledging that he'd misjudged that one, at least. "So why did you come back?"

"Ah, I almost forgot." He reached inside his jacket and pulled out the mask. "I thought you might like this." He held it out for her to take, but she didn't move, no matter how much they both knew she wanted to hold it.

"No use to you any longer, then?" she asked.

"Something like that."

"Tell me the truth, just for once. How did you know about it? About there being a map engraved on the back? No one else did."

"Not true. But that's my girl. Always seeking the answers to everything. Nothing changes." He smiled. "There was a man I knew a long time ago. He told me about it, said that it led to something worth more than rubies. And he was right, wasn't he?"

"Do you think he was talking about the statue or the shrine itself?"

"If you ask me, the *Madonna*. You saw her. But I think he probably meant the shrine. He was quite the religious sort. There was a group of them, the first Brotherhood of the Burning, if you like."

"Abdul bin Soor," she said, the name springing to her lips before the thought had fully formed.

"I knew you'd dig right to the heart of the matter," he said, sounding delighted that she'd pieced it all together on her own. "He told me that he took great pleasure in placing the whereabouts of the Moorish treasures under Torquemada's nose. You'd have liked him, I think. Clever. Quick-witted, with a wicked sense of humor. He never told me what the treasure was or where it was hidden, but I always knew it would be somewhere close to the Alhambra. It was in keeping with the games he liked to play. So now you know. Keep the mask. You earned it. And believe me, I really am sorry. If I could have found it without you, I would have."

He got back to his feet and walked to the door.

"What about the *Madonna*?"

"Beautiful, isn't she?"

And with that he closed the door, leaving her in the dark.

40

Roux was already on the flight home when Annja's call came through.

It had been a *long* day. His old bones were aching. He wanted to be in his own bed, in the château, a glass of wine in his hand, cigar tapped out on the ashtray. Content, in peace. He'd been expecting her call. He knew full well she was about to tell him Garin had escaped. He knew his former apprentice far too well to imagine a hole in the ground, no matter how deep, could thwart him.

"He's been here," Annja said. She didn't need to say anything else.

"Ah," he said. "And?"

"He gave me the mask."

"Did he, now? Fancy that. Seems like small reward for the things you've been through today, though. Is that all?"

"He knows that we know he was behind everything, that he used us and lied to us. I told him not to call again."

"Good for you. I'm sure he'll do as he's been told,

too. Until he needs something from you. What are you planning to do with the mask?"

"There's a professor in Rome, Aldo Zanetti. I promised to show it to him in person. I think he's earned the right to look at it. Plus, he wants to buy me lunch. After that, I don't know."

"Sounds like a fair exchange. For the professor, anyway."

"Without him, we would still be scratching our heads in Logroño. Garin would have been long gone with whatever he chose to plunder from the shrine."

"So what do we do about him?" Roux asked.

"We can't let him hide those things away, especially not the statue. It needs to be somewhere that people can see it, not hidden in some private collection. It should be there for everyone. That's the nature of great art."

"Leave it with me," Roux said, glad that she had given that response. "And enjoy your trip to Rome."

"Look after yourself," she said and hung up.

"You, too," he said to the empty long-distance line.

He knew what he had to do.

He brought up another name on his phone and made the call.

"Elise," he said when the woman answered, full of charm.

"Roux? As I live and breathe. Twice in as many days. To what do I owe this honor? No…wait…let me guess, another favor? I'm still explaining the last one." She wasn't laughing.

"Not this time. This one's on me. I figure I owed you."

"You do indeed, you old rogue. So how do you intend to pay me back?"

"In kind."

She laughed. "You forget, I know exactly what you're like."

"Oh, believe me, I may be old, but I never forget. I've got some information for you. Might divert some of the flak if people notice you were digging into the Brotherhood of the Burning for me."

"Go on, make my day."

"There's a container leaving out of the port of Almería on a cargo ship tomorrow. Ask me no questions and I'll tell you no lies."

"Should I be listening to this? This conversation isn't breaking any laws, is it?"

"Quite possibly. Here's the important thing. The container is registered in the name of Enrique Martínez."

"Ah, now, that's interesting. Any idea what's inside?"

"Absolutely, but I don't want to spoil the surprise. I'll say this much—the Spanish will love you. The Italians, too, I should imagine."

"That sounds very vague. Are you sure about this?"

"I can send you shipping logs, as long as they can't be traced back to me. They give the ship, date, time and the container number."

"Ah, an anonymous tip-off. No problem, if that's how you want to play it, but you could just have rung customs."

"I could have, but I owe you. I don't owe anyone in Spanish customs. Though I must admit, I rather like the idea of being in your debt."

She laughed. He liked the sound of it. Maybe he wasn't so tired, after all. It wouldn't be a lot of effort to reroute the plane to an airport not a million miles away from The Hague. "And you really won't tell me what we're going to find when we open the container?"

"That would only lead to more questions I can't answer. Trust me, you want to do this."

"Okay, I can live with that. Send whatever you have to me and I'll put something into action. I don't suppose you've got anything on Martínez's whereabouts?"

He thought about telling her and giving Garin something else to worry about, but ended up saying, "Sorry, I wish I did."

epilogue

00:00: The Port of Almería

The port swarmed with customs officers and armed police.

The threat was considered high enough to warrant extra support being drafted in. Once Elise had put the word out to Europol, everything had happened so quickly. Wheels that would usually have taken months to grease were in motion without a single squeak within moments of the alert going out. People took new leads on the activities of the Brotherhood of the Burning seriously, especially now that links to the fascist group and the courthouse bombing in Seville had been found. It was surprising the army wasn't present, too, with orders to shoot to kill. The government wanted this cancer excised from Spain at all costs.

Enrique Martínez was public enemy number one.

As the first wave of officers boarded the ship, demanding to see the manifest, a helicopter circled overhead, an eye in the sky to keep watch for anyone attempting to flee. If Martínez was here, they were bringing him in or gunning him down.

The crew was assembled on the foredeck while the offending container was located and a crane used to lift it from the cargo vessel. The ship wasn't going to be allowed to leave the port until the container had been searched and the captain had made a statement for the police. The same went for the customs officers who had checked the seals and overseen its loading.

"What's this all about?" an irritable captain demanded, but the customs officers were there to carry out their instructions, not to engage in conversation. He would have to wait his turn. The crane lifted the metal container and carried it out over the water, moving slowly, since even the officials weren't sure what they were dealing with. Eventually, the container was lowered onto the quayside, the scarred blue metal seemingly innocuous among the other thousands of containers that would pass through the port that day alone.

"Okay, let's crack this bad boy open," one man said.

In an office in The Hague, Elise just prayed that the container wasn't empty. That wasn't so much to ask, was it?

Bolt cutters were applied and at last the end of the container swung open. The contents of the simple wooden crate inside left them all breathless when it was finally prized open for all to see.

There was a knock at Elise's door.

"You've got a visitor, ma'am," her assistant said.

"Show him in," Elise told her. "I think he'd like to see this."

She heard a phone ringing. It wasn't hers. Her visitor answered on the second ring.

"Well played, you old bastard" was all the caller said before hanging up.

* * * * *

ROGUE ANGEL™

AleX Archer
BATHED IN BLOOD

The quest for youth leads only to death...
The Blood Countess is said to have murdered young, beautiful women for their blood; she believed bathing in it would preserve her vitality and beauty. Something so fantastic could only be a story. So what is archaeologist and TV host Annja Creed to make of the girl dead on the side of the road...from blood loss?

With no one willing to answer any of Annja's questions, the only way Annja can see to uncover the truth is by becoming the Blood Countess's next victim...

Available March 2015 wherever books and ebooks are sold.

GOLD EAGLE®

GRA53R

James Axler
Öutlanders

TERMINAL WHITE

The old order has a new plan to enslave humanity

The Cerberus rebels remain vigilant, defending mankind's sovereignty against the alien forces. Now a dark and deadly intelligence plots to eradicate what it means to be human: free will.

In the northern wilderness, an experimental testing ground—where computers have replaced independent choice—is turning citizens into docile, obedient sheep. The brainchild of a dedicated Magistrate of the old order, Terminal White promises to achieve the subjugation of the human race. As the Cerberus warriors infiltrate and get trapped in this mechanized web, humanity's only salvation may be lost in a blinding white doom.

Available February 2015

GOUT72R

JAMES AXLER

DEATH LANDS

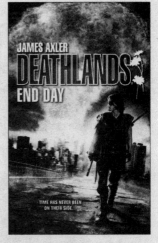

JAMES AXLER
DEATHLANDS
END DAY

TIME HAS NEVER BEEN
ON THEIR SIDE...

END DAY

Time has never been on their side...

On the heels of Magus, a Deathlands nemesis, Ryan and his companions find themselves in a place more foreign than any they've encountered before. After unwittingly slipping through a time hole, the group lands in twentieth-century New York City, getting their first glimpse of predark civilization—and they're not sure they like it. Only Mildred and Doc can appreciate this strange metropolis, but time for reminiscing is cut short. Armageddon is just seventy-two hours away, and Magus will stop at nothing to ensure Ryan and his team are destroyed on Nuke Day. As the clock ticks down, the city becomes a deadly maze. The companions are desperate to find their way back to Deathlands...but not before they trap Magus in New York forever.

Available March 2015 wherever books and ebooks are sold.